LUCA

BRATVA BLOOD BROTHERS #5

JAX KNIGHT

PROLOGUE

LUCA ORLOV

LATE JUNE - SURREY, ENGLAND - DISTRACTED

hit. What did she say?

I cleared my throat and nodded, hoping that was the correct response.

Marcie, the event planner, rambled on about her plans, but I barely registered her words. My attention was fixed on the phone in my pocket, waiting for it to ring. I nodded and kept up appearances, but my mind was elsewhere—back home, where my Bratva family and our Polish allies were under attack. The smile on my face felt like a mask, suffocating me.

Hours had passed since I'd heard from my best friend and pakhan, Mikhail Rominov. The tension built with each second, like a vice tightening around my chest. Every moment of silence from Miki gnawed at me, unravelling the thin facade of calm I desperately tried to maintain. My foot tapped lightly against the floor, a subtle rhythm of unease I hoped no one would notice.

Rubbing the back of my neck, I tried to loosen the knot of tension there, but it was no use. The waiting was killing me. I should have been there, with them. Not holed up here keeping up appearances and pretending like my world wasn't teetering on the edge of a knife.

Why hadn't Miki called yet? What the hell was happening?

God, I hated feeling this powerless.

I had faith in Miki's plan to counter the attacks, sure. But that didn't mean shit when bullets were flying and men were desperate. Anything could happen. Everything could go wrong in the blink of an eye.

Claire and Marcie chatted away, blissfully unaware of my worries. To them, their presence at Platinum—Miki's luxury hotel and spa—was all about Marcie organising the New Year's Eve event. While that was part of the truth, the real reason for their stay was to keep them safely away from the bloodshed and danger back home.

As the head of entertainment for the Rominov family's legitimate businesses, Miki had tasked me with their safety, a responsibility I took seriously. Yet guilt gnawed at me. While my friends and brothers fought, I was stuck here, babysitting.

My leg bounced, and I exhaled softly, struggling to control my rising agitation. After a decade as a Bratva enforcer, being sidelined like this was unbearable.

"Will that colour scheme work for you, Luca?" Marcie asked, pulling me from my thoughts.

"Sure, sounds great," I replied, distractedly rubbing the back of my neck. I didn't care about the colour. Marcie had good taste, and I trusted her judgement.

The two women leaned over Marcie's laptop, their easy laughter a stark contrast to the weight on my shoulders. I swirled the whiskey in my hand, untouched for the past hour. Each passing second of silence frayed my nerves further. This wasn't like me; I thrived on adrenaline and battle. Being powerless on the sidelines twisted my stomach, and I loathed it.

Unable to sit any longer, I rose from the chair, intending to clear my head with a walk. Just as I was about to speak, the phone buzzed in my hand.

Relief flooded me when I saw Miki's name on the screen. Finally!

"I need to get this," I said, trying to keep my voice calm.

Taking a deep breath, I stepped out onto the balcony of my suite. The cool night air offered little relief from the tension simmering in my chest. I hit the answer button, my eyes drifting back through the glass doors to where Claire and Marcie were still sitting chatting on the sofa.

Miki's face appeared on the screen, and I felt the weight of the worry I'd been carrying around for the last few days start to lift.

"Miki, how did it go?" I asked, frantic to learn how my friends and family were.

"It's over. They won't be bothering us again. Our guys are fine. We lost some of our Polish friends, though, and we almost lost Glowacki. He took a bullet," he replied.

"Shit!"

"Yeah, but the doc operated on him and although he isn't out of danger yet, he should be okay," Miki said, sounding tired. I didn't blame him. Defending our business and the Rominov home against our enemies would have taken its toll. Yet again, I wished I had been there to help.

"Well, that's a relief. Magdalena would be devastated if she lost her father," I replied. Hell, let's face it, we all would be devastated if we lost Glowacki.

Five years back, when Miki took over as the Bratva's UK pakhan after the Albanians slaughtered his parents, we forged an alliance. Janusz Glowacki, the head of the Polish Mafia, had just buried his eldest son, another casualty of the Albanian scum. What began as a pact for vengeance and mutual protection soon morphed into a bond of brotherhood. Glowacki wasn't just an ally; he was a good friend and mentor, guiding us younger men through the treacherous underworld. The thought of losing him? It was like losing our anchor.

"How are the ladies?" Miki asked, pulling me out of my thoughts.

"Fine," I confirmed, leaning against the cold railing. "They've no idea we are here for anything other than party planning."

"Good. The less they know, the better. You should be safe enough to return as soon as Marcie's finished the planning. I can't see there being any further danger, but nevertheless, be on guard, just in case," Miki said.

"As always." I nodded.

"Oh, and Luca," Miki said, his voice taking on a teasing quality, "I heard you were unable to take your eyes off a certain lady lawyer. How's that working out for you?"

I laughed and shook my head.

"I see that even in dire times of war, the Bratva gossip train still runs at full steam ahead. Who told you?" I asked with a chuckle.

"Ash took great delight in telling me, of course. He said you were like a dog with its tongue hanging out at the sight of a juicy bone the minute you saw Claire. Don't tell me the playboy is going to be tamed by the Ice Queen?" Miki chuckled.

"Not likely," I said, forcing a laugh at his comment, unwilling to admit just how easily that could be the case.

Miki laughed. "We'll see." His attention then shifted to someone offscreen. "Be right there," he told them, before speaking to me again. "I need to go. I'll keep you updated on Glowacki. See you when you get home tomorrow," he said before hanging up.

A wave of relief washed over me, the tension finally easing now that I knew everyone was safe, despite Glowacki's injury. He was a tough bastard, and I had no doubt he would pull through.

As I slipped the phone back into my pocket, my gaze flicked to Claire.

Ash was right. From the moment I saw her, I was drawn to her. I had only known Claire for a couple of days and, already, she was getting under my skin in a way no other woman ever had.

I wasn't quite sure how to feel about that.

Lingering on the balcony, I took a moment to study her, unnoticed. There was no denying Claire was a stunning woman. Smart and tough too. A criminal defence barrister, and according to Miki, known as *"the Ice Queen"* among her peers. I found the combination of brains, beauty, and strength utterly thrilling.

When I picked her and Marcie up from their house, it was like a punch to the gut. A visceral reaction that I hadn't expected, didn't want, but couldn't deny.

Claire's laughter bubbled up, bright and unrestrained, making me smile. She leaned toward Marcie, eyes sparkling with genuine amusement. I loved seeing her so open and carefree, letting her guard down, which I was sure from her reputation, wasn't something she did often.

My head tilted as I studied the woman who had stolen my breath from the minute I set eyes on her and made my heart quicken ever since. God, she was gorgeous. My pulse thrummed with a strange, urgent rhythm that I'd never felt before, and my body literally lit up inside when I looked at her.

Claire was irresistibly alluring, and I'd been chasing her with relentless flirtation since we first met. But I hadn't made much headway. That was unusual for me. Miki loved to tease me about my player reputation—women usually fell into my lap with ease, much to my delight. Lately, though, the thrill of casual flings had lost its edge; the emptiness that followed each encounter was starting to weigh on me, leaving me craving something—or someone—more real.

Then Claire walked into my life, and everything shifted. She sparked a need within me that I hadn't felt in a long time. Unlike the fleeting connections of my past, Claire was a puzzle I was desperate to solve. Her resistance to my usual charm only fuelled my desire to break through her defences. With her, it wasn't about playing games; it was about proving myself worthy of the challenge she presented.

I watched her profile as she laughed again at something Marcie said. Her beautiful full lips spread in a smile that made my cock thicken. Images of her kneeling in front of me, her mouth on me, doing delicious things, flashed through my mind and I groaned. God, that would feel so good. I had to make that happen.

Claire's gaze met mine, as if drawn by my thoughts. Despite her resistance, the pull between us was undeniable. I saw it in the tension of her body, the spark in her eyes. Yes, this was a challenge I craved, and I was ready to turn up the heat.

I slowly smiled, then licked my lips, feeling satisfied when her eyes widened before she quickly looked away. As I stepped back into my suite, I couldn't help my surge of excitement. The sexy lawyer might be dead set on resisting me, but I was hell-bent on melting her ice and igniting the fiery passion I sensed lurking beneath.

CHAPTER 1
CLAIRE BENSON
THE SAME DAY – SURREY, ENGLAND – NOTICING LUCA

My gaze flicked towards the balcony where Luca stood with his back to me, his broad shoulders rigid, tension rippling through the hard lines of his body as he answered his call.

Pursing my lips, I frowned, studying him as he talked on the phone. Something was going on with him, and I wasn't sure what. He had been distracted all day, which was unusual. Normally, he was very attentive and focused, but not today. Today, he had been on edge and doing his utmost to pretend otherwise. Marcie might not have noticed, but I certainly had. And that bothered me more than I wanted to admit.

Since the moment we'd met, just a couple of days ago, I'd been hyper-aware of the sexy Russian. And that was a problem—a serious one. He was the kind of trouble I didn't need. I had a knack for spotting men like him. Dangerous ones. As a criminal defence lawyer, I prided myself on that skill. I saw it in Ash when Gracie introduced us, and I saw it in Luca.

He turned his head, and I forced myself to look away

before he caught me staring. But within seconds, my gaze had flicked to him again.

Whatever he heard on the phone must have been positive, because his shoulders relaxed and the tension leeched from him. I was right. Something had been going on, but I guessed it was really none of my business, and anyhow, by the way his posture had changed it seemed like things were okay again.

I released a breath that I hadn't even been aware I'd been holding. Why was it that Luca's tension and unease had bothered me so much? I hardly knew the guy and was determined to keep it that way. So why was I so attuned to his every move and mood?

It didn't make sense. I mean, the guy was super attractive, but I had met many attractive men in my lifetime, and even dated a few. What was it about this one that made me want to see past that dangerous veneer and find out what lay beneath?

It didn't matter. I wouldn't let myself delve into his depths, no matter how tempting it seemed.

I wasn't naïve. Luca might put on a front as a legitimate businessman, but I knew he was a criminal. I'd worked hard to get where I was in my profession, driven by ambition and a refusal to let anything stand in my way, and I had plans. Working with criminals was one thing; getting personally involved was another.

Luca and his dark allure were not for me. I didn't do casual, and I wasn't looking for a serious relationship, especially not with someone tied to the Bratva. Besides, if I was, his relentless flirting—even when I shot him down— made it clear he was a player. Players don't do serious, and I wasn't about to let him play with me.

So why did the thought of it send a shiver down my spine?

Damn it! The man was no good for me. I needed to resist the pull between us.

Huffing in frustration, I tried to tear my gaze away, but it was glued to him. It was as if my eyes were intent on soaking up every inch of the stunning Russian while I could. And who could blame them? He was a magnificent specimen—tall, powerfully built, and irresistibly sexy, with an aura that radiated power and menace.

And then there were his eyes. Dark, intense, always watchful. Like a predator scanning the room, weighing his options.

I'd caught him watching me a few times over the last couple of days, and each time, the air seemed to thicken between us. It wasn't just attraction. No, this was something deeper, almost primal. It unnerved me how easily I could feel it—how easily I could see him for what he was.

Oh, this man was dangerous all right. On far too many levels.

"So, what do you think of the sexy waiter idea?" Marcie said, wiggling her eyebrows at me.

"The what?" I asked, Marcie's question finally pulling my attention away from the sexy Russian.

"Ha, I knew you weren't listening!"

"Sorry, my mind was wandering. I just needing to get out of this room for a bit, I think," I told her, hoping she hadn't noticed where my eyes had been.

"Well, I've just another email to send to a supplier and then we can call it a night if you like?" Marcie said.

"Sure, sounds like a plan," I replied. I needed another drink to take my mind off the distracting male.

"So, what was all this about a sexy waiter?" I asked, unable to keep the smile from my face.

She laughed.

"I was just saying how it would be great if we could get Ash and the other Rominov's and the lovely Luca, of course, to act as sexy waiters. You know, the ones that are topless apart from a white collar and bowtie?" she giggled.

"Oh, and we could put them in Santa hats and make them walk around with bits of mistletoe. Since the event is ticketed and the money is going to charity, I bet we'd sell out in seconds."

She laughed, snorting loudly and making me laugh in turn.

"Oh my god, I'd pay good money to see that," I couldn't help myself from responding.

"I'll bet." She winked at me, and I burst into laughter as my mind bombarded me with images of the handsome men she was referring to… especially one in particular.

My eyes drifted towards him yet again and I stared at the broad expanse of his chest decked out in a crisp white, open-necked shirt. I bit my lip as I let my imagination run wild with said images of Luca delivering me cocktails while dressed as a sexy waiter. Oh, my god.

My eyes slowly drifted upwards, and I baulked when I saw him staring back at me.

Shit. Heat rose in my cheeks and I quickly averted my eyes to Marcie's laptop, trying desperately to pretend that I hadn't been blatantly ogling him like a schoolgirl with a crush. I gulped hard. I could feel his gaze on me. Hot. Intense. Dangerous. It made my mouth dry, my pulse thunder in my ears.

He walked back inside, and even without looking at him, I could feel that smug smile of his. The one that said he knew exactly what I was thinking.

Damn, the man was too much. Too dangerous. Too hot. And way too damn tempting.

How the hell was I going to continue resisting him?

CHAPTER 2
LUCA

LATER THAN NIGHT– SURREY,
ENGLAND– THE FIRST KISS

"Oh, great, Luca, you're back. I've just finished up for the night. That's pretty much everything in place for the event. I've emailed you a copy of the plans to look at when you have time. Any questions, just ask?" Marcie said in her usual bubbly way as she packed away her laptop.

"Perfect," I replied, my eyes not leaving Claire for a second.

She wasn't looking at me. Pointedly avoiding doing so. My smirk widened as I took in the blush on her cheeks that betrayed her—she wasn't nearly as immune to my charms as she wanted me to believe. That thought thrilled me.

"Claire and I were just heading down to the bar for a drink. Care to join us?" Marcie asked.

"I'd love to," I replied, as the ladies stood to leave.

As I strode behind them, my eyes drifted over the pair appreciatively. Both were stunning, but Claire just had that little extra something for me.

In the past few days, my initial attraction had only deepened. We'd talked about everything and nothing, and I realised I wasn't just drawn to her long blond hair, those intelligent brown eyes, or that gorgeous, curvy figure. I actually liked her.

It didn't hurt that she had a sexy, squeezable ass, and I wasn't shy about appreciating it. Claire glanced over her shoulder, her eyes narrowing and her lips pursing when she caught me staring. But she didn't say a word. She just kept on walking, ignoring me just like she had every time my flirtations got too obvious.

I smirked, enjoying this little game we played. She might pretend indifference, but I saw through the act. Claire was aware of every look, every comment. Whatever this was between us, she felt it, just like I did.

"What can I get you, ladies?" I asked as I approached the bar.

"Cosmopolitan for me, please," Marcie replied.

"Same for me," Claire added.

I was ordering our drinks when a member of our reception team approached me, her expression tight with annoyance.

"Luca, we've got a situation. Some troublemakers are causing a scene in one of the rooms. They've been drinking and got a bit handsy with one of the staff who delivered their room service," she said quietly, glancing around to ensure the conversation stayed private.

"Alright, I'll handle it. I'll be right there," I replied as she headed back to the foyer.

Turning back to Claire and Marcie, I forced a smooth smile. "Duty calls. Enjoy the drinks; I'll be back as soon as I can."

———

The bar was quieting down, the last of the stragglers stumbling off to their rooms when I returned a half hour later. I nodded to the barman as he wiped down the counter, signalling for him to close up for the night.

"Where did the ladies go?" I asked.

"They headed to bed a few minutes ago," he told me, and I bit down on my disappointment.

Damn! This was our last night here, and I had longed to get Claire alone for a few minutes and test the waters. I'd only been hinting at my feelings until now, flirting, but not quite revealing the depths of my interest. Now that the trouble at home was over, I had intended to take things a step further and see where it might lead. Obviously, that was going to have to wait.

Rubbing the back of my neck in frustration, I turned to leave, planning on heading to bed myself when something caught my eye through the glass doors leading to the garden.

Claire.

Her back was to me, and I took a moment to appreciate that gorgeous bottom of hers again. The things I wanted to do to it made my cock jerk. I gulped hard and shifted to relieve the sudden pressure.

What was it about this woman, out of all the women I'd met in my life, that made me feel like a horny teenager unable to control myself?

I needed to get a grip on my libido. Exhaling sharply, I stepped to the door and stopped dead in my tracks, struck by the awe-inspiring sight.

Claire tilted her head, exposing the delicate curve of her neck, and I felt my pulse quicken. Shadows and light played across her face, highlighting the sharpness of her cheekbones and the fullness of her lips. She looked otherworldly, like some ethereal goddess wandering through the mortal realm. My chest tightened, and for a moment, I forgot to breathe.

A sense of calm washed over me as I watched her bathe in the silver glow of the moonlight. The soft light caught in her hair, turning those loose, golden strands into a halo that framed her face. Her skin glowed, every curve and angle softened by the gentle illumination. The moon had chosen her as its muse, spotlighting her so that every movement and gesture became a graceful dance with the night.

I didn't make a conscious decision to move; it was as if an invisible force drew me to her, tugging at something deep inside. Every step felt inevitable, like I was walking toward something I couldn't—wouldn't—resist.

When she noticed me approaching, I saw her tense, just for a moment, before she hid it behind a polite smile. My heart sped up at her nearness.

"I'd thought you'd gone to bed. Everything okay?" I asked, keeping my voice low and calm. Inside, I was anything but.

"Marcie has. I wanted to get some air," she replied, her tone controlled, but I could hear the undercurrent of tension.

Claire turned her face slightly, taking in the dimly lit garden grounds again. "This place is… impressive."

"It has its charms," I said, letting a slow smile tug at my lips. I could see her trying to maintain a distance, but I wasn't fooled. Her eyes lingered on me a moment too long, her breath hitching slightly when I stepped closer.

"Claire," I murmured, my voice dropping as I closed the distance between us, "I haven't been able to stop thinking about you since we met."

I saw it again, the flicker of desire in her eyes before she masked it. "This isn't a good idea, Luca."

"Bad ideas are often the most tempting," I countered,

stepping closer until the heat of her body wrapped around me. Her scent—fresh and floral—flooded my senses, making it impossible to think of anything but her.

"Luca…" Her voice wavered, but she didn't pull away. There was uncertainty in her eyes, as if she was caught between surrendering to the attraction between us and holding back.

Unable to resist from touching her any longer, I reached out. My fingers brushed lightly against her arm. Her skin was warm, soft, and I felt her shiver. She was trying to fight it, but her resolve was slipping.

I slid my hand to the small of her back, drawing her closer. She resisted for a heartbeat before yielding, her lips parting with a soft gasp. It was all the invitation I needed. I bent my head and kissed her.

The moment our lips met, it was like a fuse had been lit. The world around us vanished. Her lips were soft, her taste intoxicating, and I wanted more.

Unable to stop myself, I deepened the kiss, my hand cupping her cheek, feeling her melt into me as her hands gripped my jacket. Her lips moved against mine with a fervour that matched my own, each touch electrifying and urgent, as if the world had faded into insignificance.

But then, as suddenly as it began, it was over. Claire pulled back. Her breath was quick, her chest rising and falling as she put a trembling hand against my torso to keep me at bay. "Luca, no. We can't do this," she said in a breathy tone.

Not yet willing to let her go completely, I kept a hand wrapped loosely around her waist. "Why not?" I asked, my voice tight with emotion.

"Because of what you do," she said, her words steadier now.

My blood ran cold. "What I do?"

"I know what you are, Luca. And I can't get involved with a criminal," she replied.

A weight settled in my chest, the truth of her words hanging in the air like a dark cloud. I could deny it, but I knew it would be pointless. Claire was a smart woman and obviously had figured out there was more to me and the Rominov's than we pretended. Frustration simmered beneath the surface, battling with the longing that stirred deep inside me.

"You're a criminal defence lawyer, Claire. You work with criminals all the time. What's the problem?"

She bristled.

"I work with criminals, yes. But I didn't become a defence lawyer to get them off. I did it because I believe in the law and our legal system's principle of 'innocent until proven guilty'. It's the prosecution's job to prove guilt, and mine to ensure that evidence is legitimate, so no innocent person goes to jail. That doesn't mean I condone breaking the law. And just because I defend criminals doesn't mean I want to get personally involved with one," she said, her eyes flashing with anger.

My jaw tightened. I wasn't used to rejection, and coming from Claire, it stung more than I expected.

"I'm not just a criminal, Claire. There's more to me than that," I protested, hoping she could see beyond the surface.

She met my gaze, regret shimmering in her brown eyes. "I'm sure there is, but it doesn't change the fact that you are, and I can't condone that. I'm sorry, but whatever this is between us isn't enough for me to set aside my morals."

A flicker of desperation surged within me as I studied her, memorising the way her eyes pleaded with me to understand, to let her go. But how could I? How could I walk away from something this powerful, this undeniable? I hadn't felt anything like before. I had to see her again, had to make her understand that what was between us was worth pursuing, regardless of my shady side.

"Let me see you again," I said, my voice softening, almost a plea.

She shook her head, her expression pained. "I can't. We're on opposite sides of a line that can't be crossed."

I stared at her, frustration and longing churning inside me. I didn't want to accept it, didn't want to let her walk away. But I could see she wasn't going to change her mind tonight. She was determined, strong-willed. I admired that as much as it drove me crazy.

"Besides, I can tell you're a player, Luca, and I'm not a woman who can be played with. I won't be just another notch on your bedpost. It's best if we remain simply friends," she said, and her words hit me like a punch to the gut.

Friends? Had I just been friend-zoned by the woman whose kiss had blown my mind? Aw, hell no!

"It's true that I've enjoyed female company often in the past, Claire. I won't lie to you. But the feelings I have for you are deeper than I've ever had for anyone before," I told her, hoping she could hear the sincerity in my voice.

She didn't.

"Ha, I doubt that!" she said with a wry smile.

"It's true!" I insisted, the frustration in my voice rising as she refused to believe me.

As I watched her, the stubborn set of her jaw and the way she held herself tightly spoke volumes, and I realised she had fortified her walls, unwilling to let me in. It was clear that tonight wouldn't be the night to break through.

Reluctantly, I stepped back, letting my hand fall away from her but keeping my eyes locked on hers.

"Goodnight, Luca," she said quietly before turning away from me.

Watching her walk away, my heart clenched at the sight, and every instinct urged me to chase after her, but I stood my ground. This wasn't the end.

I wasn't the kind of man who easily gave up on something—or someone—I wanted. And I wanted Claire. Now more than ever. No matter how long it took or what I had to do, I would make her see that what we had felt when we kissed was real and worth fighting for.

She thought this was over, but I knew better. This was just the beginning.

Heading back inside, I felt the thrill of the chase coil tight within me, a burning desire I couldn't ignore. What I had told her was true: Claire was different—she wasn't just a fleeting flame. There was something about her that made me want to dive deeper, to unravel the mystery beneath her icy exterior.

That pull was dangerous. Wanting more meant stepping into uncharted territory, risking not just rejection but something deeper. In pursuing her, I wasn't just playing with fire—I was risking an inferno that could consume me completely if I wasn't careful.

My only concern was, would I survive it?

CHAPTER 3
CLAIRE BENSON

LONDON – EARLY JUNE, ALMOST A YEAR LATER – ON A WINNING STREAK

High heels clicking on the tarmac, I rushed from the office, running late as usual, and headed towards my car. Unlike most of my colleagues, who were forced to park in the nearby multi-storey, I had scored a coveted spot in the building's car park—an unexpected perk granted after my recent string of successes.

Winning a couple of high-profile cases had made me one of the most talked-about defence lawyers in London. The partners at Turner and Hanson, eager to keep me on their team, had offered me a parking space and a pay rise to ensure my loyalty. For now, my commitment was firmly with them.

As a defence lawyer, my role was to uphold the integrity of the legal system, ensuring that every case was handled lawfully and fairly. I firmly believed that the court's purpose was to seek justice, not merely to secure convictions. Every time I stepped into the courtroom, I felt the weight of that responsibility. For me, winning a case meant more than just securing my client's freedom; it was about affirming the principles of justice and due process.

Sure, there were times when the outcome felt unjust.

Clients were acquitted not because they were innocent, but due to flaws in the prosecution's case or missteps in the investigation. That was the nature of the system, and while it made my job complex, I remained committed to the idea that everyone deserved a fair trial. It was my duty to ensure the law was followed. If that meant defending someone who had committed a crime, then so be it. I focused on the bigger picture; protecting the rights of the accused and maintaining the rule of law, even when the choices felt morally ambiguous.

Each case was a reminder that justice wasn't always black and white. Navigating the murky waters of criminal defence wasn't easy, but I hoped my principles would guide me, no matter how challenging the path became.

With the highest success rate in the firm, I felt the prospect of partnership inching closer. My current leverage was solid, but I had to keep the momentum going and maintain my streak.

I threw my wig and gown onto the passenger seat with my briefcase and jumped in. Tonight was Marcie's twenty-ninth birthday party, and I had just over an hour to get home, get ready, and make it back into the City.

It was going to be tight. Really tight. But if I ordered an Uber as soon as I got home, I might just pull it off. It would cost a small fortune getting there and back, but Marcie was worth it.

Friday night traffic was lighter than expected, and for once, things seemed to be going my way. I made it home in less than an hour—fantastic!

I quickly called the Uber and jumped into the shower. Luckily, I'd washed my hair that morning, which shaved off some time. By the time the car arrived, I was dressed, makeup done, hair styled, and ready to go.

Grabbing my bag and Marcie's gift, I dashed out the door, slipping into the back seat of the waiting car. As we cruised through the streets, I leaned back, already anticipating the night ahead.

The party was being held in the VIP section of *Glitz*, one of the Rominovs' clubs. Of course, that meant Luca Orlov would be there. He was their head of entertainment, after all.

My heart thudded at the idea of seeing him again even while I desperately tried not to feel excited about that. And my lady parts certainly hadn't got the memo. I shifted in my seat, trying not to squirm in embarrassment at the wetness that was now coating my knickers at the very thought of him. Bloody hell, I needed to get a grip.

It had been almost a year since I first met Luca at *Platinum*. Marcie had been planning their New Year's Eve event, and I'd tagged along for the fun of it, never imagining I would meet the person who could have easily been the man of my dreams, except for one undeniable problem—he was a criminal. The type of man I had vowed never to get involved with.

Of course, that hadn't stopped me succumbing to his charms and indulging in a heart stopping kiss with him. I blamed the cocktails for that lapse in judgment. That was the same excuse I had at Gracie's wedding in December. And again, on New Year's Eve. It was becoming a habit—a very bad one.

I'd rejected Luca because I refused to get personally involved with a criminal, no matter how drawn I was to him. It was naïve, really, considering my cousin Gracie had married one—Ash Rominov, no less—and was now expecting their first child. Like it or not, I was tied to the Rominovs. And Luca wasn't just an employee; he was part of their Brotherhood. He'd also openly admitted to having the reputation of being a ladies' man, which only made him more off-limits to me.

It didn't matter that I was connected to the Rominov family now, or how incredible a kisser Luca was, I couldn't let myself cross that line. Luca needed to stay firmly in the friend zone. So why did my treacherous heart clench at the thought?

I shook my head and let out a quiet, exasperated sigh. What was wrong with me? How did he keep getting under my skin?

When we had first kissed, I had been determined it would never happen again. Yet, twice since, I had allowed Luca to worm his way under my defences. Each time, the chemistry between us only grew hotter, and the last time—New Year's Eve—it had happened in full view of all of our family and friends. The moment I realised what we'd done, I'd practically died on the spot, and in my panic I had pushed him away far more harshly than I intended.

But the guy hadn't given up, despite the teasing he'd endured from everyone. For months, he always seemed to turn up wherever I went. If I didn't know better, I'd swear someone—maybe Gracie or Marcie—was feeding him intel on my whereabouts.

Then, just like that, it stopped. He had gone silent on me. Gracie had mentioned he was away on business, but that had been weeks ago. I kept telling myself a relationship with him was off the table, yet I couldn't shake the truth: I missed him. His absence was a stark reminder of how much he had crept into my life and thoughts, and how much I'd secretly enjoyed having him around.

The flowers he'd sent yesterday—my first sign of him in weeks—sat in a vase beside my bed at home, their vibrant colours a striking contrast to my swirling thoughts. A surge of excitement had coursed through me at their unexpected arrival, a lifeline after weeks of silence. Even now, their presence in my home warmed my heart, and I hated that it did.

I sighed, frustration bubbling beneath the surface. Gracie had managed to overcome the Bratva issue, and seeing her so happy with Ash made me wonder: if I weren't so focused on my career, could I do the same? But I guess that was a moot point.

A romantic relationship with a man like Luca could ruin my reputation, but more than that, I feared it would shake the very foundation of my moral fibre. There was no escaping it. I needed to push my attraction for him aside and make it clear that nothing could happen between us before he pursued me in earnest again.

How I was going to do that, I didn't know.

Maybe I should take up Damien Turner's offer for dinner? Soon to become the youngest partner at the firm, and only a few years older than me, he was quite attractive, but mixing business with pleasure was always a dangerous game.

Or perhaps I should seek a distraction tonight? Dating someone else would surely send Luca the message that we weren't meant to be. But as much as it might solve my problem, the very idea filled me with dread. I hadn't been interested in another man since I met Luca. He was just so hot, and that kiss had left an everlasting impression. Damn, I had it bad!

My heart pounded, my core clenching as I remembered his lips and hands on me. God, it was going to be hard seeing him again and not giving in. I had to keep my distance. Because once he got too close, my resistance would crumble, and I'd be putty in his hands.

I shook my head in frustration. Clearly, finding someone

else to take my mind off Luca wasn't the solution. I needed to find another way to exorcise the maddening man from my thoughts. As for tonight, I would keep my distance. There was nothing else for it.

Closing my eyes, I took a steadying breath before stepping into the club, determined to make it through the night without breaking my vow.

Surely, I could manage that?

CHAPTER 4
LUCA

LONDON – SAME DAY – RUSHING HOME

My favourite playlist blasted through the speakers as I drove along the motorway back to London. I'd been sorting out a staffing issue at Platinum, which took longer than I'd anticipated, and now I was running late.

As I drove, my thoughts drifted to Claire, as they always seemed to do these days. After weeks of forced separation, I was finally going to see her again tonight, and the anticipation was a tight knot in my chest.

I hated being away from her, but it was necessary.

For the last couple of years, we and our Polish allies had been under constant attack from various enemies. After we'd wiped out the ones responsible for the attack on the Rominov family home, which we referred to as the Estate, and our drug lab—the same night I first kissed Claire—we discovered a network of men orchestrating the chaos behind the scenes.

One by one, we dismantled them, until we reached the man at the top. A corrupt politician and member of the UK government, Timothy Evans-Hughes, with a personal vendetta against the Bratva, intent on making us suffer.

But it wasn't just about us—he was a twisted bastard in every sense. His company, *Darkest Desire Productions*, catered to rich degenerates who paid to hunt men and women for sport. Even as criminals, there were lines we wouldn't cross, and murdering innocents for profit was one of them. It was something we couldn't tolerate, especially when women were concerned.

There was no doubt that he'd needed to be stopped. But we had to tread carefully. Taking him down directly would have jeopardised our public image as legitimate businessmen.

That's where our friend Anton came in. He got me in as a bodyguard, and I bided my time, earning the MP's trust while we planned his downfall. Marcie's position as the event planner at one of his garden parties provided the perfect distraction and gave us the opening we needed to pull off a heist and gather enough evidence to bring him down.

We handed it to the authorities anonymously, and the MP was hit with multiple charges, including murder. But, of course, the prick managed to get bail. Now he was tagged and under surveillance, unable to leave his home thanks to the reporters swarming his doorstep. In essence, he was under house arrest.

I'd gone underground the moment the authorities moved in. Although I'd been careful, disguising myself as much as I could during my time with the MP, it was safer to lie low at the Estate, where I'd grown up and still had rooms, just in case. If the MP ever discovered who I was, he'd undoubtedly seek revenge.

Now that he'd been formally charged, and I had things other than my identity to worry about, I was finally back to my usual routine—and it felt damn good to be out in the world again. Back to my life, and back to Claire.

Shit, I frowned as I saw the long queue of traffic up

ahead. By the looks of things, it could be hours before I got to see her.

Frustration coursed through me, but I refused to let it sour my mood or dampen my anticipation. I'd been longing for this night, and nothing was going to stop me from getting there and spending time with the sexy lawyer I couldn't stop thinking about.

Soon, I told myself, taking a deep breath. It didn't matter if I was late, as long as I got to see her.

The traffic continued at a slow pace while thoughts rushed through me.

Tonight was Marcie's birthday party, and I still had to swing by my apartment to grab her gift before heading to the venue, *Glitz*, our newest club.

For once, I was looking forward to being a guest there rather than running the show.

With the help of Miki's brother Ash, my assistant manager, Suzie, had been running everything in my absence. But tonight was her first big test on her own. I was confident she'd handle it without a hitch—she was more than capable.

Assuming all went well, I planned to hand over more responsibilities to her in the near future. And once the MP's trial date was confirmed, I had a long-overdue holiday in mind—time with my family back in Russia. I needed the break. And I intended to take Claire, my Little Miss Sexy Ass, with me; despite her current resistance to my charms, I was still hopeful that soon she'd be putty in my hands.

After the sexy lawyer rejected me following our first kiss last year, I'd made it my mission to show her how good we could be together.

Before I had to go away, I'll admit, I'd practically turned into a stalker. Gracie or Marcie would mention where Claire was going to be, and like clockwork, I'd show up. I was obsessed—an addict needing a hit of her any way I could get it.

I tried everything to prove that beneath my player exterior —and despite the whole criminal thing—I was a good guy, someone worthy of her trust, maybe even her heart. We'd shared two incredible moments of intimacy since, but she still couldn't admit that what we had was special.

Yet, with every minute we spent together, every intimate moment we shared, the connection between us only deepened —no matter how much she tried to deny it. Her refusal to see me as anything more than a friend because of my criminal roots and reputation as a player, was soul-destroying.

Having been born into this life, I'd never had a choice about being part of the Bratva. My dad was Bratva and a good friend of Maxim Rominov. So, when Miki's dad brought their family to the UK to establish a branch of the Bratva here, my dad was tasked with being his second and mentor, and so my family came with them.

Since Miki took over as pakhan, things had changed. We'd built our legitimate businesses and offloaded the more overt criminal activities these last few weeks in favour of more covert ones. Leaving such a lifestyle behind wasn't easy, but like the Rominov family, I was trying hard to find a way out of it, and my plans were starting to fall into place.

As for my player's past, well, that was over. It had been the moment I'd laid eyes on Little Miss Sexy Ass. I couldn't get her out of my head. She was the woman I wanted, nobody else compared. But the constant rejection was wearing me down.

While I was away, I went cold turkey and had time to think. I made a decision—if I couldn't change Claire's mind by the time I left for Russia, I'd do something drastic. Maybe I'd take her with me, whether or not she agreed. A little break away together—forced or not — might be exactly what she needed to finally give in to my charms. But that was Plan B, and I had a lot of mileage yet in Plan A.

Claire wanted me—I knew that much. She just didn't want to admit it. Tonight was my chance to get close to her again, and I intended to make the most of it. It'd been weeks since she last saw me. Had she thought of me as much as I'd thought of her? I could only hope.

Maybe the time apart had worked in my favour. Absence makes the heart grow fonder, right? A grin tugged at my lips. Tonight, I'd get her to dance with me, and if she had missed me, maybe I'd get another taste of those sweet lips. And maybe, this time, we'd go further.

The thought of that sent my pulse racing and made my cock thicken. She had no idea how much I wanted her, but this attraction went beyond the physical. I wasn't just after a quickie or a one-night stand. Claire was different, and I wanted something more—a hell of a lot more. Something real and lasting.

Before meeting her, the idea of a long-term relationship had never seemed likely. Finding someone who could handle both sides of me had always felt impossible. And it wasn't just about my criminal and legitimate lives. There were two distinct sides to my nature: the calm, charming man I showed the world and the darker, more possessive side that craved control. Especially in the bedroom.

But that didn't mean I wanted someone I could walk over. No, I respected women too much for that. I needed a woman with strength, one who could hold her own, but who would also submit to me when the moment was right. And my Little Miss Sexy Ass? I was convinced she was that woman. I could see it—her strong, no-nonsense persona during the day, and then, at night, her yielding to me in all the ways I'd been imagining for months. The thought of her surrendering, trusting me enough to give in, had been driving me insane.

So, my mind was made up. Tonight, I'd make another move—because accepting that she would never be mine wasn't just gut-wrenching; it was downright impossible. The thought of walking away from her twisted something deep inside me. I couldn't let it happen. One way or another, I would make Claire mine. I couldn't imagine a future without her.

I had ambitions, and I was determined to focus on them—to become the man I'd always wanted to be, not the one shaped by being Bratva-born. But I was just as determined to have Claire at my side when I did.

Several hours later, I pulled into the underground car park, my thoughts still churning with plans and hopes for the future as I killed the engine. The lift hummed softly as I stepped inside, pressing the button for my floor. Pushing aside my swirling emotions, I focused on getting ready for the night ahead—one that could change everything.

CHAPTER 5
CLAIRE

LATER THAT NIGHT – MARCIE'S PARTY

After flashing my invite to the bouncers on the front door, I squeezed my way through the crowds and headed for the VIP area where two of the Rominov's men were standing guard. Vlad, the one I recognised, nodded in acknowledgement, moving aside to let me in.

Marcie was already there, sitting at a table, glass of bubbly in hand, chatting loudly with Gracie, her sister-in-law Sonia Rominov, and Mikhail Rominov's fiancé Eilidh. All three were in varying stages of pregnancy and holding what looked like soft drinks. Poor them. I smirked. They might not be able to enjoy alcohol tonight, but I sure as hell was going to.

As I approached, Marcie squealed in delight, grabbing me and planting twin cheek air kisses that made me chuckle. Clearly, I wasn't the only one planning to get tipsy—she was well on her way. It was her birthday, after all, so she had every right to overindulge if she wanted to.

"Happy birthday, birthday girl. Where do you want me to put your gift?" I asked.

"Over beside the bar," she said, gesturing vaguely.

"Great, I'll grab myself a drink while I'm at it. Want anything?" I asked, knowing it was probably a dumb question.

"Hell yeah! Hit me up with a double shot of tequila. Actually, just bring the bottle, and we'll do a round of shots," she said, flashing a wicked grin.

"You really want to go there this early?" I asked, raising a brow. If Marcie was breaking out the tequila now, something was definitely wrong. Tequila was our go-to when we wanted to get plastered, but it usually meant we were drowning our sorrows. Which could only mean—man trouble. "Don't you think you should pace yourself a bit?"

"I'll be fine. Just planning on making the most of my birthday," she said, taking a sip of champagne.

"Everything alright?" I asked, watching her closely.

"Fine," she said, nodding and smiling. But the smile didn't quite reach her eyes, and the tightness in her expression was impossible to miss.

Most people wouldn't notice she was faking her enthusiasm, but I did. We'd known each other too long and been through too much for me to miss the signs. She'd been so excited about this party, but something was definitely off. As I turned towards the bar, I spotted the likely cause: Anton DuPont, standing nearby, talking to Vlad.

Damn. What had he done, or more likely *not* done, now?

Anton was a close friend of the Rominovs, but that's not how Marcie had met him. About eighteen months ago, she'd had a stalker—someone who met her at an event she'd planned and became dangerously obsessed. Things escalated quickly, to the point where she was terrified to leave her house. Derrick, her assistant, had connections, and he brought in Anton, who'd just opened a security firm. He protected her, the stalker was caught and jailed, and ever since then, Marcie had been head over heels for him. But Anton kept rejecting her. Yet, whenever he was around, he couldn't stay away.

The mixed signals had been driving Marcie crazy, and I guess tonight was no different. It was time that stopped.

Huffing in annoyance, I was about to go rip him a new one when it hit me—Marcie and I were dealing with the same problem, just from opposite sides. Here she was, obsessing over a guy who wouldn't get involved, while I was refusing to get involved with a guy who seemed obsessed with me.

Anton had friend-zoned Marcie, just like I'd friend-zoned Luca. Of course, I had my reasons, but I wondered what Anton's were. Marcie wasn't a criminal, and she wasn't someone who played around. What was his deal?

Maybe I should ask him. But as I dropped off Marcie's gift and headed for the bar, I thought better of it. Interfering in someone else's life only invited them to interfere in yours, and I didn't need that. No, whatever was happening between the two, they'd have to figure it out themselves.

Grabbing a bottle of tequila, some salt, lime, and shot glasses, I returned to the table. I might not be willing to get involved, but I'd sure as heck help Marcie through it—line up the shots and hold her hair back when the tequila inevitably came back to haunt her. After all, that's what best friend's did.

Several shots later, I felt a pleasant warmth spreading through me. Marcie's face was brighter now, her smile goofier, her eyes a little unfocused.

A shadow fell over us as we downed another shot, and I looked up to see Anton. He kissed Marcie on the cheek.

"Happy birthday, Marcie. You look beautiful. I hope you like my gift," he murmured, handing her a small box.

"Thank you," she said, smiling widely at him.

I missed the rest of their conversation as Gracie turned to let me know she was heading to the bathroom. When I looked back, Anton was turning to leave, Marcie grabbed his arm, asking him to sit with us, but he made some excuse I couldn't hear and headed off towards the Rominov men.

Marcie watched him go with a sad smile and eyes filled with longing. Yep, we were both hooked on men we couldn't have—me because I wouldn't date the guy, and Marcie because he wouldn't date her. What a pair we were.

"Are you okay, honey?" I asked, my eyes searching her face in concern.

She nodded, huffing heavily, and closed her eyes.

"He's a bloody fool if he won't take a chance on a wonderful woman like you," I said, squeezing Marcie's hand as I shot daggers into Anton's retreating back.

Marcie opened her eyes and forced a smile before grabbing the last of our tequila shots, and downing it.

I sighed. Marcie was completely obsessed with Anton, but I wasn't sure he was worth it. Not the way he'd been acting. It was okay for him not to feel the same way about Marcie as she did about him, but it wasn't okay for him to keep sending her mixed signals.

"I know he was your hero, Marcie, but to be honest, he's been acting like an arse since," I said, unable to keep my thoughts to myself any longer.

"No, he hasn't; it's my fault that I can't get over him. He told me right away that he didn't want a relationship," she replied, annoyance evident in her voice.

"It's not Anton's fault that I have a massive crush on him." She sighed, and my heart went out to her.

"You've always had a thing for the military type," I said, trying to lift the mood slightly.

"Hell yeah. Who wouldn't? All that muscle and danger?" She smiled wickedly and winked. "You have to admit, Anton is gorgeous."

"Hmm," I replied. Yes, the guy was good looking, but not my type.

"Oh, I forgot, you prefer the tall, dark, and dangerous type who hides his danger behind a charismatic smile," she said, smirking and wiggling her eyebrows at me.

"Ha, ha." I replied, huffing in annoyance at how true that was despite how much I denied it. The mention of Luca had me scanning the room, unable to stop myself from searching for his presence.

"Looking for the man himself?" Marcie said in my ear, startling me and making me nearly jump out of my skin.

"What? No, I was just taking in the atmosphere," I denied, pursing my lips in displeasure when she grinned knowingly at me.

Turning away from her I continued my perusal of the room, biting back my disappointment at not finding who I was looking for. While I didn't want to be with the guy, I did love to look at him, and I couldn't deny the little thrill of pleasure the thought of seeing him again gave me. Though I'd never admit that to anyone. Especially not him.

Where the hell was he? Why wasn't he here?

A heavy sigh coming from beside me dragged me out of my musings. Glancing at Marcie, I could sense the downward spiral of her own thoughts by the dejected look on her face.

Damn it, this was her night, and I wouldn't have her depressed. It was her time to celebrate, and that is exactly what we'd do, and damn those men. Squeezing her hand I said, "Let's get you another drink and mingle a bit. You're the star of the night!"

We spent the next couple of hours chatting with the other

guests. Soon, it was time for the buffet to open. Marcie gave a quick thank-you speech, managing to avoid slurring too much, which was impressive considering how much she'd drunk. To counter the effects, I made her eat some of the buffet.

Stuffing my face with tasty little pastries, I scanned the room for what must have been the thousandth time, searching for Luca. He still hadn't shown up, and while I should have been over the moon about it—since it made staying away from him easier—I felt sick with disappointment instead.

As my gaze flitted around, searching for him, I noticed Anton's furtive glances our way. I was pretty sure Marcie wasn't oblivious to them, either. Why wasn't he willing to admit his attraction to her? I didn't get it. Marcie didn't have the issues that Luca came with; she was a great catch. He really needed to man up. What was stopping him?

Marcie sighed heavily, and I'd had enough.

"We're off to the loo," I whispered to Gracie, who was deep in conversation with the others. Grabbing Marcie's hand, I dragged her with me.

Once inside the VIP bathroom, I turned to her. "What's going on with you and Anton? Spill!" I wasn't going to interfere, but she clearly needed to talk.

"Obviously, I told Anton how much I liked him not long after we met, and he said he didn't want anything more than friendship. Fine, I accepted that—I really did, Claire. But ever since he kissed me on New Year's Eve, he's been sending mixed signals. I finally plucked up the courage to ask him out again last week, and he rejected me. Then, at Derrick and Nick's engagement dinner the other night, he kissed me again—and it was great. We were both panting when he broke it off, but then he mumbled something about it being a mistake and bolted. He couldn't get out of there fast enough," she said, her voice trembling on the verge of tears.

"Aw, babe, I'm so sorry!" I said, hugging her tight.

"What's wrong with me, Claire? Why doesn't he want me?" Marcie sobbed, and in that moment, I could have throttled Anton with my bare hands.

"Nothing. There is absolutely nothing wrong with you, Marcie. This is all on him. You are a strong, independent, successful woman—a great catch. If he's too blind to see that, then he doesn't deserve you. Now, dry your eyes and fix your makeup. This is your night, and I refuse to let him ruin it for you!" I said firmly.

She sniffled, nodding as she blew her nose before dabbing at her eyes with a tissue.

"Seems we're both doomed to obsess over guys we can't have," I sighed, shifting from foot to foot as my need for relief became urgent.

"Got to pee," I called, darting into the cubicle.

As we touched up our makeup, I turned to her, determined to lift her spirits.

"It's your birthday. Screw those guys and their issues. Let's dance, have some fun, and get absolutely plastered," I said with a wicked grin.

"Hell yeah!" she replied, grinning from ear to ear. "Let's go tear this place up!"

<h1 style="text-align:center">CHAPTER 6</h1>
<h1 style="text-align:center">LUCA</h1>

THE SAME NIGHT – FINALLY ARRIVED

finally got to the party several hours late, and after a brief word with the guys on the door, I headed into the VIP lounge.

"We were beginning to worry about you," Anton said.

"The situation at Platinum took me longer than expected and then I got stuck for a while in traffic," I replied.

"Have you checked in with the guys yet?" he asked.

"Not yet, I'll catch them later," I told him. "How is Suzie handling things?"

"Great. There have been no issues. Are you still planning on opening your own business?"

"Yeah. I've been discussing things with Trent and hopefully we'll be able to launch in a few months," I said, grinning.

"How is Miki taking the fact you won't be around as much to be his errand boy?" he teased.

"Ha, fucking, ha!"

"He's fine about it. I'll still be acting as Head of Entertainments, I'll just be delegating more and promoting some new managers to take over where needed. Got to keep everything in the family. But now things with our enemies have died down, and we've started offloading some of the problem areas of our business, he is more than happy for me to branch out. Besides, if things go dark again, he knows I'll always have his back. Just like you," I replied, and he nodded.

"Where's the birthday girl?" I asked.

Anton pointed over to the table where Marcie and Claire were slurping on cocktails. My heart skipped a beat as I stared, letting my eyes feast on the woman who was the star of all of my fantasies. She was fucking gorgeous! The soft curls of her long blond hair made me want to wrap my fist around them as I slammed my mouth down on hers and ran my other hand over that delectable bum while grinding her against my cock.

"Those two have been knocking them back tonight. Tequila shots and now cocktails. It's a wonder they're still standing," he said with a smirk.

"Headaches all around in the morning then." I chuckled unable to take my eyes off Claire. I gulped and ran shaky fingers through my hair. God, the effect that woman had on me should be illegal. Bloody hell, I needed a drink.

"Yeah, they are both going to have one hell of a hangover. Especially Marcie. You missed her thank you speech and the buffet, but there are still some leftovers at the back of the room, if you want any. And you can leave your gift over there too," Anton said, taking a swig of my beer.

"If you are lucky, maybe Claire will be inebriated enough to let you kiss her," he teased.

"Fuck you. Maybe that's what Marcie needs to do with you then. Get you drunk and you'll finally admit how much you want her!" I taunted in return.

"I'm heading to the bar. I'll grab you a beer while I'm there," I called over my shoulder chuckling as he muttered "Arsehole." One of these days, the guy was going to have to admit that he was as obsessed with Marcie, as I was of Claire.

As I placed the gift bag next to the already large pile of presents on the table, I couldn't help but chuckle at Marcie's birthday cake. It was shaped like a chiselled male torso, with a tight shirt clearly meant to be part of a military uniform—one that revealed a very defined chest, the kind a male stripper might wear.

That was so Marcie. She'd made it no secret that she had a thing for military men. Or ex-military men, and one in particular. My gaze settled on Anton, still standing at the balcony pretending he was watching the dancefloor below and not Marcie. For a man who had been in the Special Forces and was used to subterfuge, he was doing a piss-poor job at hiding it.

He had it bad for her, too. Unfortunately, something had been holding him back. I wasn't sure what. None of us guys could figure it out.

Anton had a troubled past, having grown up with an alcoholic father. His mother had died when he was young, leaving him and his twin sister with their dad who couldn't cope without her. He had taken to drinking, and although he wasn't a mean drunk, he had been neglectful. So, he and his sister Louisa had generally had to fend for themselves and Anton quickly took on the role of her protector.

Just after we had moved to the UK, Anton and Ash met at school and became inseparable. As a result, he and Louisa spent a lot of time hanging out with us at the Rominov estate where we all lived.

We'd seen how hard things were for them and how seriously he took his role and wanted to help. With no other family to help him, we'd created one for him, forming a pact so that he would know we all had his back and would protect him and his sister. Of course, Anton's pride wouldn't have allowed him to accept our help directly. So, Miki and I created the Bratva Blood Brothers with him, Ash, Romi, and Marko. We cut our fingers and merged our blood and formed a pact in which we all pledged to protect each other, our families and especially our sisters.

In that way, whenever Anton or Louisa needed help with anything, we did whatever was required and just said it was our duty as part of the pact.

Unfortunately, it didn't work quite as well as we'd hoped and when he was in his last year of school, Louisa got in with the wrong crowd and became distant. She started seeing an older guy behind our back and he was bad news. Within a few weeks, she had gone missing.

By the time we tracked her down, she was already an addict, living in Manchester and selling herself for her next fix. The asshole had been pimping her out.

We had killed the fucker; he was one of our first kills, and we had brought her home. Miki's dad paid for her to go to rehab. She had been successful, and later ended up going to college to study graphic design. We'd all believed her when she said she was doing fine. But sadly, the lure of heroin was too much and Anton found her in the bathroom of her flat, having taken an overdose.

It hit us all hard, but especially Anton who blamed himself for not knowing she was back on drugs. A couple of weeks after she had died, his dad had passed away, and Anton had joined up.

He had needed to get away from things for a while, he'd said. We would have preferred for him to stick around, but respected his decision and we stayed in touch. Finally, after spending almost nine years in the military, he'd come home and opened his own security firm.

But his time in the military had hardened him, and he rarely smiled these days, except occasionally around Marcie when her bubbly personality wormed its way under his defences and he couldn't pretend he was a robot.

It was obvious to anyone looking that he was smitten with her. Yet, he resisted the pull, saying he didn't want a relationship.

Just like my Claire was with me, I thought ruefully. I knew the reasons Claire was reluctant to take a chance on me, but I couldn't understand why Anton had a problem doing so with Marcie. It was an enigma. I'd tried talking to him about it. All of us guys had, but he just closed up and told us to mind our own business. So, we did.

It saddened me to watch the pair of them pining for each other and yet not coming together. I truly hoped that they would sort it out just as avidly as I hoped that Claire and I would.

Sighing, I shook my head, ridding myself of my gloomy thoughts. I was here to fight for my chance with Claire, and I needed to focus on that.

Turning towards where I'd last seen her, I frowned. She was no longer there. Neither was Marcie.

Damn it. I needed to find her. Grabbing a couple of beers at the bar, I headed back to Anton to find out where my elusive Little Miss Sexy Ass was.

"Here you go," I said, passing him a beer.

"Thanks!" he said, taking a swig.

"Where are the ladies?" I asked, scanning the floor below.

Anton gestured towards them just as Claire glanced up in our direction. She saw us but quickly looked away again. Hell! My sexy lawyer was playing hard to get once more. Not that I'd expected anything different. But watching her deliberately turn her back on me only heightened my resolve.

Eyes narrowing, I silently accepted her challenge. Tonight, Claire was in for a surprise. I was going to break through that wall she'd built between us, smash it to pieces, and hopefully reduce it to dust, so it could never be rebuilt. If it was the last thing I did.

I was still staring at her when Anton tensed beside me.

"Problem?" I asked before noticing what had caught his attention. Two guys were sidling over to Claire and Marcie. They asked them to dance, and the ladies accepted. Oh, hell no!

Leaving my drink, I glanced at Anton and we headed towards the dance floor to get our women.

Within seconds, we'd tapped the guys on the shoulder and gestured for them to leave. One of them went to protest, but I stepped forward and literally growled at the asshole. Eyes narrowed and fists clenched, I waited for him to get the message.

Thankfully, he did, and I didn't have to cut the bastard's hands off for daring to touch my woman. I doubted Claire would have liked that.

My woman! Hmm, I knew that technically she wasn't mine, and I didn't have any right to feel so possessive, but I couldn't help it. In my heart, she was mine, and that was that. She just didn't know it yet, but if my plan worked tonight, she soon would.

I pulled her close.

Her soft curves fit perfectly against me, and I was already getting turned on. I could tell she was a bit tipsy as she looked up at me with that same unguarded expression she'd had the last time I held her. I smiled, then leaned in for the kill.

Should I be taking advantage? Hell no. But was that going to stop me? Again, hell no!

Her lips opened for me, and I delved inside her hot mouth. Our tongues tangled together as we explored each other, and she moaned. The sound had my cock straining against my pants, and I groaned with pleasure.

Claire brushed up against me, clearly as turned on as I was. Yes! I mentally gave myself a high-five. Her response elated me, but it wasn't enough. I wanted more—needed more.

Breaking the kiss, I grabbed her hand and tugged her off the dancefloor, through an employee-only door, and straight into my office before I could even think about what I was doing.

Pushing her up against the wall, I pressed my body close to hers and kissed her again. I loved the feel of her in my arms. It felt like she belonged there, giving me another reason to believe we were meant to be together.

She was so responsive, lost in the moment, and I couldn't help but take things further.

Letting one hand move down and then up under her dress, I pushed her lacy knickers aside and rubbed her clit. The wetness coating my fingers made my cock stiffen. Fuck, she was so wet for me.

Unable to stop myself, I slipped a finger inside her tight pussy, and she moaned into my mouth again. That was all the encouragement I needed to add another, thrusting deep inside, fucking her pussy with my fingers as I fucked her mouth with my tongue.

God, she felt incredible.

I was rock hard, my cock screaming to replace my fingers and bury itself into her until she screamed my name.

I wasn't going to push her that far tonight, however, I *was* going to make her come.

That thought had me thrusting my fingers faster in and out of her tight channel, while I used my thumb to apply pressure to her clit at the same time. She was lost in her passion and her hips moved involuntarily up to meet each thrust. With every kiss and plunge of my fingers, my Ice Queen was beginning to thaw, and the beast that lived inside of me roared in the knowledge that whether or not she wanted it, Claire melted under my touch.

My Little Miss Sexy Ass rocked against me, while I murmured Russian endearments in her ear. I'd never enjoyed anything so much in my life as I did the feel of her in that moment. She was panting hard, her head thrown back against the door, while I nibbled on her neck and continued my assault against that icy wall within.

It wasn't long before I felt her breathing change, and her channel tightened. She gasped and cried out as she came. The sound made my whole body shiver, and I almost followed her with my own release, just barely holding myself back from messing my pants. The only thing that stopped me was the thought that when I came for her, it would be either in her hot, wet mouth or buried deep in that tight, wet pussy. Nothing else would do.

I shifted to look at her, watching the elation on her face as the waves of her orgasm swept through her. My eyes widened as I took in her flushed cheeks, swollen lips, and dilated pupils. I'd never seen a more beautiful or sensual sight.

With one last circle of my thumb, I reluctantly removed my fingers and brought them to her mouth. I smeared some of her juices on her trembling lips, licked the rest from my fingers, then buried my hands in her hair, fisting it like I'd imagined doing earlier, and smashed my mouth against hers.

The sweet-salty flavour of her spreading between us as we kissed made my cock jerk painfully. Still rock-hard, it was desperate for release, but I pushed the sensation away. One day soon, it would get what it wanted. But not today. It was bad enough that I'd taken this much advantage of her when she had drunk so much. I wouldn't take anymore. Giving her pleasure in this state was one thing, taking it was something else entirely. A step too far.

Not that she was so drunk she couldn't say no. I'd never have done anything if that had been the case. But she was enough under the influence that I knew her inhibitions were lowered and while it had allowed me to get this far, that was where I'd need to stop.

But not quite yet.

"Your juices taste great, babe," I murmured, still staring into her eyes and pressing my hips against her. There would be no mistaking how she affected me. I might not be going to press the situation tonight, but I would leave her under no illusion about how much I wanted her.

She didn't push me away. In fact, she didn't do or say anything, just stared at me, her chest heaving against mine as she struggled for breath.

I knew I should back off now, but I couldn't. One last kiss, I told myself before my lips met hers again.

Claire groaned again, and her hands went round my neck. We kissed deeply, and I lifted one of her legs up just enough to allow my cock the pleasure of rubbing against her core.

One hand went into my hair while her other slid between us. Before I knew what she was doing, she had my pants open and her hand on my dick.

I was so hard that her touch was both pain and bliss. A hiss escaped me, my eyes rolling back at the sharp, exquisite pleasure.

She gasped, yanking her hand back like she'd touched a live wire. Her body stiffened as she pressed her palms between us, breaking the kiss.

"Sorry!" she stammered, her cheeks flushed with embarrassment. I guessed she thought she'd hurt me.

"Babe, it's fine," I said, grabbing her arm gently. "I don't need anything from you tonight, Claire. Just giving you pleasure was enough."

But she shook her head and pulled away again. "No, I mean I'm sorry. This is wrong. It can't happen."

Ah, fuck. My blissful high came crashing down, my cock deflating as her words hit like a punch to the gut. I stepped back, putting some distance between us as I bit down on the hurt and disappointment. Still, this was my chance to convince her otherwise, and I wasn't giving up yet.

"Babe, after what we did, you can't deny there is something strong between us. I think we could be great together. We can take it slowly, keep things quiet. Whatever you want. Just give me a chance to prove we belong together."

"We're not right for each other," Claire replied, but I could see the uncertainty in her eyes.

"We could be," I protested.

Taking a step closer again, I held her face in my hands and stared into her eyes so she could see as well as hear the conviction in my next words.

"You know me well enough now to know I'd do anything for you. I haven't been with anyone since you came into my life, and I don't want anyone else. Just you. And as far as being Bratva goes, I'm trying to get out of that life. Please, Claire, give us a shot?" I beseeched.

Tears sprung to her eyes, and she pulled away from me.

"I'm really sorry, Luca!" she cried before rushing out of the room.

My heart hurt as I watched her go. She glanced back just before heading out into the main club, and I didn't miss the regret and confusion in her eyes. I wanted to chase after her, but I refused to force my obviously unwanted attention on her anymore. At least not tonight.

Instead, I stood rooted to the spot, trying desperately to keep a lid on the anger and hurt that crashed through me like a tidal wave.

I'd come into the evening filled with hope, and while I'd finally got past first base—and it had been bloody brilliant—it felt like we'd taken yet another step back. She was still running from us, still in denial, and it was bloody infuriating.

Unable to stand still any longer, I stomped along the staff corridor and out the back exit. There was no way I was going back inside. I couldn't face her again right now, and I wasn't in the mood for small talk or teasing from the guys. They'd see my emotional state and immediately know the reason: Claire. They all knew that any time I lost my cool, it was always because of her. In my current state, if anyone said the wrong thing, I might just kill them.

The best thing I could do for everyone was clear my head, and the best way to do that was to go for a drive. Thankfully, I'd only had a few sips of beer, so a drink-driving charge wasn't on the cards.

My Little Miss Sexy Ass was stubborn, but so was I, and once I set my mind on something, I always got what I wanted. And I wanted Claire. She might have run from me yet again, but at least she'd go to bed tonight with the memory of coming on my tongue, and she couldn't deny the pleasure she'd taken from it. I'd send her flowers tomorrow and start my pursuit in earnest again. Now that I'd had a taste of her and watched her come undone, there was no way I was giving her up. Not for anything.

As I drove through the empty streets, taking the long way home, frustration simmered beneath the surface, but a gnawing dread began to take its place. I couldn't shake the feeling that the night had more in store for me than merely another rejection from Claire. I just hoped I was wrong.

CHAPTER 7
CLAIRE

LATER THAT NIGHT – WHAT HAVE I
DONE?

Tears threatened as I glanced over my shoulder. The raw emotions displayed on Luca's face nearly sent me to my knees. The sight of that strong, powerful, gorgeous male looking at me with a mixture of anger, frustration, and downright desolation in his eyes, made me ashamed.

What the fuck had I done?

How had my vow to keep my distance crumbled so easily the moment he'd wrapped his arms around me?

Back in the main club, I headed for the ladies' room. Thankfully, it wasn't busy, and I hurried into an empty cubicle, locked the door, sat on the seat, and cried.

As Marcie and I danced with those two guys, I'd hoped it would elicit a reaction in Anton. How could I not have realised it would do the same for Luca? Or had I? Perhaps deep down that was what I'd wanted.

Damn it! Why the hell couldn't I leave well enough alone? I wasn't the type of woman to lead men on or play games. Yet, it appeared, subconsciously at least, that's exactly what I had done with Luca. Maybe even been doing since we'd met. God, I felt like such a cow.

All this time I had been promising to keep my distance, telling him we weren't meant to be, yet letting him have a bit more of me each time we got close. Like I was dangling a carrot on a stick, keeping him interested just enough to bolster my ego, when I had no intention of following through on the subtle promises my actions hinted at.

Shock and shame coursed through me. Was that really the type of woman I was?

I shook my head. No. I didn't play with people's hearts. I'd simply made mistakes due to the effect he had on me. That pull was undeniable. He was right about that. There was definitely something strong between us. But if I wasn't willing to overlook his criminal connections, then I had to do better. He deserved better.

This had to be the end of it. After tonight, there could be no more mistakes. So why did that thought make me cry harder?

Big, fat, ugly tears ran down my face, and I sobbed. My mind was in turmoil. I was supposed to be focusing on my career, yet here I was hiding out in a toilet crying over a man I kept insisting I didn't want.

Even as I thought that, my body protested—my nipples hardening and my core clenching as I remembered the feel of his hands and lips on me.

Would it really be so bad to give Luca a chance? Why did the thought of continuing to deny what we had feel like I was making yet another mistake? Perhaps the biggest one of my life.

Covering my mouth with my fist, I bit back the scream of frustration that threatened. I was so confused.

Grabbing some toilet paper, I dabbed my eyes and blew

my nose. Sitting here crying wasn't helping me. Sorting through my feelings when I was drunk really wasn't the answer. I'd need to make a decision about Luca, once and for all. But not tonight.

After splashing my face with water, I reapplied my makeup. This was Marcie's party and the last I'd saw her she was dancing with the man of her dreams. I wondered how that had worked out? Had she finally got that kiss she'd coveted for so long? Or had he done a better job at keeping his distance than me? It was time I found out. She'd either be having the time of her life in Anton's arms, or crying her eyes out in a corner.

As Marcie's best friend, it was my job to make sure she was okay, and I wasn't doing a very good job of it. Pushing aside all thoughts of my shameful actions with Luca, I pulled up my big girl panties and headed out in search of my friend.

It didn't take me long to find her. She was dancing on top of the table where we'd been sitting earlier under the watchful eye of Anton. It was impossible to tell what had happened between them on the dance floor, but he hadn't run at least.

Gracie, Sonia, and Eilidh were sitting, chatting around the table next to the one Marcie was using as a dance floor. They'd lasted longer than I'd expected. With them all being pregnant, I had thought they'd have gone home by now.

Gracie waved at me and I gave her a little wave back before grabbing a drink and heading her way. As I approached, I couldn't help but notice how happy they all looked. Happy and pregnant. They were each partnered with a Rominov. I guessed the Rominov boys had strong little swimmers. I sniggered as I found myself wondering if the Orlovs did, too.

Don't go there! I told myself firmly. Nevertheless, my

eyes drifted to each of their bellies and a warm glow travelled through me.

I was standing beside, Melissa, watching Marcie's table dancing antics when her fiancé, Marko Rominov, headed our way. As he whispered in her ear, I slipped away.

Eilidh got up on the table with Marcie and Miki appeared within seconds behind her, no doubt trying to ensure she didn't fall in the same way Anton was doing for Marcie. I wondered if Luca would do the same for me? Shit, I needed to stop thinking like that.

"Claire, get up here," Marcie slurred when she finally noticed me.

Her enormous grin lifted my mood, and I scrambled up to dance beside her. I laughed hard when she pretended to use me as a pole, shimmering up and down me and pursing her lips as she sent what she probably thought were flirtatious glances at Anton, which in fact just looked ridiculous in her drunken state. Oh my, I was going to be hung over tomorrow, but Marcie was in for the hangover from hell.

God, I was being such a shitty friend. I should really get us both some water. I climbed down unsteadily and headed to the bar. As I gulped my mineral water, I held up a bottle to Marcie.

But she wasn't having any of it. She shook her head, and the motion made her fly backwards. Shit, I took an automatic step forward even though I wasn't in a position to catch her. Luckily, Anton was.

"I think that's enough dancing on tables for you, birthday girl," he told her before sitting her down. I gave him the bottle of water as he sat down beside her and he held it up to her mouth.

For a guy who said he wasn't interested in her, his actions and body language certainly suggested otherwise.

Just like me with Luca. I sighed and closed my eyes, feeling suddenly exhausted.

Unfortunately, Marcie was way beyond the stage where water was of any good. A few sips, had her retching and vomiting all over herself. Oh no, that was so bad!

"I'll take her home," Anton announced. I was about to insist I take her instead, but she passed out and he lifted her into his arms, uncaring that she was covered in sick. He looked at me and I nodded, fighting back a grin when Marcie started to snore.

Anton looked down at her and smiled, and the look on his face made my heart clench. It was such an "aw" moment. Marcie let out a louder snort and Anton chuckled before grabbing her bag and carrying her out, bridal style. I grinned as I watched them leave. The guy could protest his feelings all he wanted to, but there was no denying that he had it bad.

She was going to be so embarrassed in the morning. Or probably tomorrow night, after her hangover started to subside enough to let her feel anything other than its effects. Effects I was already starting to feel myself.

I wasn't worried about Anton taking her home. In fact, I thought it might be the best result of the night. I knew that not only would he take good care of her, but it might even make him drop his guard a little. Maybe even enough to admit to his feelings. I certainly hoped so.

After they left, everyone else began to get ready to leave, too. Derrick, Marcie's assistant and our good friend, came over with his boyfriend Nicholas and offered me a lift. Nicholas was one of Anton's men and hadn't been drinking as he was working in the morning. I gladly accepted, and we packed up Marcie's gifts so we could get them to her tomorrow.

I was just saying goodbye to the women and Miki when Trigger ran over to us.

"Luca's been arrested!" And suddenly, I was completely sober.

CHAPTER 8
LUCA
STILL THE SAME NIGHT – ARRESTED!

I opened the door and stepped inside, thinking about a quick shower, seeing to my unruly appendage, which was back at full mast after my thoughts during the drive home. My mind inevitably returned, again and again, to Claire and what we'd done in my office—then the bed.

As I entered my bedroom, I stopped dead. *What the fuck?!*

Unable to believe the sight before me, I shook my head in denial. There was blood all over my bed and a naked woman lying spread-eagled, tied to it.

Her hair was over her face, but I recognised the tattoo on her hip. It was Julie. My ex! *Oh shit!*

Shock washed over me. Without thinking, I rushed to the bed to check if she was dead. As I reached her side, I slipped on something and fell forward, barely catching myself before landing on top of her. *Jesus!*

Pushing aside her hair to check for a pulse, I grimaced at the sight of her throat. There was no doubt—she was dead. Now I had blood on my hands and up my arms.

Fuck, fuck, fuck!! What the hell was I thinking? I knew better than this!

I was panicking. *I never panicked.* Tonight's situation with Claire had messed me up more than I'd realised. This was bad. *Really fucking bad!*

It took me a minute, but the shock finally subsided enough for me to pull out my phone. Normally, I'd call Miki first, but since he was likely still at the party and might not pick up, I called Trigger, knowing he was working tonight.

Just as I waited for him to pick up, someone pounded on the door. *Aw, shit!*

"Police! Open up!" a voice shouted.

I froze. Grabbing my phone, I dialled Trigger's number again.

"Luca, what the fuck are police cars doing in front of your building?" he asked as soon as he picked up.

"It's Julie—my ex. She's dead on my fucking bed. Murdered. Tell Miki, I'm about to be arrested," I said frantically, hurrying to the door.

"Police! Open the door!" the voice shouted again.

"Coming!" I called and rushed to open it.

As soon as I did, several officers barged in. They took in my appearance and the bloody trail of footprints I'd made from the bedroom. Two officers grabbed me while another followed the trail.

"Aw, shit!" he muttered, gingerly retracing his steps as he tried not to contaminate the crime scene further.

"We've got a dead woman, tied to the bed, throat cut," he said, his voice holding a thinly veiled thread of disgust.

"You're under arrest," one of the officers holding me said as he cuffed my hands behind my back and led me out to the awaiting police car.

Fuck, I'm in so much trouble!

CHAPTER 9
CLAIRE
EVEN LATER THAT NIGHT – TAKING LUCA'S CASE

"Everyone, wait here!" Miki ordered, before he and a few of the guys disappeared through an employee-only door with Trigger. Privacy, I assumed, while they figured out what the hell was going on.

My stomach churned. What had Luca done? I had no idea, but I prayed it wasn't something serious. As I glanced around at the shock and concern etched on everyone's faces, I felt bad for them—but I couldn't help but be relieved I wasn't involved in whatever this was.

No one was talking, no one speculating out loud. That was how I knew most of the people here were criminals. Normally, there would be gossip, wild guesses flying around about what the man himself had done. But instead, we just stood there, waiting for Miki to return and either explain or dismiss us.

After what felt like forever, Miki came back with Ash and motioned for me to join them in a quiet corner.

"Claire, I know you don't want any involvement in the family's criminal activities, and I respect that," he began. "But our lawyer had a heart attack a few nights ago. He's still recovering. You know he's elderly, and I've been trying to find a replacement, but so far, no luck. Could you help with this? Just for now?"

Shit. This was exactly what I'd been trying to avoid—the very reason I wouldn't get involved with Luca. The conflict of interest, the risk to my reputation if I ever had to defend him for something illegal. I glanced at the crowd of faces around us and felt a wave of nausea.

"I'm sorry, but I don't think that's a good idea," I stated firmly.

As much as I liked them all—especially Luca—I couldn't get sucked into the Bratva's world. A few months ago, Miki had approached me with an offer. He'd told me his lawyer was retiring, and he needed someone to head up the legal practice, handling both corporate and criminal law. He'd wanted me to be that person.

The idea of running my own firm had been tempting. If it had been a legitimate operation, I would've said yes in a heartbeat. But the reality was, it wouldn't be. Right or wrong, I still believed in the black-and-white nature of the law. Either you did things above board or you didn't. I couldn't straddle both sides.

Lately, several lawyers and police officers had been exposed as corrupt. Even a government MP, one of the Rominovs' enemies, according to Marcie, had been caught. But surely they were a minority? I still believed that the UK legal system was among the best in the world, thanks not only to its laws, but to the people who upheld them. I wasn't going to let myself fall into corruption. I'd vowed that to myself, and that hadn't changed.

"Please?" Miki persisted. "I really appreciate it. Just until we find someone else?"

I shook my head, but he cut in again.

"This isn't Bratva business. I know you don't want to be involved in that, and I'm not trying to rope you into it. This is about Luca. He's been arrested for murder. He's innocent. He needs a good defence lawyer, and you're one of the best. I know you don't want a relationship with him, but if you care about him at all—help him."

My heart clenched at the concern in his eyes.

"Innocent?" I whispered.

"Yes," he replied.

"How do you know?" My voice was barely audible.

"Because the victim was a woman. She was killed in his flat. There's no way Luca would do something like that."

His conviction was unwavering, and I found myself pausing.

"Please, Claire," Gracie chimed in, giving me her classic puppy-dog eyes, hands clasped in a pleading gesture. She always did this when she wanted something from me. I sighed, knowing I couldn't say no to her.

"Alright," I conceded. "But I'm only stepping in until your lawyer is back on his feet, or you find someone else. That's it."

"I appreciate it!" he said, nodding in agreement.

Miki nodded, gratitude clear in his expression. "Thank you."

We made our way to the police station where Luca was being held. Along the way, Miki filled me in on what they knew so far.

It was even worse than we'd thought—rape and murder. My breath hitched. No… No way!

Surely he hadn't?

As soon as the question crossed my mind, I dismissed it. Of course not. Luca might be many things, but he wasn't a rapist, and he'd never hurt a woman. I was sure of that.

Despite everything, Luca and his Bratva Blood Brothers had high morals when it came to women. They believed women were to be loved and protected. I knew that much from Ash, who'd reassured me when Gracie started seeing him. Gracie had also told me about Krissa, the Rominovs' oldest sister. She'd been raped and murdered a couple of years ago. It had devastated the family. I couldn't imagine any of them doing something similar to another woman after what they'd been through.

So, despite my initial reluctance, I resolved to help. Not just for Luca, or the Rominovs, or even Gracie—but for the woman who'd been murdered. She deserved justice. And justice meant finding the actual killer, which started by not letting an innocent man take the fall.

Besides, no matter my earlier protests, deep down, I knew I could never leave Luca to face this alone. I just hoped I wouldn't regret it.

CHAPTER 10

LUCA

EARLY HOURS THE NEXT MORNING –
CHARGED WITH MURDER

After arriving at the station, the cops processed me before shoving me into an interview room. Detectives Rollo and Williamson tried to pry information out of me, but I knew the game too well to fall for that. I may never have been arrested before, but we'd all been schooled in exactly how to handle such situations just in case. Every question they threw at me got the same response: "No comment." I requested a lawyer, and after about half an hour of circling the same empty routine, they finally gave up. I was led to a holding cell, and left to sit and wait in this tiny, windowless box.

By now, Miki would know about my situation. Trigger had received my text just as the police were at my door, and I knew he'd wasted no time alerting the others. So, it was just a matter of time until a lawyer arrived, and I'd have to run through the interrogation again—this time with legal backup. If they charged me after that, I'd be taken to court on Monday and have to apply for bail.

Would it get that far?

I sighed. Yes, I'd no doubt it would.

The reality of it made my skin itch. I shifted on the hard bench, my shoulders tense, and rolled my neck to work out some of the stiffness. Someone had framed me. The dead woman lying in my flat, my ex Julie, was nothing more than a pawn in someone's twisted game. My gut told me it was the MP—he'd found out who I was. We had anticipated the possibility, but apparently we'd underestimated just how badly he wanted revenge. The MP was already buried under a mountain of charges; we assumed he'd be too busy wriggling out of those to bother coming after us.

We had been wrong.

A man like him couldn't be taken lightly. Desperation makes people dangerous, but this guy? He was something worse—a full-blown psychopath. Maybe a sociopath. I wasn't sure which, but either way, the result was the same: he was capable of anything. And now, he'd had me arrested for murder.

The dull hum of distant voices and clanking doors were my only company. This boredom was unbearable. I really didn't relish the prospect of being stuck here much longer. Worse was the idea of going to jail. Danger? That I could handle. No doubt I'd thrive in it, like always. But the thought of losing my freedom? That crawled under my skin in a way nothing else could. The confinement would be a special kind of hell.

I was the Head of Entertainment for the Rominov's for a reason. People were my world. The buzz, the pulse of life around me, were like my life's blood. Miki always said charm was my superpower. He was right. Making people do what I wanted came easily. There was nobody I couldn't charm. Well, except Claire. My Little Miss Sexy Ass. She was a special case. Stubborn as hell—and I loved her for it.

Loved her?

Those two words made my heart stutter, panic filled me and a cold sweat prickled across my skin. I dragged my hand down my face. If anyone was watching, they'd think I was starting to crack under the pressure of a murder charge. But this panic had nothing to do with that. It was Claire—my feelings for her ran deeper than I'd even realised, and that left me shaken.

What the hell was I going to do? The weight of everything pressed in on me, harder with each breath. Claire hadn't wanted me because of my ties to the Bratva. What would she think now? A murder charge, involving a woman I'd once been with—it was a disaster. This would remind her of my past, my reputation as a player. One more nail in the coffin of whatever I'd hoped we could have. After this, she'd be even less inclined to open her heart to me. And I didn't think even my Plan B would change that.

Devastation threatened to overwhelm me. My heart had recognised Claire as mine from the moment we met; I just hadn't realised it had given itself fully to her at the same time. I'd known her rejection would cut deep and my heart would hurt if I failed to win her. But I'd expected it would heal with time, along with my battered self-esteem. Now, I wasn't sure how the hell I was going to cope with losing her. Something, I'd never truly believed was an option until now.

Leaning forward, I braced my elbows on my knees and buried my head in my hands. My fingers curled into my hair as I fought the urge to scream, to lash out at something—anything. But there was nothing in the cell to vent my frustration on, and even if there was, it would only give the cops the satisfaction of thinking they were getting to me.

With nothing to do and trying desperately not to succumb to my worries about Claire, I turned my focus onto the reason I was here. Julie Wilson was only ever supposed to be a one-night stand. Yet the woman had pursued me relentlessly. Grief-stricken over the loss of Miki's older sister, Krissa, and in need of comfort and distraction, I found myself letting it become something more. I'd known Julie was troubled, but I'd foolishly believed I could help her. Losing Krissa had hit all of us Bratva Blood Brothers hard, just as losing Anton's sister, had all those years before.

Each of us suffered from feelings of guilt at our failure to protect and save her, and we all dealt with it differently. My way was to try to help Julie. Of course, I hadn't known the extent of her troubles then or just how highly strung she was. Julie was a highly functioning heroin addict with several mental health challenges. By the time I realised that she needed more help than I could possibly give, she'd become obsessed with me.

When I tried to end our short relationship, she became difficult, taking to stalking me and my staff, turning up wherever she thought I'd be, begging for cash to fund her habit or for me to take her back, and threatening to kill herself if she didn't get her way. Eventually, Miki and I had forced her to go to rehab. I'd used money from one of our shell companies to pay for it so people didn't know of my involvement, and then I'd cut ties. That was about eighteen months ago, and I hadn't seen or spoken to her personally since.

She'd been at the clinic for almost a year, and between coming off the heroin, getting her mental health assessed, and taking properly prescribed medication, she'd been well on the road to recovery. After she'd been discharged, Miki had kept tabs on her and ensured that she found work with a temporary employment agency, and the last we'd heard she was doing great and had obtained full-time employment as a secretary with a small law firm.

So, how the hell did she end up dead in my bed?

Sighing heavily, I stretched out on the hard bench of the holding cell and closed my eyes, trying to ease the stress headache that was starting to build. As soon as my eyes shut, images of Julie's blood-drenched body assaulted my mind, and I felt sick. I couldn't believe what had happened, and that I was being charged with doing such a horrible thing. It pained me that any woman should be hurt like that, but I couldn't help wondering, why her? I'd been with quite a few women between breaking up with her and meeting Claire. So why had she been chosen as the victim? And how did they even know about her connection to me in the first place? I rubbed between my eyes; there were so many questions and no answers.

I'd need to think through things logically. I might be innocent of Julie's murder, but I needed to prove it. The law might say, 'innocent until proven guilty,' but I still had to be able to deny these allegations with more than just words.

Just as I was thinking of that, I heard footsteps approaching, and a second later my cell door was opened.

"Lawyer's here!" the gruff duty sergeant stated.

Glad of the chance to get out of this box, I jumped up and followed him into a small interview room.

I stepped through the door and stopped. It was Claire.

My excitement at seeing her so soon was overshadowed by the gravity of the situation, yet my heart sped up at the sight of her. The pinched, annoyed expression she wore while scanning the charge sheet made me want to kiss it right off her face. The thought of her relaxing against me, making those adorable little moaning sounds she always did when we kissed, sent a thrill through me.

Fuck, I had it bad!

My cock hardened as illicit thoughts raced through my

mind. *Not the time!* I reminded myself. I needed to rein it in; this was hardly the moment to get worked up. Considering the serious charges against me, sporting a hard-on in for my sexy lawyer would definitely give the detectives more ammunition to use against me. Not to mention the whole morality of the situation. Getting turned on by Claire at a time like this, no matter how gorgeous she was, was highly inappropriate, definitely wouldn't impress her, and on top of that, was just all kinds of wrong!

My internal monologue seemed to work, and the strain against my pants lessened. Thank fuck!

When the sergeant closed the door behind him, Claire turned and smiled at me, and just like that, the strain returned.

"How you holding up?" she asked.

I gritted my teeth against the pulsing below and forced myself to conjure the image of poor Julie to tame the beast again before answering.

"I'm okay, but feeling sick to my stomach about what happened to Julie," I confessed, my voice laced with sincerity. "I didn't do this, Claire, I swear!" The urgency of my words hung in the air; I needed her to believe me. She knew I was a criminal, and she'd know that meant I had done some bad things in my life, but the thought of her believing I could harm a woman cut deep.

Her nod of understanding brought me relief. "I know, Luca. However, we need to get you out of here, and then we need to figure out who did this. Someone is obviously setting you up," she replied, her determination shining through.

"I agree!" I nodded, feeling a flicker of hope at her conviction. She smiled, a light breaking through the darkness of the situation.

"This is going to be a long night," she said, her brow

furrowing slightly, grim determination flickering behind her gaze.

Several hours later, I had officially been charged with the rape and murder of Julie Wilson, and we found ourselves back in the interview room.

"Well, at least that part is over. I'll meet you at court on Monday afternoon for the bail hearing," Claire said as she prepared to leave.

"Thanks, Claire. I really appreciate this," I replied, my insides knotting as she looked back at me, her tired nod resonating with unspoken worries.

Watching her leave, I braced myself for the return to the cell. Hours stretched ahead, filled with the unsettling silence and the gnawing worry about what was going to happen.

CHAPTER 11
CLAIRE

OVER THE WEEKEND –PREPARING FOR THE BAIL HEARING

Exhaustion loomed heavy, my eyes were sore and dry, my mouth stale. God only knew what my breath smelled like. I'd been here for hours, and the few cups of coffee I'd had to counter the effects of the alcohol at Marcie's party had long worn off.

"Well, at least that part is over. I'll meet you at court on Monday afternoon for the bail hearing," I said, stuffing my notepad in my bag and trying to mask the weariness in my voice.

"Thanks, Claire. I really appreciate this," Luca replied.

I nodded, unsure how else to respond. I'd agreed to help, and I believed in Luca's innocence. But still… being dragged into this mess was exactly what I'd been trying to avoid. The gnawing frustration crept back as I thought about it. I hadn't wanted to do this, yet here I was.

My head throbbed with the familiar warning of a hangover. I needed water—gallons of it—some painkillers, and sleep. Lots of sleep. Especially since I had another bail hearing before Luca's on Monday and had to prepare for both. As I walked away from the interview room, I couldn't ignore the feeling of Luca's eyes on me. The intensity of his gaze lingered, burning into my back as he was led in the opposite direction, back to his holding cell.

I hated the idea of him locked up all weekend. Trapped in that cold, sterile cell. But there was nothing I could do—not until Monday. The only small comfort I had was that I would get him out then.

As I rounded the corner, Miki and Vlad were waiting for me in the reception. A flicker of warmth eased through me at the sight of Miki. He hadn't needed to stay, but he had. Concern etched into the lines of his face, and it was clear he wanted to know how Luca was holding up. His worry for Luca was palpable—both a best friend and a boss.

"You look exhausted," he said.

"I am," I replied, stifling a yawn.

Vlad handed me a bottle of water and I smirked when he very nearly forgot himself and smiled as I thanked him. Vlad always seemed very serious, but I'd caught a sparkle in his eye now and then and figured, deep down, the man was hiding a soft heart under a serious façade. A bit like me.

"He's been charged, I take it?" Miki asked.

I nodded, taking a long swig of water.

"We'll talk in the car," Miki said, glancing towards the cluster of officers behind the desk.

In the SUV, the silence hung heavy between us until we pulled away from the station.

"So, how's he doing?" Miki asked, turning his head towards me.

"Okay, bored and upset about Julie, but holding up," I replied, resting my head back.

Miki nodded, his jaw tight. "And the charges? How bad is it?"

I sighed, rubbing my temples to ward off the impending

headache. "Honestly? On the face of it, it looks bad. His ex, a woman obsessed with him, found dead in his bed? Spread-eagled, needle in her arm, throat slit? The police find him covered in blood? It's a hell of a picture to paint."

A beat of silence passed between us before I added, "But we know he's innocent. We'll figure this out. Right now, we need to focus on getting him out on bail. Once we have a proper time of death and the autopsy report, we can work on establishing his alibi. One step at a time."

Miki exhaled slowly, the tension easing just a little. "I know what happened between you two, Vlad told me. I don't know what's going on with you both, but thanks for helping us out."

"There is nothing between us," I told him a bit too sharply. He raised an eyebrow, obviously not fooled. "But like I said, I'm happy to help until you can arrange someone else."

"I'll see you at court on Monday then," he said when we pulled up outside my place.

"Yeah, I'll prep over the weekend. See you then," I replied. As I opened my door, I turned and gave him a little wave before I went inside.

Dropping the files on my bedside table, I chugged more water and swallowed some painkillers. The exhaustion finally overtook me as I changed into my pyjamas and crawled into bed.

I closed my eyes, pushing thoughts of Luca, court, and work aside. Tomorrow would be another day to deal with the chaos. Tonight? Tonight, I just needed sleep.

———

I slept well into Saturday evening, the remnants of last night's drinks weighing heavily on my body. Ordering a greasy, cheesy pizza was my attempt at damage control, followed by a glass of red wine—because 'the hair of the dog' was always my go-to fix.

As I chewed through several slices, I tried to shake off the guilt that hung over me, matching my hangover. I re-read the charge sheet, then scrolled through the emails. As expected, the police report was there, a grim summary of everything collected so far—evidence that didn't do Luca any favours.

But it wasn't until Sunday morning that my head cleared enough to focus. Feeling guilty for wasting the previous day, I woke early, opened my laptop, and started making notes. Even though I wouldn't be handling Luca's defence beyond the bail hearing, I couldn't just leave things half-done. Anything I pulled together now might help whoever took over, be it Miki's lawyer or someone else. They needed to hit the ground running.

Julie Wilson—the woman at the centre of this nightmare —had been a part of Luca's life briefly, more than a year ago. He'd told me about her issues, her stint in rehab. Miki had kept tabs on her afterward. She'd landed a job, seemed to be doing well. So why was she found dead with a needle in her arm?

Was she back on heroin? Or was this part of a setup? Why inject her? Why the needle at all? Had she willingly gone to Luca's apartment, or had someone else brought her there? Too many questions, none of them easy to answer.

The autopsy hadn't been done yet. These things took time. Still, the preliminary report put Julie's death somewhere between ten and midnight. Oddly enough, that was exactly when the police had shown up at Luca's, after receiving a report of a disturbance.

Luca said he'd arrived at the party around nine-thirty. He left forty minutes later, just after I had stormed out. He went for a drive, then headed home—just in time to find her body and have the police barge in behind him. And just like that, he didn't have an alibi.

It was likely my fault. He hadn't said it, but I knew the truth. He'd left the party because of me, to clear his head after I'd rejected him. If I hadn't run off, would things be different? Would he have stayed at the party, in plain sight, with an alibi? I could've been his alibi.

The guilt crept into my chest, tightening like a vice. The guilt crept into my chest, tightening like a vice. I set my pen down, rubbing my temples as a wave of nausea hit me. My rejection had led to this, hadn't it? God, I was a cow.

Stop it, Claire. This wasn't helping. Luca driving around didn't automatically damn him. If we could pinpoint the time of death, then maybe we could find an angle, some way to account for his time. Failing that, he would need to go to trial, and proving his innocence would be much harder.

Right then, I vowed to help. I couldn't handle his defence personally beyond Monday, though, because doing so would create a conflict of interest, considering I was part of the reason he'd been driving around in the first place.

We hadn't known that, of course, when Miki had asked me to represent Luca and I'd only ever promised to represent him for the initial stages. But I couldn't step aside completely now. I'd assist the lawyer in charge of his case, whoever they were, and together we'd clear his name.

First things first, there was a bail hearing to get through—routine, simple. So why was my gut twisting like it knew better?

CHAPTER 12
LUCA

MONDAY AFTERNOON – THE BAIL
HEARING

oredom was gnawing at me. With nothing to do but think, I leaned my head back against the cold wall of the holding cell, fighting the pull of exhaustion. Every time I closed my eyes, Julie's lifeless body flashed before me—her bruised skin, the way she'd been discarded like trash. The rage hit me in waves, tightening my chest. My fists clenched as I fought the urge to scream. It was impossible to think of her final moments without wanting to tear apart the bastard responsible.

But I needed to push that anger down. I had to focus.

My mind went back to the moment I found her. There had to be something I'd missed. The police were building a case, and I needed something solid to fight back. The scene played over and over in my mind. Her clothes had been stripped, her body laid out, no blood on the floor. But I'd slipped—on what? It wasn't blood. Whatever it was could be important, and yet, it slipped away from me like smoke. Why couldn't I remember?

Julie's murder reeked of the MP's revenge. It had to be him. The timing was too perfect. But who had he sent to do his dirty work? Who had called the police, conveniently ensuring they'd show up just minutes after I found her? And how had they known I'd returned to my flat that night? I'd gone dark after the MP's arrest, staying off the radar at the Rominov estate. I'd only just returned to my flat the night before. Who knew I was back?

Could we have another traitor? No, I didn't think so. So, who else would have known I was back home?

The thought burned through me. Someone had been watching, waiting. They knew I'd be at the party and come back to the flat after. My mind went to building security. Most of the guards had been there for a long time and the company they worked for prided itself on their professionalism and discretion. It's one of the reasons I bought a flat in this building. In my line of business, and with the amount of women I'd had coming in and out over the years, such concerns were a necessity.

It helped that I was generous and tipped frequently to ensure things remained that way. However, there was one guy who was fairly new. He'd arrived not long before I went in as the MP's bodyguard. I hadn't checked him out the way I normally would and hadn't gained his loyalty yet. A mistake that had likely cost Julie her life.

Thinking about it, he wasn't even at his post when I got home. Conveniently on a break, or so the police report said, just before the police arrived. And then there was the security footage—wiped out by a sudden system failure. Another coincidence? Too many things lined up too perfectly.

I'd make sure Claire and Miki were looking into the guard, the company, all of it. Marko was likely already on it, but I'd be damned if I didn't double-check. This wasn't just about clearing my name. It was about getting justice for Julie.

But for now, I had to sit here, helpless. The hours

dragged on, each second adding to the knot of anxiety in my gut. I needed to be doing something, not pacing in a cell, waiting for a system that wasn't designed to favour men like me.

Finally, the door opened, and they came for me, the heavy silence shattered. As I was led upstairs, my wrists cuffed to the officer beside me, I scanned the room. Claire was there, waiting. Seeing her steadied me, even if just for a moment. She hurried toward me as soon as our eyes met.

"Sorry I couldn't get in to see you, but I can't foresee any issue with bail, so we can talk things over after you're out," Claire said just before a voice shouted, "All rise!"

Everyone stood as the judge entered.

I had attended court before, watching members of the brotherhood face charges, but this time, I was the accused. It was a new experience—and one I didn't like at all.

An overwhelming sense of dread washed over me. I was right to feel that way. Less than ten minutes later, I was being escorted back down to the cells, awaiting transport to jail. I hadn't got bail! Despite Claire's protests about my clean record, the judge remanded me into custody.

Miki shouted, "We'll get this sorted!" as I was taken down the stairs.

Claire met me in the interview room a few minutes later. "God, Luca, I can't believe you got remanded. I've never failed to get a client out on bail before with no prior convictions. I don't understand how they can justify this when that fucking MP is out on bail, accused of numerous crimes!" She shook her head in disbelief.

"It is strange, but I guess someone wanted me locked up," I told her grimly.

She started pacing, biting her bottom lip. "I didn't want you to go to jail. You've been deliberately set up, and now this! It's obvious someone is out to get you—likely that MP. But why jail you? Why not just kill you?"

"You know about him?" I asked her, wondering how.

She gave a slight grimace. "Marcie told me about it. And just for the record, I don't condone you guys dragging my friend into your family business. But she's a big girl I guess. Anyway, she told me what was going on. Although, it was only after talking to Miki that I discovered where you've been all of these weeks." She glared at me and I smirked.

"Did you miss me, babe?" I waggled my eyebrows at her and grinned.

"No, not in the least," she stated, huffing and mumbling something like, "infuriating man," under her breath.

I laughed. "I think you protest too much."

"And I think you should be taking this more seriously," she huffed again.

Her pacing stopped, and she faced me, anxiety flashing in her eyes. "What is even the point in setting you up like this?"

"Probably for some warped sense of revenge. After his arrest, I lived at the Estate, ramping up security. When I went out, I was surrounded by people, making it hard to reach me. Friday was the first day I went anywhere alone and the first time I returned to my flat. I guess someone had been following me, waiting for the right moment to strike. And without an alibi for the time of death, it was easy for them to pin this on me."

"I'm sorry, Luca. If I hadn't run out on you at the party, you might not be dealing with this right now, and that poor woman might still be alive!" She looked distraught.

Fuck, I hadn't meant for her to blame herself.

"It's not your fault, babe," I said, pulling her into my arms. "The people responsible are the MP and whoever he got to carry out his plan," I murmured against the top of her head as I hugged her tightly.

"I don't want you to go to jail, Luca. I'm scared something will happen to you!" She tilted her head up at me, and I wanted to kiss her then, but I held back, unwilling to take advantage of the situation. I wanted Claire to want me for me, not out of guilt.

"Don't worry about it, Claire. I'll be fine," I said, smiling reassuringly.

She nodded, taking a deep breath before stepping back. I tried to ignore the feeling of loss that accompanied her withdrawal and focused on her next words.

"This case has so many holes in it. I'll help your lawyer, and together we'll get you out at the pre-trial hearing," she said, her confidence palpable.

"I know you will, Claire. You're a great lawyer, I'm sure you'll blow the case wide open." I smiled at her, grateful for her support and secretly thrilled at the prospect of spending more time with her, regardless of the circumstances.

I was in the worst position of my life, feeling guilt for Julie's death. I shouldn't have felt happy about spending time with Claire, but I couldn't help it. The desire I had for her overshadowed everything else.

The interview room door opened, and a police officer walked in. "Time to go!"

As they cuffed me and led me away, I glanced back just in time to catch a glimpse of Claire sashaying down the corridor in the opposite direction. I had maybe a second to enjoy the view before they pulled me out the door and shoved me into the waiting prison van.

Jail didn't bother me—I'd survived worse. What gnawed at me was being denied bail when everyone expected otherwise. For three judges to vote against it, at least two had to have been threatened or bought off. Despite the gravity of the charges, I was a first-time offender and not considered a flight risk. Bail should have been a given.

I'd been set up—that much was clear. But I thought the trial itself would've satisfied the MP's thirst for vengeance. If he just wanted me dead, he could've had his man waiting at the flat, ready to end it there. Blocking my bail was something else. A message. A reminder of his reach, of the power he still wielded. He wanted us to know he was pulling the strings—he could get to us anytime, anyway. The MP wasn't just after blood. He wanted us to suffer first.

Maybe it was also about keeping the remnants of the Broxys and Malia Boys loyal to him. Most of them had survived because they were already locked up during the attacks. And they'd love nothing more than to take out one of their enemies—me.

Whatever his agenda, one thing was clear: I'd have to watch my back. Jail was always dangerous for Bratva. But now? Now it was a death sentence.

And I'd just walked right into it.

CHAPTER 13
CLAIRE

My heart pounded, and every step away from Luca was a test of sheer willpower. My jaw ached from biting the inside of my cheek, holding back the scream threatening to break free as I watched him being led to jail. I'd failed him.

I had barely made it to the courtroom in time, rushing from another case, my chest tight with panic until I saw him. Relief washed over me the second he appeared, composed in a sharp suit, even after a weekend in that god-awful holding cell. Miki must have arranged it—his own clothes had been taken, blood-soaked evidence. Seeing him, looking so unaffected, standing so strong and handsome, made my knees weak. All weekend, I had done nothing but think about him, worry about him.

Everything had gone as expected. Until it hadn't.

Bail denied.

Shock hit like a punch to the gut. It was beyond outrageous. My client was made an example of, sacrificed to appease the media's obsession with serious offences and bail. These were the same three judges who had granted the MP bail, a man with an extensive list of charges—assault, kidnapping, murder, and a ton of evidence against him. And yet, they remanded Luca, a man with no criminal record, charged with a single count of rape and murder, on circumstantial evidence. Un-fucking-believable.

I could hardly wrap my head around it. These judges had either caved to the media storm as they said, or they were corrupt. Either way, my belief in the justice system had taken another hit. There were too many people meant to uphold the law who were proving to be corrupt—at least half of them worse than the so-called criminals I'd dealt with so far. It was getting harder to believe in what I once held so highly.

As I walked towards the exit, anger and shame coursed through me. I'd never failed to get a client bail before, and I sure as heck didn't want to break my record with Luca—a man I cared for more than I should.

Guilt threatened to take me to my knees. This was my fault! He'd gone home to his flat because of my rejection, leaving him with no alibi when I couldn't resist his allure but refused to commit.

When I spoke with him just now, I'd found it hard to contain my worry. The prospect of him being in jail was terrifying. I knew the kind of things that could happen in prison.

My stomach clenched. If I hadn't been such a stupid bitch, he might have stayed at the party and been accompanied home by me, or he could have come to my place—either way, he would have had an alibi for the time of Julie's murder. The poor woman may still have been killed, but at least Luca wouldn't be accused of it, and the MP wouldn't be getting his revenge so easily. This was a bloody mess, and I couldn't shake the feeling that my actions had made things worse for him.

Luca told me it wasn't my fault and tried to comfort me. That only made me feel worse. I should have been the one to comfort him.

I had it bad for the sexy Russian. When he held me in his arms, putting my feelings over his own, I'd wanted to kiss him right then. But I stopped myself. Why? Because I was still hung up on his criminal status—not the stuff he was accused of, but the things I knew he'd done for real. Why couldn't I get past that?

Shit, I needed to push aside my confusing feelings for Luca and focus on what had to be done. Those feelings could be dealt with later. For now, it was more important to confront the battle ahead to win his freedom. With that thought at the forefront of my mind, I pushed aside my unprofessional desires and put my professional head back on.

"This case has so many holes in it. I'll help your lawyer, and together we'll get you out at the pre-trial hearing," I had told him, though I wasn't sure how easy that was going to be.

As I stepped out of the courthouse, Miki and his brothers were waiting with Anton. I hurried over and gave them a quick run-through of my conversation with Luca.

Miki assured me he'd see to Luca's safety. I assumed that meant he'd either get his men—if there were any currently in jail—or his allies to watch Luca's back. I was glad of that, but it didn't reassure me. Where there were allies, there were also enemies, and the MP obviously planned to make use of them. The thought of Luca being hurt sent shivers of despair through me.

However, I appreciated that Miki would do what he could to keep Luca from harm.

"I told Luca I'll help your lawyer—or whoever else you appoint—with this. I want Luca free, and I'll do everything I can to make that happen," I told the men.

They nodded and murmured their thanks.

"Great. I was hoping you would say that. In fact, I took the liberty of letting Bradley know you'll be assisting him. He's a good man and an even better lawyer. He's served my family well over the years and told me he wouldn't let anyone else defend Luca. But with his ailing health, he'll be glad of your help," Miki said, smiling.

I wasn't sure how I felt about working with a lawyer who had been on the payroll of the Bratva for years, and I wasn't sure I would agree that he was a "good man" in my opinion. But under the circumstances, there was nothing for it. I wouldn't let Luca stay in prison any longer than necessary, and I wouldn't leave his freedom to chance, so I was willing to put my prejudices aside on this occasion and work with the man.

"I'm in court all day tomorrow. Set up a meeting for me with him first thing Wednesday morning," I stated, before heading off to get my car. As I walked away, a sense of purpose filled me. I would do whatever it took to free Luca; his future depended on it.

CHAPTER 14
LUCA

WEDNESDAY – THE ATTACK!

Returning from the mess hall, I strode up the stairs towards the dull metallic walkway which led to my cell, forcing calmness into my gait despite the anxiety knotting my insides. The air felt thick, almost suffocating, as if the very walls were closing in around me. A hit had been put out on me, and I could practically feel the weight of the target on my back. A fellow prisoner had casually dropped the news for the price of a smoke, his eyes glinting with the thrill of gossip and turning my world upside down in an instant. My heart raced, each beat echoing in my ears like a countdown.

With no Bratva or Polish Mafia allies by my side, I relied on tenuous connections and friends of friends for backup. None of them had a real stake in my survival. We had slowly offloaded many of our more overt criminal activities, first scaling back our drug production, then shifting responsibility for the route through the UK we'd once run for our pakhan in Russia. This pivot toward more white-collar crime kept our people out of prison, a strategic move that would make our lives safer in the long run. Yet, right now, it left me stranded and vulnerable in this hostile environment, where every corner could hide danger.

I didn't scare easily, but being trapped here was suffocating. Control had always been my safety net, the one constant in the chaos, but it was slipping through my fingers. Every instinct told me I needed to get out—soon. Doubt gnawed at me; was I strong enough to survive this? My muscles tensed, bracing for whatever was coming next, the sense of danger growing thicker with each passing second. It wasn't just anxiety. It was instinct.

The walkway emptied quickly. I scanned for the officers —they were gone. The shift in atmosphere hit like a gut punch. A figure lunged from the shadows, shoving me into a nearby cell, where another two guys waited.

Thrown off balance, I stumbled, but managed to stay upright.

The first thug, the one who had pushed me into the cell, grinned as he approached. "Someone wants you dead, mate, and they're paying a lot for it. A nice little nest egg when I get out of here!" His bravado was laughable.

Smirking, I replied, "You'll have to earn it first."

The mouthy arsehole lunged, his fist flying towards my face. Blocking the blow easily, I countered with my own. Blood burst from his lip and sprayed across the room as his head jerked to the side. A guy with a nose ring came at me from the side. I quickly spun, kicking him, landing a solid strike to his gut and sending him flying backward.

The third attacker, a guy with long red hair, closed in from behind; a quick sidestep and an elbow to his solar plexus sent him doubling over. A swift blow to the back of his head brought him down.

"Oof!" Nose ring kicked me in the stomach, and I doubled over, winded. Then they were all on me. Blow after blow rained down, sending me first to my knees, then to the floor. Shit, this was bad. If I stayed down here too long, I'd be done for. I had to get back on my feet, and soon.

Huddled on my side on the floor between the metallic bunks made that difficult. Lying there in the tight space, I held my hands up, doing my best to fend them off, while I looked for an opening. The blows continued, one striking my temple and almost making me see stars. The urge to vomit my lunch threatened as I took several kicks to my gut.

The idiots laughed, thinking they had me. But these guys were chancers. Big and brutish, full of confidence that their size gave them, but no actual training. Unlike me.

The red-head learned that quickly when my knuckle hit him in the jugular, forcing his head back and stealing his breath. Unable to breathe, he fell back, gasping for air.

With him out of the way, I turned onto my back and head-butted the mouthy arsehole looming over me. Stars danced in my vision, but it did the trick, knocking the guy out. I pushed him off me just as Nose Ring's punch landed on my jaw, making me bite my tongue.

Fuck, that one hurt!

The metallic taste of blood filled my mouth and I spat. I rallied in time to see another fist coming my way and dodged it. Grabbing the side of the bunk, I got to my knees in time to block yet another punch, then a kick. The mouthy arsehole was back, but I was already scrambling to my feet. Now, I needed to stay up.

Mouthy was still knocked out, but the other two came at me with vengeful eyes.

"You're going to die now, you Russian fucker!" Red-head shouted. He came at me, throwing wild punches. I smirked and dodged them easily. This was starting to become fun.

As they tried to land more blows on me, I parried them

all, ducking and twisting my body in a fluid motion as I danced around them, grinning and enjoying the game, while trying to get closer to the door.

A sharp kick to the back of my leg knocked me off balance, and I was grabbed from behind. The mouthy one I knocked out was back. Dumb fuck! Using him for leverage, I brought both legs up and kicked the red-headed fucker in front of me. He crashed into the wall, hitting his head and going down, out cold.

Then I dived backward and rammed the guy behind me against the wall. The air rushed from his lungs and his hold loosened. I spun and grabbed his head, bringing my knee up quickly and breaking his nose. Mouthy screamed and fell to his knees, holding his bloodied face.

Nose Ring roared in fury at the sight of his friend crumpled on the floor and ran at me brandishing a shiv.

Shit, he'd upped the ante. Time to stop playing!

Sidestepping and grabbing his hand, I turned, forcing his arm down and before pulling him towards me and punching him in the jaw. He grunted. He might not be a trained fighter, but the fucker was strong.

Focused on my struggle for control of the shiv, I didn't notice Mouthy coming at me from the side again, pulling another shiv, until it was almost too late. Holding tight to the arm of the first knife-wielding attacker, I brought my right leg up and kicked the second. The blow sent him off balance, but the shiv sliced into my lower calf before he could recover.

Rage coursed through me, and I bellowed in fury. Twisting back around to Nose Ring, I ripped the bloody thing from his nose, making him scream in pain as I tossed it to the ground and kneed the fucker in the stomach. Clutching at his nose, he dropped the shiv and sunk to his knees. A punch to the head, and he was knocked out.

I spun to face Mouthy again, rushing me with another shiv. We grappled, each trying to get control of the weapon. Sweat poured off me as I fought to keep the thing from sinking into my stomach.

A noise had me turn my head in time to see Red-head rejoining the fray, pulling yet another shiv. There was no way to avoid him and my heart sank. I twisted and turned as best I could, trying to make it harder for him as he lunged.

But before he could strike, an unknown guy charged into the cell, tackling him to the ground. Another man entered and seized the one I was grappling with, pulling him off me enough for me to land several punches. It took a few hits, but the brute finally went limp, and the guy tossed him aside and extended a hand out for me to shake.

Panting with anger and exertion, I eyed it warily but didn't take it. He smirked and retracted it.

"Sean O'Brien, at your service," he said with a wink and a mock bow. "That's my cousin Finley," he added, gesturing to the other newcomer, standing silently beside him.

I frowned, maintaining my fighting stance. The only O'Brien's I'd heard of hailed from Manchester, and I hadn't dealt with them directly.

They had just helped me out, but could they be trusted? Who knew? But I wasn't in the mood to trust anyone right then.

"A mutual acquaintance from Glasgow sent me," Sean insisted, backing off when I showed no sign of relaxing my posture.

"Explain!" I snapped, feeling tired and battered. My ribs ached, and I was bleeding. No time for cryptic bullshit!

"Jim McArthur!" he blurted. "But this isn't the place to talk; let's get out of here!"

Nodding, I agreed, and we headed back toward my room.

Sean shook his head. "First, you should get patched up!" He urged me toward the nearest officer.

"What the fuck happened to you? You look like you went a few rounds with Tyson Fury," the officer said with a smirk. He'd disappeared along with all the others when the attack went down, he knew exactly what had occurred.

"Don't remember," I said. I was no fucking snitch, but I would report the attack because it might prove useful later.

"Knock you out, did they?" his grin widened.

"Something like that," I said, staring at him.

"You won't have seen them then?" His smug grin made me itch to punch it off his face.

I stared hard at him, saying nothing, until he gulped and finally wiped the smirk off his face. "Nope."

He nodded, avoiding my eyes and not looking quite as fucking smug anymore. Fucking arsehole!

"I'll write up a report. Let's get you to the doc," he said before escorting me to the medical room.

A short while later, my wound was dressed, and I'd received some painkillers. Returning to my cell with an ice pack for my swollen eye, I reflected on my luck. Despite the blows I'd taken, only bruised ribs, a shallow knife wound, and a badly swollen eye remained. The question lingered—how long could that luck last without proper allies? Outside my door, the two Irish guys awaited me, along with several others scattered along the walkway.

Sean stepped forward, his gaze steady. "You ready to talk?"

I nodded, a cautious optimism flickering in my chest. Could these guys be the allies I desperately needed?

CHAPTER 15
CLAIRE

I t had been two days since Luca was remanded, and I kept myself busy by taking some annual leave to assist Miki's old lawyer, Bradley Kozlov, with preparing his case. Recovering from a heart attack and double bypass surgery, he looked frail, sitting in bed, forced there by his wife, who insisted that bed rest was "doctor's orders." His ashen complexion made him appear tired, yet his eyes sparkled with life.

Despite my reservations about working with him, he turned out to be the most charming person I'd ever met—so knowledgeable.

"You seem to remember everything," I said in awe as he recited details from past trials and verdicts effortlessly. His sharp mind impressed me, and I could hardly keep up with the wealth of information he shared.

As we took a short break for tea, I decided it was time to learn more about the man behind the Bratva façade. I couldn't shake the nagging curiosity about how he ended up in this position.

"Kozlov is Russian, right?" I asked.

"It is, indeed, young lady," he smiled warmly.

"When did you come to the UK?"

"I was born here. You see, my father fled Russia during the Second World War. He had been forced to fight for a cause he didn't agree with and hated every minute. He was part of the occupying forces in Poland, and as soon as the war ended, he came to the UK. Later, he met my mother and made a home here," he replied.

"Is that how you became Bratva? Were you born into it like Miki and the others?"

"No, my dear," he chuckled. "There was no Bratva when I was born—at least not in the UK. They came much later. I had already passed the bar and been a lawyer for some time before I even met Miki's father."

I tilted my head, curious. "How did you meet Alexi Rominov?"

"Ah, that's a story worth telling," Bradley said, leaning back in his chair. "We first crossed paths at a charity golf tournament, paired with mutual friends. Over the course of the day, we shared our views on the chaos in the Russian community here."

"What kind of chaos?" I asked, sensing a deeper story.

He sighed, nodding thoughtfully. "Infighting, power struggles. It was a mess. But Alexi? He was sent here to restore order, and he succeeded, even if it took time."

His expression turned serious as he continued, "But it wasn't until one fateful night that our connection deepened. My son got into trouble after a night out, finding himself in a precarious situation with the local authorities."

"Oh no," I said, my heart racing at the thought.

"Yes. It was nothing too serious—just drunk and disorderly and vandalism. But he was studying medicine at the time, and it threatened his scholarship."

"That would have been a problem," I said, a wry smile on my lips.

"Exactly," he nodded. "That's when Alexi stepped in. With a few discreet calls, he ensured my son faced only a slap on the wrist rather than serious consequences, allowing him to retain his scholarship." His relief was palpable.

"That must have meant a lot to you."

"It did, and we became good friends after that," he said, his eyes sparkling with mischief as he leaned closer, as if about to share a secret. "We played golf regularly, even though he wasn't very good. I must admit, I often played badly to ensure he won. The guy needed all the help he could get," he chuckled, and I couldn't help but laugh.

"Ha, I heard that, old timer. Dad said it was the other way around," Miki's voice came from behind me, causing me to jump in surprise. The rascal had snuck up on me while I was engrossed in conversation with Bradley.

Miki smirked at my reaction before turning toward his lawyer. "That's what I let him think," Bradley replied, and Miki chuckled.

"Just popped in to see how you were doing. May sent me up," he said, producing a bottle of Scotch. "Brought you something to enjoy once you're back on your feet again," he added, his gaze warm as it swept over the older man.

"Oh, wonderful! Macallan. My favourite. Thank you, son," Bradley said, and my heart warmed at the closeness these two shared.

"What do you think of Claire, old timer? She's almost as sharp as you. Bet she'll keep you on your toes," Miki teased, glancing my way.

I felt my cheeks flush at the sudden attention.

"Indeed. And a beauty too. Brains and beauty. What more

could a man ask for? No wonder Luca's set his sights on her," Bradley replied, a mischievous twinkle in his eye.

The heat in my cheeks deepened at the revelation of Luca's interest in me.

"If I were forty years younger and not madly in love with my May, I'd give him a run for his money," Bradley said, winking, and I laughed. The man was incorrigible.

Shaking my head, I picked up my cup and took a sip.

"And speaking of love, how is your young lady?" Bradley asked Miki.

I watched intently as Miki's expression transformed into a happy glow I'd only ever seen when he was with Eilidh.

"Great. The best thing that's ever happened to me," he replied with a grin.

Eilidh had been a police officer in Scotland before learning that her corrupt colleagues had killed her dad. She'd met Miki somehow; I didn't know the ins and outs of that story. What I did know was that he'd somehow saved her life, and they'd fallen head over heels. She'd left the force and was now engaged to him—a Bratva pakhan. It was a strange situation, but I guessed that discovering her colleagues were corrupt and had committed such a heinous crime would be enough to turn anyone off the law.

"Have you taken a look at Luca's case?" Miki asked, his tone growing more serious.

"Yes, and there's a lot of work to do, but I have no doubt that, together, Claire and I will get him out of this predicament."

Miki nodded.

"Well, I have a meeting to get to, so I'll leave you two to finish your tea and get back to work. I'll check in with you both tomorrow. In the meantime, if you need anything, let me know," he said before disappearing.

Bradley watched him go with a gentle smile.

"He's a good boy, that one," he said before turning to me. "Now, what were we talking about before he arrived?"

"You were telling me how you became a Bratva lawyer."

"Ah yes, we remained close friends for the next few years, but when Alexi's lawyer was killed by a disgruntled husband—he was a ladies' man, you see, particularly partial to married ones—he offered me the job. I knew him well by then and respected him greatly, so I didn't hesitate. The fact I was feeling undervalued by my firm at the time, overlooked for a promotion yet again in favour of a partner's son, only sweetened the offer. Alexi made me feel like I mattered again."

I smiled as he continued.

"Since then, I have helped with everything they've needed, whether in a commercial law capacity for their business interests or in a criminal capacity. I must admit it has been more commercial these days, especially since Miki took over and has been turning to more legitimate sources of income. There has been less need for me to attend criminal court, and I have to say, I much prefer that."

Bradley's mouth tilted in a smile as he watched me closely, trying to gauge my response, no doubt fully aware of my own issues with the situation. Finally, I nodded slowly, filled with an understanding I hadn't expected. My initial caution about working with him faded, replaced by a newfound respect for the man who was deeply embedded in a world I had always viewed with suspicion.

"Shall we get back to work, then?" he said, patting the bed. I nodded happily and climbed up beside him.

"Now, don't get too close, dear. I'm a happily married man, and we don't want May to get jealous," he said, trying hard to keep a straight face.

Laughing, I shook my head at his silliness. "Stop your nonsense. We have serious work to do," I told him in a prim voice, making him chuckle.

"That we do, dear. That we do," he agreed.

I adjusted my laptop, making sure he had a clear view of the screen. His gaze shifted from the playful glint of our banter back to the details on the monitor, and I could see his focus sharpening. There was no mistaking the seriousness of what lay ahead, even if we'd allowed ourselves a brief moment of levity.

"Right, let's get to it. Let's start with the holes in the prosecution's case," I said.

We spent the next couple of hours discussing and listing all the inconsistencies with the prosecution's case. The Crown Prosecutor Service was citing this as a crime of passion.

The story they were trying to concoct was that although Luca claimed to not have seen Julie since she went to rehab, they'd supposedly reconnected recently. Even though he'd taken a restraining order out on her due to her erratic behaviour, and they should not have been anywhere near each other, the prosecution argued that the pair had got back together before the evening of her death. They claimed that he left Marcie's party early to return to his flat and meet with Julie, hoping for sex. But things hadn't gone to plan. They asserted he'd drugged and restrained her, sexually assaulted her, and then slit her throat.

Yet, there were no witnesses to their meeting, and no mobile calls or messages to corroborate that. The CCTV in Luca's building was apparently broken that evening—how convenient, especially when it had been working fine all day. And why didn't the night shift security guard see her? He claimed to be on his dinner break when Luca returned, so he couldn't confirm what time he'd returned or that he'd been alone. Another coincidence? I didn't think so.

So, how and when did Julie arrive at the flat? And how did she bypass security? Also, why were there no fingerprints on the needle? But why would he do that yet still leave the needle in her arm? She'd been raped—but no semen or condom had been found. Where was the condom? And the poor woman's throat had been slit. What happened to the murder weapon? The prosecution asserted that Luca must have wiped the prints off and disposed of the evidence prior to the police's arrival. But how could he? None of that made sense. In fact, it was ridiculous.

"So many holes," I mumbled as I read through the list we'd made.

"Yes, dear."

"And who was the anonymous caller?" I huffed in exasperation.

"And why would the police break down the door based on such a call when there was no sign of a disturbance when they got to the flat?"

"The report says they heard a scream from inside and so broke down the door when it wasn't answered. Even though a man had shouted he was coming? How could they hear a scream when Julie was already dead? That seems very suspicious."

"Exactly. It might be prudent to look into the officers that came to the scene, my dear. Perhaps they were just overzealous and wanted a chance to break down a door. Or maybe they wanted to ensure that they had proper cause to search Luca's home. After all, if he'd come to the door and not had blood on him, they wouldn't have had any cause to go inside if there were no signs of a disturbance and Luca denied any had taken place. Especially not based on an anonymous call which might simply have been somebody trying to make a nuisance of themselves."

I nodded in agreement. So many things didn't add up. There were major gaps in the prosecution's case, and much of it stank of police malpractice, possibly even corruption. The thought soured my stomach. I would do my utmost to exploit the flaws in the case, expose any unlawful or overzealous behaviour by the police, and shed doubt on the prosecution's theory, in order to secure Luca's freedom.

Bradley's eyes were heavy by the time we had made our notes.

"Okay, we've done enough here. I'll make a start on gathering the evidence for Luca's defence," I told him. "I'll come by again tomorrow to discuss whatever I find. In the meantime, you need to rest," I said, giving the old man a peck on the cheek. He was already snoring lightly by the time I'd packed up my laptop and left his room.

Back in my car, I placed a quick call to Marko. He agreed to get me all the information he could on the security guard and the company he worked for, check the building's security system to see if it had been tampered with, and look for any means of giving Luca an alibi for the time he was driving around.

After grabbing a sandwich for lunch, I headed to the courthouse. I needed to discuss another case with the prosecutor involved. My client was prepared to accept a deal and plead guilty to a drunk driving charge if the more serious assault charge against him was dropped.

Once we'd agreed to the terms, I submitted the required documentation to make it happen, then called the client to let him know the outcome before his trial date, which was scheduled for the following morning.

As I was leaving to head to the jail to see Luca, the Crown prosecutor for Luca's case approached me with the pre-trial information. I was relieved to see my friend and mentor, Elizabeth Traynor, also known as Lady Frost, she would preside over the preliminary hearing and the High Court trial, should it reach that stage. I knew she would be fair and reasonable.

"Ah, the woman I wanted to see!" a voice called, and I looked up to see the very woman hurrying towards me.

"Elizabeth!" I smiled, giving her a kiss on each cheek as she leaned in.

"Claire, my dear, a word if you have time?" she gestured for me to follow her into a nearby empty office.

"I see you have a copy of the pre-trial for the Wilson murder case," she said, eyeing the document in my hand.

I nodded, ready to respond, but she cut me off. "Good, then you'll see that I'm presiding over it and expect it to go my way," she declared firmly.

"Your way?" I echoed, confused.

"Yes, Claire. Luca Orlov has powerful friends. However, those friends have made enemies. People more powerful than them, who wouldn't hesitate to protect their interests, even at the expense of justice. I wouldn't want you to find yourself in a position where your career, or worse, is on the line."

"My career?" I asked, feeling a knot tighten in my stomach. "Are you saying that my position could be compromised just by assisting Bradley with Luca's case? Or worse, that my safety is at stake for merely doing my job?"

Was this a test? Or an actual warning? As the judge, Elizabeth's role was to oversee proceedings fairly. I'd always believed she did that, but now I sensed I might be wrong, and I didn't like the direction this was heading.

"Claire, sometimes the law has to bend. The Rominovs

are significant players in this city, and so are their enemies. You need to tread carefully. You don't want their enemies to become yours. I expect you to take this matter seriously." Her voice dropped to a low, conspiratorial tone, making my skin prickle.

"Of course, I will," I replied. "I always look out for my client's best interests."

Her gaze softened slightly. "You always do, Claire. You've made your mother proud. But remember, sometimes the law doesn't work as it should. Evidence can be manipulated, and alliances can shift. You never know who might come knocking when the stakes get high, or what might be required of you."

"Are you suggesting I break the law?" I shot back, feeling my defensiveness rise.

She raised a hand. "No, no! I'm not implying that at all. I simply want you to be aware of the larger picture. Understand how things operate. Know that the outcome is sometimes beyond our control and there are times when it is prudent to extract yourself from problematic situations."

I swallowed hard, sensing the weight of her words. "Thank you for your advice, but I assure you I will remain ethical and I have no intention of withdrawing my help in this case."

"Very well, Claire. Just remember, it's a dangerous game we play. Protect yourself," she stated firmly, before returning to the corridor.

Staring after her, I frowned, unable to fully grasp the meaning behind her veiled warnings. A knot tightened in my stomach. What was she really suggesting? Could I trust her? For the first time in my life, I doubted it. The weight of her words lingered, making me question everything I believed about the justice I was fighting for.

After a moment to collect myself, I returned to my office, my heart racing with renewed determination. I had to protect Luca and ensure he was exonerated—whatever it took.

CHAPTER 16
LUCA

LATER THE SAME DAY - MAKING NEW
ALLIES

s we stepped into the cell, Sean claimed the lower bunk like he owned it, while Finley leaned against the wall by the door, his arms crossed, casual but watchful. They both looked relaxed, but I wasn't about to let my guard down. I'd seen plenty of men smile right before they stabbed you in the back. I stayed by the door, feet planted, my hands loose at my sides, ready for anything. Sean's easy smile didn't quite reach his eyes. I could respect that; life was dangerous in our world, and trust took time to build. He'd be measuring me up just as much as I was him.

"Here's the deal. We came from Northern Ireland a few months back, my dad's looking to carve out some territory in London now that there's a bit of an opening, if you know what I mean," he grinned.

"Our mutual friend Jim MacArthur clued him up on things and told him you'd been remanded and would need some help in here. We're both on remand ourselves for a bit of a scuffle, but this isn't our first time in the nick. So, Jim asked us to keep an eye on you."

Nodding slowly, I crossed my arms, my gaze sharp. "Uh

huh, and what's in it for you, exactly? Not that I don't appreciate it of course."

Sean didn't even hesitate. "Simple. My dad wants an introduction to your pakhan. Make the intro, and we've got your back."

My gaze shifted between the two of them. An introduction to Miki? That could be arranged easily enough. As for the 'opening' Sean had hinted at, he wasn't wrong. We still needed someone to take over the remnants of the drug trade we'd inherited after we took down the Malia Boys and Broxys. And if Jim vouched for them? Maybe the O'Briens were exactly what we needed.

"Jim planned on doing the honours, but when he heard of your predicament, he thought us having your back might be a good way for us to prove our worth, so to speak. Get us an intro, put in a good word, and your ass is safe while you are in here. Otherwise…" Finn's smirk widened, but the edge in his voice was clear.

The way he let that sentence hang in the air? It wasn't just a joke; it was a test. My fists clenched, ready for whatever came next. I wasn't some scared newbie they could intimidate. If they wanted to play games, I'd be more than happy to show them just how dangerous I could be.

Sean let out a sharp laugh, breaking the tension. "Finn, stop messing with him!"

Finn's face split into a cheeky grin, and he winked.

"We do want that intro, but don't worry. Your ass is safe, mate. Just… maybe don't drop the soap in the shower. You're a pretty boy, Finn here might take a liking to it," Sean said grinning, his eyes sparkling with mischief.

"Feck off!" Finn snorted, before good naturedly punching Sean in the arm.

Their back-and-forth eased the tension, and I couldn't

help but chuckle under my breath. They had the look of trouble, sure, but my gut told me there was something genuine beneath all the bravado. Maybe I wasn't as alone in here as I'd thought. With these two watching my back, I might just get through this.

"Done!" I said, sticking my hand out.

"So, Finn and me, like to do a bit of bare knuckle boxing. You got any good Russian fighters on your team? We should set up a match," Sean said.

"One or two. I'm sure Vlad would be up for a round with one of you. Pretty sure he'd wipe the floor with you in seconds too," I teased, though I wasn't sure I was wrong. Vlad was one hell of a fighter.

"Sounds like a challenge to me, Sean," Finn said.

"Hell, yeah, when we get out of here, let's get it set up," Sean replied.

"I'll see what I can do," I told them, finally relaxing in their presence.

Within minutes, we were talking about everything but prison and the weight on my shoulders lightened just a bit.

———

About an hour later, I was called out to see my lawyer.

Since I knew Bradley was still recovering from his heart op, I was hoping it was Claire, and my heart skipped a beat as I saw her sitting there waiting for me.

"What the hell happened? Are you okay? Who did this?" Her voice cracked as she scanned my bruised face.

"I'm okay, Claire," I said pleased to see how my appearance affected her. Seeing her worry over me, her guard down for once, made every bruise worth it.

"Did you file a report? Did you tell them who did it?" she cried again.

"Yeah, I reported it to get my stitches. But I didn't grass on the bastards. I'm no snitch, Claire."

"Besides, it's just a few bruises. Nothing to worry about, babe," I kept my voice steady, trying to ease the worry in her eyes.

She sighed heavily and chewed at her lip. "And the person behind the attacks, was that who I suspect?"

I nodded. There was no point denying it.

"What if it happens again? What if you're not so lucky next time?" she asked, looking distraught.

"I've got backup now, Claire. You don't need to worry about that," I said softly, locking eyes with her.

Seeing her concern brought an unexpected warmth to my chest, and the fact that she didn't flinch when I called her babe gave me a sense of satisfaction I hadn't anticipated. But beneath that satisfaction lay an unsettling awareness of how misplaced my emotions felt in such a dire situation.

Was it really right to feel this way, to welcome the chance to be near her because of this crisis? I loathed the circumstances—nobody deserved to meet such a tragic end as Julie had. But as I sat there, I couldn't help but feel a thrill at the knowledge that Claire was here with me. She was navigating the depths of one of the darkest times in my life, offering her support and care, and I found myself savouring every fleeting second of her presence.

Whether or not it was morally right, I was going to use this time to continue my pursuit of my Little Miss Sexy Ass, and maybe at the end of all of this, she'd decide that I was not just worth defending, but worth loving. Surely, something good had to come out of this terrible nightmare?

Over the next hour, we talked through the details of my

case. Between the holes in the prosecution's case and the assault to add weight to things, Claire sounded confident she'd get me out at the pre-trial next week.

Regardless, I sensed she was holding back. Something was bothering her.

"What's wrong, Claire? What's got you so worried?"

She looked at me. "Nothing. It's fine," she said too quickly.

I leaned back, crossing my arms, eyes locked on her. I wasn't buying a word of it. Others might not see through her stern countenance, but I could, and I knew my Little Miss Sexy Ass was not being truthful with me.

She smiled, but it didn't reach her eyes. My gut twisted. Something was wrong—very wrong.

"Claire, tell me," I demanded, my voice low and firm as I looked her in the eye.

"Damn it, Luca. You always see through me."

Claire started pacing, and all I wanted was to pull her close. But I couldn't—not with the cameras and prison officers watching every move.

"If I tell you, promise me you won't panic," she said. Of course, her saying that made me want to panic, but I did my best to hide it.

"Just tell me, Claire," I said.

Sighing heavily, she sat back down and told me about her conversation with Elizabeth Traynor.

"The more I go over it in my head, the more awful it seems. I'm not sure what she meant by expecting it to go her way, though I assume she expects me not to fight for your release. Do you think the MP has got to her, and she's scared? Or is she corrupt?" she asked, a slight quiver in her voice betraying her upset at the idea.

"Either sounds possible, babe. But my money is on the latter. Has she ever given you reason to doubt her before?"

"No, never." Her eyes filled with unshed tears as the truth sunk deep.

"She was a close friend of my mum's; I've known her all my life," she said. Then her face took on a look of horror.

"Do you think that means my mum could have been corrupt too?" she asked, her voice thick with anxiety. I recalled the stories Claire had shared about her mother, a dedicated officer with the London Metropolitan Police Force, whose life had ended abruptly when her car skidded off the road during a storm last January. I could see the shadows of doubt creeping into Claire's eyes, a fear that threatened to unravel the memories she held dear.

"No, babe. I'm certain she wasn't. This woman may be corrupt, or she could have been coerced; we really don't know all the details yet. But your mum's integrity isn't in question here."

She nodded, but her lips trembled and she quickly swiped at a single tear.

God, I wanted to hug her. I fisted my hands, furious at this Traynor woman and how with a few short words she'd rocked the very foundations of Claire's belief in her whole world.

Claire bit her lip as I continued. "Your mum brought you up to fully believe in the justice system and those who enforce it. I doubt she would have instilled such a strong belief in you if she hadn't believed that herself. Don't let any of this tarnish your mum's memory."

My words seemed to calm her, and she smiled in relief.

However, I wasn't calm. I maintained the outward appearance of it, but inside, my guts were twisting. I needed to make sure my Little Miss Sexy Ass was protected. Claire could be in real danger. So could Bradley and his family.

Who knew what the MP had planned? I needed to make sure they all remained safe.

"Claire, your safety is the most important thing. Bradley's too. I want out of here, but not at the expense of any of you getting hurt. Call Miki and tell him what happened, and do whatever he says for you to stay safe," I told her firmly.

"I can't do my job properly if I'm being followed about all the time," she said angrily.

The cute frown and pursed lips made me long to kiss her. God, how I ached to kiss her. As soon as I got out of there, that was one of the first things I vowed I would do. I shook my head and forced my thoughts back to her safety.

"Miki will ensure your security is discreet, but I won't budge on this, Claire. You need to be protected. I won't risk anything happening to you. I couldn't live with that," I told her truthfully.

She gulped and looked me in the eye before quickly dropping hers.

"These people are dangerous, Claire. Promise me you'll be careful. Let Miki handle your security. Do what he says— no arguments."

"Okay," she said softly, with a weary slump of her shoulders.

"Time's up," the prison officer said, and Claire reluctantly packed her notebook away. She turned to me, her eyes shimmering with worry. "Be careful, Luca. I couldn't bear for anything to happen to you either."

"I will, babe. Don't worry about me. Just make sure you do what I said. Talk to Miki and follow his instructions, and I'll see you soon."

As she left the room, my heart raced with a mixture of hope and dread. Claire was everything I never knew I needed, and the thought of losing her sent a shiver down my spine. I wouldn't let that happen—whatever it took, I'd protect her.

CHAPTER 17
CLAIRE

"Time's up," the prison officer said, and I reluctantly packed up. Tears threatened to spill as I faced the harsh reality of leaving Luca trapped in this cold, dangerous place. The thought of something happening to him again made my stomach churn.

"Be careful, Luca. I couldn't bear for anything to happen to you either," I told him, and I meant every word. The man had got under my skin and there was no denying the fact that my heart wanted him even if my mind was still reluctant to agree.

"I will, babe. Don't worry about me. Just make sure you do what I told you. Talk to Miki and follow his instructions, and I'll see you soon," he replied as I left the room.

When I first saw the state of his bruised face, I was desperate to go to him and hold him tight. The watchful eyes of the prison guards monitoring the cameras were all that held me in check.

The past hour with Luca had been a whirlwind of emotions. After my conversation with Elizabeth, I grappled with her veiled threats, struggling to maintain control. Each bruise on my sexy Russian's face deepened my turmoil.

We suspected the MP might try something since Luca hadn't been granted bail, but I had hoped the guy wasn't behind that, and it was down to the judges caving under the media pressure. Knowing that wasn't the case frightened me.

Rage coursed through me. How dare anyone lay a hand on Luca?! Elizabeth's implications only added to the danger. The thought that the MP had not only framed Luca but was manipulating the very system I believed in to secure his conviction sickened me.

Why not simply wait for a moment of vulnerability to eliminate him? Did the MP really need to have Luca behind bars to carry out his plan? What was the purpose of murdering Julie and framing Luca for it? Was this all part of a twisted game to dismantle his reputation and send a warning to the Rominovs while also exacting revenge?

There was so much more to this than I understood. The rationale behind the MP's actions was lost on me, but one thing was clear: he was a dangerous psychopath, and I had no intention of delving into his twisted psyche.

Regardless of his reasons, he wouldn't win. And neither would Elizabeth.

The prosecution's case was flimsy at best. Given the assault Luca had endured, it would be nearly impossible for the judges to deny bail without facing serious backlash, even amid the media storm.

Despite what Elizabeth wanted, I'd get Luca out of prison next week and then I was going to help Bradley get my guy off these charges, no matter what.

Oops, my guy?!

I was still teetering on the fence with that one, yet

thinking of him as "my guy" felt undeniably right in that moment. Damn, I was still so bloody confused.

Shaking my head, I pushed my uncertainty aside. Now wasn't the time to dwell on my tangled love life and my feelings for Mr Sexy Kisser.

Nodding goodbye to the prison officer at the external door, I headed toward my car.

As I approached, something felt off. Shit, my tires were flat! Both front lights were smashed, and someone had keyed the side.

Fuck! This was the bloody prison car park. How had this happened?

I returned inside to file a complaint. Ironically, the camera that should have covered the car park had been repositioned to face another direction, leaving no footage of the vandalism. Of course, there were no witnesses either.

As I left the building again, I got a text: *"Back off, or you'll be next!"*

My blood ran cold. Shit just got real. The vandalism to my car was an unmistakable warning, and I suddenly realised just how much danger I was in. If they could reach me in a prison car park, they could get to me anywhere.

Luca was right, I needed protection. I gave Miki a quick call and then arranged a tow truck.

Within half an hour, Vlad arrived just as the tow truck pulled up next to my car. After arranging for my car to be taken to my local garage, Vlad took me back to mine.

"Pack a bag. Miki wants you to stay at the Estate until this is over," Vlad said, his voice as gruff as ever.

"Hell, no!" I shot back, crossing my arms defiantly. "All I need is a bodyguard."

"Claire, you received several threats today. You need

protection. Miki wants you with us where you can be looked after properly. This isn't up for debate."

"I don't need to be babysat in some mansion! I have a job to do. I can take care of myself—just someone to watch my back is all I ask." My frustration bubbled over, flushing my cheeks.

"Look, I get it. You're tough, but this isn't something you can handle alone. They got to you in a prison car park. You could be a target anywhere. You're safer with us."

His calm demeanour only made my annoyance flare more. "I've faced threats before. I won't hide away like some damsel in distress!" My heart raced with indignation; my life was spiralling out of control, and I hated it.

"Then take it up with Miki. He's the one calling the shots here, not me. Just know he wouldn't suggest this if it weren't necessary."

"Fine!" I retorted, voice sharp. "I'll call Miki and give him a piece of my mind!"

I dialled Miki's number, my heart pounding as I braced myself for the conversation.

"Claire," Miki answered, his voice calm yet firm. "Are you safe?"

"I'm fine, but I don't appreciate being treated like a child. I don't need to stay at the Estate. I can handle this on my own." Even as I said the words, I knew I was being foolish. Miki was right, I just wasn't ready to accept that yet.

"Your car was vandalised, and you received a threatening message. You need protection, Claire."

"Protection? I'm not some fragile thing that needs coddling." My voice strained with the effort to maintain my composure.

"Luca would want you to be safe," he replied, a hint of steel in his tone.

His mention of Luca sent a jolt of annoyance through me. "You think bringing him into this will make me comply? This isn't about him!"

"It is about him. He can't protect you right now, but I can. Staying at the Estate is the safest option. You'll have guards, and you can still work from there. Plus, Gracie is here; I know she'll feel better having you close, especially given the circumstances."

I inhaled deeply, the weight of my situation pressing down on me, and let out a rush of breath. He had me.

"Fine, Miki. I'll stay, but only because I want to help Luca and don't want to worry Gracie."

"Thank you, Claire. Your safety is my priority, and I'll ensure you're well taken care of. I promise."

I hung up, frustration and resignation heavy in my chest. I loathed feeling forced into actions I didn't want to take, yet deep down, I recognised their necessity.

Not long after, I found myself settled in a room at the Rominov family estate. I was right where I didn't want to be, yet part of me felt oddly relieved. The added security of the estate allowed me to justify my stay by spending more time with Gracie. But beneath that, a knot of dread twisted in my stomach. The shadows encroaching around us felt darker, and I couldn't shake the nagging sensation that my safety—and Luca's—hung by a thread.

CHAPTER 18
LUCA

OVER THE NEXT FEW DAYS –
PRELIMINARY HEARING

After Claire had left, worry clawed at me for the rest of the day. Would she do what I asked and call Miki?

My sexy lawyer could be stubborn. She liked to act tough, but underneath she was a pussycat. No doubt she'd think she could protect herself, but she couldn't take on our world alone. Like it or not, she needed protection.

I hated that I couldn't protect her myself, but I would bloody well make sure Miki did. Of course, knowing my Little Miss Sexy Ass, she'd likely fight him on it all the way. A flash of warmth ran through me at the thought of her getting her claws out, and I smiled, but concern quickly wiped the smile off my face. Despite how tough my woman thought she was, she had to listen to Miki.

She would? Wouldn't she? *Not unless she believes she's in real danger*, the annoying little voice in the back of my head said.

Damn it! I needed to call Miki and make sure he knew she'd been threatened.

Before I could think about it, I found myself at the door to Sean's room.

"Luca, everything okay?"

"You got a phone?" I asked, keeping my voice hushed as I entered his cell.

"Sure. What's the problem?"

"My woman's in danger and I need to make sure she's being properly protected," I replied.

He nodded and tossed a phone my way. "Have at it. You can keep it tonight, give me it back in the morning," he said.

"Thanks."

I returned to my room just in time for lockdown. As the door closed, shutting me in for the night, I was glad I had a cell to myself.

Settling into my bunk, I dialled Miki.

"Who the fuck's this?" he asked, suspicious of the unknown number.

"It's me. Borrowed the phone from an Irish guy. Sean O'Brien. Him and his cousin Finn have got my back in here. They moved from Ireland recently. Their dad wants to carve a niche in London and wants a chat. Apparently, Jim will vouch for them. You heard of them?"

"No, but Jim left a message saying he'd arranged protection for you and he'll call me tomorrow, so I assume he'll enlighten me then. I'd called him since we don't have anyone inside and neither does Glowacki. I didn't want you in there without backup," he replied.

"Thanks. I knew you'd get something organised. Did Claire call you? She needs protecting. She's being threatened by the judge who'll be handling my case."

"Yeah, she did. But there's more," he said, a grim edge in his tone. "Her car was vandalised in the prison parking lot."

The words hit me like a punch to the gut. "What?! Is she okay?"

"Pissed off, but safe. I've got her staying here with us. However, she also received a threatening text telling her to back off, or she'd be next. Marko traced it back to a burner phone, so we've no idea who sent it."

Guilt clawed at me. This was my fault.

"Make sure she stays away from the prison," I urged, my voice tight. "I can't trust her safety if she comes here before the pre-trial."

"She's safe at the Estate," Miki assured me. "I've got Vlad assigned to her at all times and when he's not there, Trigger, or one of us, will be. Got a couple of guys on Brad, too."

I let out a breath I hadn't realised I was holding. The knowledge that she was under Miki's protection kept me grounded. But my thoughts spiralled back to the threat looming over her.

"Good. Just make sure they stay discreet, she won't like the fact she's got bodyguards trailing her every move, no matter how much it's for her own good. She's likely to act up if they cause a scene or make themselves too obvious. She needs to be protected despite herself, I can't lose her, Miki."

"I've got it covered, Luca, just concentrate on your own safety and I'll take care of Claire. I don't want anything happening to either of you," Miki replied, his voice steady but laced with urgency.

"I'll see you at the pre-trial hearing. Keep your head down until then," he said before the phone went dead.

After he'd hung up, anger pressed down on me like a ton of bricks. That fucking MP needed to be dealt with. His trial was set for three months from now; and it couldn't come soon enough. No doubt the arrogant bastard still thought he'd find a way out of his charges, but he wouldn't. There was far too much evidence against him. Also, Marko was about to hit the final nail in his coffin, by sending the prosecutor a whole new set of evidence we'd managed to uncover after we'd sent the first lot.

There was no doubt about it, he was going down. Once convicted, he would likely end up in Belmarsh or Wakefield, where some of our allies had connections in place to ensure he was taken care of. I wouldn't rest until that was sorted. The need for revenge on the fucker was nearly driving me crazy.

———

The day finally arrived, and I was taken over to the court for the preliminary hearing. Sean and Finn said a quick goodbye before I left. They didn't expect me to return, and I hoped they were right. I'd been safe with them backing me up, but both were up for trial next week, and rumour had it they'd get out. If they did and I didn't, it would mean I'd be back to square one—open to attack again.

The Irish Mafia had a couple of other guys in on remand, too; they'd been around helping watch my back, but I didn't know them as well. I wasn't about to rely on them. No, I needed to get out today.

Claire was there with the rest of the gang—even Marcie and Derrick had shown up. Seeing my Bratva Blood Brothers and friends there, rooting for me, felt good.

My Little Miss Sexy Ass gave me a small smile. She looked worried, and I hoped it was just the fact she had to face her corrupt mentor today, not because she thought I wouldn't get bailed after all.

The judge entered, and Claire began presenting my case

for revoking remand and granting bail. She reiterated her previous arguments but emphasised the recent attack against me as further justification.

"The refusal to grant bail to my client after his arrest resulted in an attack that left him with several injuries, one requiring stitches, putting his life in serious jeopardy. I am requesting bail again and assert that, under these circumstances, there is no valid reason for it to be denied."

The judge's expression soured, her eyes glinting dangerously as Claire pressed on.

"I must remind you that, given the current media scrutiny facing the Crown Prosecution Service, denying bail in this instance could provoke even greater interest. The public was outraged when a judge granted bail to an MP accused of multiple counts of kidnap, rape, and murder, with compelling evidence against him. It would be even more concerning if the same judge denied bail to a businessman facing only one count of rape and murder, where the evidence is flimsy at best."

It was a bold move, and I couldn't suppress a smirk. My woman knew exactly where to strike. She was playing hardball. Elizabeth Traynor's eyes narrowed as she stared at Claire, clearly displeased by this unexpected turn of events.

Claire held her ground, meeting her gaze defiantly. A silent exchange passed between them before the judge glanced down at her paperwork, scribbling notes. I caught the faintest hint of a smirk on Claire's lips—a barely there expression, but I saw it. She knew she'd won.

My Little Miss Sexy Ass had a competitive streak, and she played to win. It was one of the many things I loved about her. A wicked thought crossed my mind, and I bit back my own smirk as I awaited my fate.

The judge was caught between a rock and a hard place.

Granting me bail would anger whoever had insisted she refuse it in the first place, while refusing it would open her up to media scrutiny, possibly exposing her own corruption. She was bound to lose either way. I found myself wondering what she feared more—the MP or the media.

A couple of minutes later, I had my answer. The trial was set for six weeks from now, and bail was granted.

Yes!

Claire beamed at me, and I grinned back. I wanted to kiss her right there, but that would have to wait. As I'd promised myself before, as soon as I got out of here, that's exactly what I was going to do.

I was escorted back downstairs for my release to be processed. Thank God. I couldn't wait to reclaim my freedom, and once I had it, I intended to hold on tight.

When I was first remanded, I knew being locked up would be hard, but I didn't realise just how suffocating it would feel, even with the O'Briens around. I knew I never wanted to return. They say, "Don't do the crime if you can't do the time," but my dad and Miki's had a better saying: If you're going to commit a crime, don't get caught.

Being born into the Bratva meant avoiding crime was impossible, making that motto a far better guide. Sure, not committing any would be ideal, but the likelihood of that was almost laughable. Still, shifting our focus from illegal dealings to white-collar crime would certainly ease the burden.

Miki would still call on me when needed, but with less overt criminal activity on the table, that demand would decrease significantly. Especially after we finally got rid of the MP. Then maybe Claire could see past my Bratva connections.

Suddenly, Miki's push to legitimise us took on a whole

new significance. I needed to encourage him to ally with the O'Briens and offload as much of our dirtier business as possible.

My future with Claire depended on it. As I waited for my belongings, a swirl of hope and anxiety filled me. I longed to hold her close, to make her feel the depth of my absence, but a nagging worry crept in—would she still resist the undeniable bond between us?

No, I refused to let that happen. Her name was etched into my very being. I belonged to her, and she belonged to me. I would kiss her until she could no longer deny what we shared. My resolve solidified; the moment I laid eyes on her again, I would stake my claim in the most passionate way possible.

CHAPTER 19
CLAIRE

Bail had been granted. Relief washed over me, and I beamed at Luca. He grinned back, making my insides melt. God, the man was gorgeous! The scowl on Elizabeth's face said it all. She didn't like being put in her place, but if she was going to play with the law, then she deserved no less.

I wasn't called the Ice Queen for nothing, and if she thought she could intimidate me—well, screw you, Lady Frost. This newer, younger, better version is out to get you! And I'd learnt from the best: her.

Elizabeth Traynor had once been a figure I admired—a force to be reckoned with, the epitome of a woman who clawed her way to the top in a world dominated by men. I'd been inspired by her growing up, watching her in court as a young barrister, studying every cutting remark and icy glare, hoping one day to be half as formidable. She was proof that a woman could hold power and command respect without losing her edge.

Now, all I saw was a woman who'd sold her soul for influence, hiding corruption beneath that frosty veneer. Lady

Frost wasn't the role model I'd once idolised; she was a warning—a reminder of the cost of ambition when you start playing dirty. And today, I'd shown her that she wasn't untouchable.

As I gathered the defence paperwork, the courtroom around me began to empty, leaving me in a bubble of my own thoughts. The crisp rustle of paper grounded me, a reminder that this wasn't just another case—this was Luca's life on the line. The echo of my heels against the marble floor was the only sound that filled the silence as I walked to the prosecution office, but inside, my mind was anything but quiet. I'd just bested Elizabeth Traynor—Lady Frost herself —in a game she thought she'd mastered. And it felt damn good.

But as the adrenaline of victory began to fade, thoughts of Luca took over. His grin from across the courtroom had sparked a flutter in my chest that was impossible to ignore. For so long, I'd kept him at arm's length, convinced that getting involved with him was reckless, foolish—dangerous.

Recent events had shaken that conviction. The so-called pillars of justice, people I once held in high regard, had shown their true colours. Elizabeth and the MP—two people I once believed were the epitome of power and respectability, people who should have been upholders of the law and defenders of the legal system—were nothing more than empty shells wrapped in lies and corruption.

Luca was complicated, but there was something unmistakably genuine about him that set him apart. Unlike Elizabeth or the MP, who cloaked their corruption in the trappings of respectability, Luca's world was layered in shades of grey. His public persona as a Russian businessman was polished and refined, but it wasn't a lie—it was a necessary mask in a world where wearing your true face could get you killed. Yet beneath that facade, Luca wasn't hiding his flaws; he was simply navigating the reality he was born into. He never pretended to be virtuous or played the victim. He didn't try to justify his choices with excuses or self-righteousness.

Where others schemed in shadows, Luca stood firm in the light he allowed himself. His life had been built on violence and loyalty—two forces that often dictated his actions—but he didn't dress them up as anything else. It wasn't just the crimes he committed that defined him; it was the fierce protectiveness, the unwavering loyalty to those he cared about, and the unapologetic way he fought for what was his. In a world full of masks, Luca was at least honest about the lines he'd crossed, and that was more than could be said for most. He was flawed, certainly, but he was also real, unfiltered, and fiercely protective of those he loved.

The sound of rustling paper snapped me back to the task at hand and the black-and-white text of Luca's case staring back at me. All those legal arguments were just formalities, a means to an end. It was hard to believe that something so clinical held the power to determine the future of someone like Luca—a man whose life was anything but black and white.

Yet, as much as the legalities mattered today, the real battle was taking place inside my head. Could I really accept him, knowing everything he was? The violence, the bloodshed, the Bratva ties that defined so much of his existence—these were things I'd been trained to condemn, not embrace.

A deep breath steadied me and I flipped through the remaining forms, barely seeing them as my thoughts continued to race. Luca had never hidden who he was. He'd hurt people, crossed lines, and broken laws that couldn't be bent back into shape. But he also fought for his family, stood by his word, and protected what was his. There was a code in that, twisted as it might be—a kind of honour that Elizabeth and the MP would never understand. They were the reason I had believed in the system, and now, they were the reason I was questioning everything. Luca was better than them, not because he was a saint, but because he made no pretence about his sins.

Just a few scant months ago, I would never have believed it possible for me to seriously consider a relationship with Luca, no matter how attractive he was. But the more I learned about the world I'd dedicated my life to, the more those judgments felt misplaced. The court system I'd believed in was flawed, tainted by people who wore the right suits and said the right things, but were just as dirty as the men they condemned. And Luca? He didn't pretend to be clean. Not to me. He was honest in a way that none of them could ever be.

The folder snapped shut with a decisive thud, my decision solidifying with it. No more pretending. No more hiding behind excuses or clinging to fears that had long since lost their hold on me. Luca was more than a client, more than a reckless fling. He was the man who looked at me and saw past every defence, every carefully constructed barrier. He saw me—the woman who was more than just her career, more than the Ice Queen title she'd earned. And maybe, just maybe, that was worth risking it all for.

As I walked through the foyer, I caught sight of Miki talking to Glowacki near the exit, their conversation a low hum that blended into the background. They were waiting, just like me, for the doors to open and for Luca to walk through them. But this time, it wasn't just a legal victory I was anticipating. It was the chance to finally let down my guard and see where this could lead.

My gaze drifted to the doors as my heart raced at the thought of Luca on the other side. Today wasn't just about Luca walking free; it was about me stepping into the unknown. The old Claire, bound by rigid rules and unyielding principles, would never have entertained this risk. But today, I wasn't that woman anymore. What mattered was that Luca was real in a way no one else was. He didn't need to be perfect; he just needed to be him.

The thought of seeing him, touching him, feeling that electric pull between us again made my breath hitch. He'd be out soon, and I'd let him know that I was ready to give us a chance and see what came next. And as much as I feared the risks, the thought of letting him go scared me more. Would we really be able to make a go of things? I'd no idea, but one thing was clear: I wanted to find out. I was done running from it.

The courtroom's walls, usually a place of certainty, now felt like a threshold to something new, something I was finally ready to embrace. Luca was more than just the Bratva enforcer with a dangerous past—he was the man who'd fought his way into my heart, whether or not I'd wanted him to. And today, for the first time, I was ready to admit that he was worth the fight.

CHAPTER 20
LUCA

As soon as I was bailed, I made my way to the front of the courthouse. Everyone was waiting for me in the foyer, and I received hearty back slaps and handshakes from the guys, and a warm hug from Marcie. Claire stood off to the side, a smile lighting up her face.

"Be back in a few minutes. I need to confer with my lawyer!" I told Miki, smirking as I grabbed Claire's hand and pulled her down the corridor.

My eyes landed on the disabled toilet, and I grinned as I quickly ushered her inside, locking the door behind us. Turning us around, I stripped off my jacket, removing my tie from the pocket where I'd stuffed it earlier.

"What are you doing?" Claire asked, sounding uncertain as I unbuttoned her suit jacket and slipped it off her shoulders. Dropping it onto the floor with mine, I slowly backed her up against the door.

"Exactly what I've been dreaming of doing for days, while I was locked up with nothing much to do but think about you. Dream about you. Fantasise," I told her, licking my lips. "Now, be a good girl and let me show you how much I've missed kissing you, touching you."

Claire's breath hitched at my words, and her eyes widened. A thrill ran through me. I'd always suspected that my sexy lawyer, the Ice Queen herself, who loved to dominate in the courtroom, would secretly long to submit in the bedroom. She was my perfect match, after all.

"Luca, everyone is waiting outside. We can't…" I cut her off, claiming her lips in a kiss, as I pinned her against the wall, deliberately trapping her hands between us, holding them with one hand while my other gripped her arse. I ground against her, letting her feel the effect she had on me.

When she moaned, the sound almost brought me to my knees. This is what I needed, this is what I'd spent so many nights longing for.

Without breaking our kiss, I removed my tie and wrapped it around her hands, quickly tying them together, and thrust them above her head. Holding them in place with one hand again, I lowered my other to her blouse and popped the buttons.

Once they were undone, I pulled the cloth open and squeezed her lace covered breast. She arched into my touch and I smirked. Plucking at the nipple beneath the fabric, I teased it until she groaned.

Breaking off the kiss, I pulled the cups of her bra down, exposing the most luscious tits I'd ever seen. My mouth watered at the sight and my cock jerked its approval.

Bending my head, I latched on to one, licking and sucking hard on the dusky pink bud before turning my attention to the other.

My cock was getting harder by the second and I groaned as I pulled away just enough to look into her face. Her lips were swollen, her eyes half closed with lust, and she was panting hard. I'd never seen a sexier sight.

All sorts of dirty thoughts ran through my mind, but this wasn't the place to do all the things I wanted to—no, needed to—do to her.

I'd pulled her in here with me for a reason. As I'd waited for my release papers, I'd made a plan. One I hoped would appeal to my Little Miss Sexy Ass's competitive nature.

Would she accept my challenge? God, I hoped so.

After working on my case and finding her world was no longer the black and white one she'd thought it to be, I hoped that she would be more willing to take a chance on us.

"I have a proposition for you. I think we can be great together and I want you to be mine. I want to give you everything Claire, and I will, if you just let me."

She went to say something, but I put a finger to her lips, cutting off. I didn't want her to say no, I needed to convince her to give me my chance.

I was pretty sure by the way she responded to me in general that I only really needed one night with her to show her how good we could be together, and I'd do anything to make that happen.

Staring into her eyes, I slipped my hand up her skirt, she wore hold-ups, and the tops of her thighs were bare. The feel of her silky soft skin sent a shiver of pleasure down my spine and straight to my cock, which throbbed painfully in response.

Claire gasped as my fingers brushed over her lace covered mound. I groaned deeply and closed my eyes in ecstasy at the feel of the dampness there.

Fuck, that felt good. I loved that she was wet for me and it spurred me on.

"I'll make a bet with you that I can make you come twice in

the next ten minutes, here, now. If I can, you will spend the night with me, no holds barred, giving yourself to me completely, and I will show you just how great we can be. I'll make it so good that you will never want to leave me," I whispered in her ear, before pulling back to look her in the eye again.

Sliding my fingers inside the cloth, I rubbed her clit. She cried out and bit her lip, her eyes fluttering closed as I continued to move my fingers over her. My Little Sexy Ass was so responsive to my touch that it made me hopeful that I could make it happen, make her mine.

"And if I can't, I will leave you alone and never bother you again," I said, blowing on one nipple then the other, smiling when she shivered in response.

As her breathing grew harsh, I nibbled on her neck, kissing, licking, and sucking her there, while my thumb circled, and pressed, against the source of her pleasure. As her juices coated my fingers, I slid two inside her. She gasped and rocked her hips up to meet them as I thrust in and out.

The tightness of her channel made me long to bury my cock deep inside, but that wasn't my plan. Not yet. If I was lucky, I'd get to fulfil all of my fantasies with her in the future and my cock would be constantly kept satisfied, but right now, it had to wait.

"Do you agree to the bet?" I asked, my voice thick with passion as I whispered the words against her lips.

When she only groaned and leaned into my kiss, I dipped my head back to her breasts, nipping and tugging gently on her nipples, as my fingers sped up their rhythm. I needed her to agree. The last thing I wanted was for her to regret what we were doing and deny what we had again. I had to get her to agree to the bet.

As her panting increased, I dipped my head to her breasts

again, my tongue circled one nipple then the other, while my thumb circled her clit.

"Babe, answer me," I whispered.

Watching her face as she slowly rocked her hips against my hand, I couldn't believe that she was finally allowing me to touch her in this way again. When she ran from me last time, I thought this day might never come.

My lips crashed down on hers, and I pulled her tighter against me, needing to have her as close as possible. She wasn't going to run this time. Never again. I'd make her see she was mine. But she still hadn't agreed.

Claire's half-closed eyes were filled with passion. She was lost in her lust, moaning and squirming as I increased my passionate assault on her body. I knew it was unfair to manipulate her this way, but to get my chance with her, I would do anything, even if it meant not playing fair. Then I reminded myself of the old saying, *"All's fair in love and war!"*

Pulling back, I looked into her eyes, the passion I saw there took my breath away, but there was a hint of something else too. Was that a glint of mischief?

My eyes narrowed, and I grinned, was my sexy little lawyer playing hardball with the player? Lifting my eyebrows in question, I waited for her response.

Claire still didn't say anything, just smiled and leaned up to kiss me hard. So, she was playing then. I chuckled. It looked like she needed a lesson in submission. Game on, baby girl!

Her eyes were closed, and she rocked against me, panting. She was close to coming, but she wasn't being a good girl. She wasn't going to get her reward until she told me what I wanted to hear.

"Look at me, Claire," I demanded, and her eyes snapped open.

"Do you agree to the bet, Claire?" I asked, more forcefully this time. When she still didn't respond, I withdrew my fingers. She mewled a protest.

"Oh no, naughty girls don't get rewarded. Now be a good girl and answer me. If you want to come, you need to agree to my terms."

Chest heaving, she gulped and nodded.

"I need your words, Claire. Tell me you agree!"

"Yes!" she gasped, and I grinned.

"Good girl! Now, you get to come. Now, I'm going to make you see stars. Twice," I told her as I reinserted my fingers and got to work on fulfilling my promise.

A few seconds later and she came moaning my name against my lips.

"That's the first one," I said with a satisfied chuckle. "Time for another."

CHAPTER 21
CLAIRE

THE SAME DAY – PLAYING WITH THE PLAYER

Another? He really was intending to get me off again? Hell yeah, bring it on!

When my sexy Russian first suggested he could do that, make me orgasm twice in ten minutes, I had to admit, I didn't believe him. But within a couple, he'd achieved the first and by the way my body was continuing to respond to his very thorough exploration, I thought he might actually succeed.

"If anyone can, Luca can," the little thrilled voice in my head squealed.

Still, I had refused to give in to his bet. Why? Because I'd already been willing to give us a shot. He hadn't needed to come up with this elaborate scheme to make me. I'd been about to tell him that when he stopped me from speaking, no doubt thinking I'd refuse, and set about in earnest trying to convince me. I moaned into his mouth, masking the giggle threatening to spill out and give my game away. The Player thought he could manipulate the Ice Queen? Not a chance.

Mr Sexy Kisser might easily thaw me out with his lips, but he had to learn that manipulating me wasn't something

I'd let him get away with. At least not often. Controlling me in the bedroom? Hell yeah! But while I loved submitting to his domineering ways—especially when he growled "good girl" in my ear—he'd better understand that it stopped there.

So, I kept quiet, letting him try to earn what I'd already been willing to give. It was so much fun watching him work for my answer, seeing that flash of uncertainty every time I held back. Luca's lips smashed against mine, and he devoured me like a starving man, teeth grazing and tongue demanding. My body was already singing, heating up under his touch, but the best part was knowing I had him exactly where I wanted. His hands gripped my waist, pulling me closer until there was no space left between us, and every breath, every gasp, felt like proof of the fire burning between us.

"God, I've missed these lips. You're such a great kisser," he murmured, voice thick with desire.

"You too," I moaned, unable to hide the pleasure coursing through me. It was true—the man was one hell of a sexy kisser. That was what had made him so difficult to resist. I'd been holding my ground until the moment he first claimed my mouth, and after that, no amount of stubbornness could save me. The second our lips met, I'd been his. I just hadn't been ready to admit it until now.

My core still throbbed from my last orgasm, my hips arching up to meet his fingers as they rubbed my clit and thrust inside me, relentless and unyielding. Luca kissed me deeply, his growl vibrating against my lips and sending shivers straight down my spine. My legs buckled, my knees nearly giving out, but he held me steady, pressed tight against the door, my hands pinned above my head. Without him anchoring me, I would've melted into a puddle at his feet.

A wicked smirk played at the corners of his lips as his tongue dived deeper, exploring every inch of my mouth. He knew exactly what he was doing, knew he'd hit my Achilles heel when another low growl escaped him, louder this time, rough and primal. My eyes fluttered shut, rolling back in bliss as I surrendered to his control.

The man had Henry Cavill vibes pouring off him— broad, commanding, and dangerously sexy. Each growl, each thrust, made it impossible not to give in. My body was on fire, and every move he made only turned the heat up higher.

Oh, my god! What this man could do to me with just his voice, let alone those wickedly skilled fingers, defied all logic. No one had ever made me come so easily, so utterly undone, the way my sexy Russian did. And those lips? That kiss? I was hopeless against him.

When Luca sank to his knees in front of me, and his mouth replaced his thumb, I knew I was done for. There'd never be anyone who could live up to my Mr Sexy Kisser. He'd stolen my heart and branded me, body and soul, with his searing passion.

Luca's hands gripped the sides of my knickers, tugging them down in one smooth, determined motion. I stepped out of them without hesitation, my skin tingling at the brush of his touch. In a flash, my skirt was shoved up to my waist, and one of my legs was draped over his broad shoulder. I gasped, my pulse racing as he positioned me exactly where he wanted.

Groaning, he licked my slit and sucked on my clit. My fingers gripped the door hook for dear life. Luca's moans as he went down on me with gusto, had me panting with need so strong I was sure if I didn't cling to the hook, tethering myself to the room, I'd end up soaring through the roof and into space, never to come back down again.

Moans and pants filled the air around me and I knew I

was close. He was going to do it. He was going to make me come again.

"Life isn't black and white, Claire. You know this. Come dance with me in shades of grey," he whispered as the waves of my second orgasm crashed through me, stealing my breath and cleansing my mind of all thoughts except Luca.

That did it. My world shattered as I broke apart, crying his name.

As my breathing slowed, Luca brought his lips back up to mine and kissed me again. I could taste myself on him and it almost made me come again. Dear lord!

"That's two. I win!" he stated with a giant grin.

"Yes hotshot, you win!" I laughed unable to stop myself at his smug look.

Shaking my head, I smoothed down my skirt and buttoned my blouse as Luca washed his hands and then wiped my thighs and pussy with some toilet paper. My heart melted even further at his tender care of me.

Picking up our jackets, Luca gave me a quick peck on the lips before helping me on with it. Realising I was knickerless, I frowned, looking down at the floor.

"Looking for these?" he said, twirling them around a finger.

I tried to snatch them, but he lifted his arm out of my reach.

"Uh uh, these are mine now, babe," he said smugly before pocketing them.

"Give me those back!" I cried, but he just laughed, picked up my laptop bag, grabbed my hand, and tugged me out of the toilet.

My gasp of indignation at having to walk around commando style was met with an amused chuckle and I was about to demand he return them when I saw the others still waiting for us. The knowing looks and smirks making it clear they knew exactly what we'd been up to.

I'd never live this down. My cheeks flamed, and I was glad they didn't know about Luca's little trophy. Yet, I wasn't truly embarrassed, rather I was filled with excitement that I'd finally agreed to be with Luca and everyone knew.

Marcie took in my flushed face and turned to Luca with a grin. "About time you got your leg over!" she cried.

"He didn't!" I claimed indignantly, enthusing my voice with all the primness I could. Luca's face fell. Did he expect me to deny us to our friends? Did he think I would go back on our agreement?

My lips twitched. "Not yet anyway. But he promised me a night of no holds barred sex, so let's go home," I said with a wicked grin as I met the eyes of everyone there before turning to Luca. His eyes were wide with shock, but he quickly got over it and grinned, tugging me into a tight embrace and planting a big smacker on my lips.

"Damn right I did," he smirked and grabbed my hand, holding it tightly all the way back to the Estate.

My heart soared. There was no way this man was letting go of me, and I was more than happy with that. As we drove the distance back to the Estate, we smooched in the back of one of the SUVs.

There was a convoy of them. Everyone else had bundled themselves into the others, leaving us alone in ours. Except for Vlad. He drove, but after we started making out like horny teenagers, he quickly closed the partition, hiding us from view.

My hand lowered to Luca's crotch, and I rubbed the bulge there, rewarded by a deep, pained groan. His cock was so hard, it had to hurt.

Licking my lips, I started to pull down his zip.

"No, babe. Not yet."

"But you're in need, honey," I protested.

"I can wait, babe. I have plans for us when we get back to the Estate. So many plans," he told me, gently moving my hand away. His words sent a gush of wetness to my pussy and I squirmed.

God, hurry up! my inner voice screamed. We needed to get home soon, or I was going to explode.

CHAPTER 22
LUCA

THE SAME DAY – PUNISHMENT AND
PLEASURE

Miki was waiting for us when we stepped out of the car. Everyone else had thankfully gone inside and wouldn't be witness to the painful, desperate look on my face as I willed my cock to behave. When Claire had wanted to ease things off for me, I'd almost let her. But I'd spent ages planning all the ways I'd make love to her when I had the chance and I was determined to fulfil those plans. So, I held off. But now I was at the end of my tether, barely able to think straight due to the throbbing pain in my cock.

"We need to talk. We've lots to discuss," Miki said as we got out of the car.

"Later, much later," I shouted, rushing past him, pulling Claire behind me.

Miki's deep chuckle resonated behind us. Oh, I would never stop hearing about this. And after all the ribbing I'd given him and his brothers, and all of my protestations that I wouldn't follow in their footsteps, gagging after a woman, I would deserve the teasing.

We practically flew up the stairs, almost stumbling in my haste to finally get Claire into my bed, where she belonged.

"Hey!" Claire protested as I tugged her in the opposite direction to the guest wing.

"My room, babe!"

As soon as we reached my room, I pushed open the door and hurried her inside. Grabbing her, I kissed her hard until we had to break apart just to breathe. I loved the way this woman tasted, and I loved how she kissed me back with just as much hunger, meeting my intensity without hesitation.

But I wanted more. Tonight was to be no holds barred, and I wasn't about to waste this chance she was giving me. She walked towards my bed and turned to face me, eyes dark with anticipation.

"Strip," I commanded, slowly removing my jacket, keeping my gaze locked on her.

She didn't move, just watched me, her mind clearly turning over thoughts she didn't voice. I wasn't about to let her find an excuse to back out, not when I'd finally got her here, so I reminded her of our deal.

"You promised to spend the night with me—no holds barred, giving yourself to me completely. Remember, sweetheart? And you told everyone about it. You can't back out now."

"I did, didn't I?" she said, a slow, sexy smile spreading across her lips. "And I don't have any intention of backing out."

"So, strip," I ordered again, my voice firm.

She shivered, and I knew she liked my domineering side. Little Miss Sexy Ass wanted to submit, and I was more than ready to let her. For good measure, I added, "Don't make me tell you again, sweetheart. Be a good girl. Naughty girls get punished." I let the smirk spread across my face as I watched her reaction.

Another shiver ran through her, followed by a chuckle as she slipped off her jacket, tossing it aside. I pulled off my shirt, and she smiled widely, watching me as she removed hers.

My shoes were next, followed by hers, then my socks. She started to undo her skirt when my gaze dropped to her chest.

"The bra," I growled, staring at her luscious tits as she followed my command. My cock throbbed hard, almost doubling me over in pain when her breasts spilled free as she loosened the straps and removed the bra completely.

My hands flew to my belt, and I undid it and pulled down my zip, before slipping my hand into my trousers to stroke myself. God, the pain in my engorged shaft was almost unbearable.

Little Miss Sexy Ass playfully twirled her bra on one finger before tossing it at me. I caught it, smirking, and threw it aside with the rest of our clothes. Without taking my eyes off her, I started to remove my trousers, eager to claim what I'd been waiting for so damn long.

She licked her lips, her eyes widening as she watched them fall to the floor. Her hands worked to remove her skirt, but she never took her eyes off me. I could see her breath quickening, just like mine. She was openly ogling my cock, straining against my tight boxer briefs, and I loved it. The way she couldn't tear her gaze away, how she clearly liked that I was hard as fuck for her—it drove me wild.

My cock throbbed, making its impatience clear, jerking at the sight of her skirt falling away, leaving her in nothing but her hold-ups. Her nipples were hard, her chest rising and falling with each rapid breath. I couldn't hold back a groan at the sight of her, stunning and ready.

This tandem strip was turning us both on beyond belief.

Hooking my thumbs into the waistband of my boxers, I slowly pulled them off. As my hardness sprung up to greet her, she gulped. Our gaze travelled over each other as we panted hard at seeing the other naked for the first time.

She was so gorgeous. Pre-come dripped from my cock and my hands ached to touch her, but I fisted them, denying myself. *Not yet. Soon!*

Breathing deeply, I forced myself to remain where I was. No matter how badly I needed this, I wasn't going to let it rush me.

Her eyes lit up as she saw how badly I wanted her and how hard I fought for control. She bit her bottom lip, making my resolve almost buckle, and reached down to remove her stockings.

"Leave them on!" I snapped, panting hard.

They were as sexy as hell, and I wanted to keep her in them for a bit longer, to feel them as her legs wrapped around me. Soon, I reminded myself, not quite yet.

There was something I really wanted to do to her first. I planned on driving her wild tonight, and I knew just how I wanted to start.

"On the bed, on your knees, facing the headboard," I commanded, my voice leaving no room for hesitation.

She obeyed immediately, and I sucked in a breath at the sight before me—her naked, sexy ass exposed and ready. This was what I'd been fantasising about for months, ever since she first rejected me. I knelt on the bed behind her, still resisting the urge to touch her, but barely.

My breathing was coming in short, harsh gasps now, and I knew I couldn't hold back for much longer.

"You've been a naughty girl, Claire," I said, my voice low and commanding. "Rejecting me, keeping me waiting for this moment for almost a year. Denying us all this time. I'm going to punish you for that, babe. Twelve good, hard spanks, six on each cheek to make up for it."

I was going to light up that sexy ass of hers, make it burn, the way she made my cock burn. Then I was going to fill her up, over and over again, in every way possible, until she combusted with pleasure.

Claire gulped hard and looked at me over her shoulder. I caught a glimpse of hesitancy in her eyes, but she didn't move.

She was being such a good girl.

"Don't worry, babe, I'll make sure you enjoy every minute of it," I told her as my palm came down on one cheek. One quick hard slap to her bottom and she gasped.

Reaching between her folds, I rubbed and her clit as I leaned down and kissed her bottom right where my hand had been.

Another spank, to the other cheek this time, then I massaged it before rubbing her clit again. I repeated my actions, each time giving her a good, hard slap, reddening her sexy bottom before taking time to play with her clit and kiss or massaging the sting away.

Sweat broke out all over her body and she cried out, her body jerking, each time I spanked her luscious cheeks. The wetness between her legs and her moans when I touched her there told me that my sexy lawyer was enjoying it as much as me. Little Miss Sexy Ass definitely had a hot ass now, I silently chuckled.

By the time I'd finished her punishment, she was a quivering wreck, and her pussy was soaking from the little bit of pain with maximum pleasure I bestowed. I gently stroked her, feeling the heat in her cheeks and admiring the redness.

She arched her back, pushing her bottom up towards my hand in silent invitation, and I smirked. I knew she wanted to be filled, but that would happen, many times tonight but not right now. My cock couldn't take any more waiting and since it was about to burst, I wanted it in her mouth. She wouldn't get it inside that sweet pussy until she begged.

Leaning over her, I nibbled on her neck and whispered in her ear.

"You're such a good girl, Claire. You took your punishment so well. Now it's time for your reward," I told her before lifting her hands off the headboard and turning her to face me and pushing her gently to her knees on the floor. "Suck me!" I demanded, sitting on the bed and bringing my cock to her lips.

Her cute pink tongue flicked out and licked the tip of my cock, and that was almost my undoing. Hissing in pleasure, I breathed deeply and squeezed the top, forcing myself to hold off, just as I'd been doing throughout Claire's punishment.

Little Miss Sexy Ass licked my length a few times, each stroke of her tongue sending jolts of pleasure through me. Then she took me into her mouth, and my eyes rolled back in my head. The feel of her hot, wet mouth wrapped around my cock was better than any of my fantasies, and I'd fantasised about it more times than I could count.

She gripped my cock in one hand, stroking my balls with the other, sucking me in a way that made it impossible to think straight. My hands tangled in her hair, holding her gently as I let myself get lost in the sensations she was giving me. Her lips were locked around my hard shaft, moving up and down with a rhythm that was both maddening and perfect.

This was such an exquisite torture. My cock longed to release down that sexy throat, moaning around it. But I'd promised myself I wouldn't come until I was buried balls deep in her pussy and that before I did so, she'd be wild and begging for me to fuck her.

Oh, but she is so good at this!

How the hell was I supposed to hold out?

CHAPTER 23
CLAIRE

THE SAME DAY – GIVING LUCA A
CHANCE

Luca was close, teetering on the edge of release, but doing all he could to avoid it. Lord, the man had an amazing level of control.

It was truly surprising, considering he'd been painfully hard for so long and practically dragged me up the stairs to his room. I'd half expected him to throw me over his shoulder like a bloody caveman when I wasn't going fast enough, and we almost stumbled. I'd been hard pressed not to laugh at his eagerness, but I'd held back, knowing just how desperate he was.

Miki hadn't had the same reservation and his loud chuckle told of future teasing Luca and I were both likely to have to endure. Still, I couldn't bring myself to care. Not when I was just as eager to sample our no holds barred night of sex. And what a night it was turning out to be.

My bum stung as I kneeled on the floor in front of where he sat on the bed, my nipples were hard, my pussy wet and clenching with need.

I'd never been spanked before, but I had to admit, it was thrilling. Who knew I would love the exquisite mix of pleasure and pain? I chuckled. Luca, I suppose. Lord, that man knew exactly what turned me on and right now, hearing his pleasurable groans and seeing his eyelids flutter and his eyes roll back, well, that was certainly doing the trick. I had never really enjoyed giving head before, but it turned out with Luca it was different. Giving my Mr Sexy Kisser pleasure was just as enjoyable for me as receiving it.

To think he'd actually thought I would turn down a bet that promised a couple of orgasms and a night of incredible passion with the sexy man afterwards. Ha! As if! Even if I'd still been in denial about us, I wouldn't have turned that down. What grown ass woman in her right mind would?

Still, he didn't have to know that. Not yet. Let him still think he had to convince me more. I was far too busy enjoying that to let him in on the secret. I grinned wickedly around his hardness.

He tasted good. As I moved my head up and down, enjoying the feel of him in my mouth, I took in the rest of his body. He was bloody stunning. And how much did he have to work out to maintain that physique? The six-pack abs that were every man's dream, and every woman's. The muscular arms and legs which showed his strength, the strong jaw and dreamy brown eyes and that soft dark hair. God, he truly was the full package.

And what a package he had. I silently sniggered. It was proving quite the task to take him all the way in my mouth. Luckily, I didn't have much of a gag reflex, but the sheer size of him made my jaw ache. Not that I was complaining. Who'd complain over a big cock and a guy who knew what to do with it?

Of course, he was yet to prove that, but the way he was going, it was not something I was concerned with. My pussy clenched, reminding me it needed to be filled, and I moaned loudly, squirmed and sucked on Luca's cock harder in response.

Thankfully, he got the message.

Grabbing me, he hauled me up and threw me onto the bed, lunging over me, notching his cock at my entrance.

Oh, hell yeah! But just when I thought he would enter me, he stopped.

"Luca!" I protested, and he chuckled.

"I know what you want, babe, and I'll give it to you. Soon," he said with a wicked grin.

Seemingly out of nowhere, his tie appeared in his hands and he wrapped it around my wrists then stretched my arms up and fastened the ends to the metal headboard.

With me at his mercy again, those sexy lips of his sprinkled kisses all over my body deliberately avoiding the parts I wanted his mouth on the most.

"God, you are the sexiest woman I've ever known," he said, his eyes travelling over me with such raw lust, I almost came just from his look alone.

"Please, Luca," I begged, thrusting my breasts at him when he kissed his way down my chest intent on avoiding them again.

Smiling, he licked his lips and latched on.

Positioning himself, he wrapped my stocking clad legs around him and rocked his hips slowly, letting his cock slide back and forth across my clit, but pulling back every time I lifted my hips to meet his, not allowing me what I desperately craved.

My moans filled the room as he teased me mercilessly, rocking against me as he licked, nipped and sucked my breasts and body all over my body, until I was a hot squirming mess. Sweat coated my body, and I felt like I was burning up.

"Fuck, Luca, please, no more teasing. I need you, please!" I begged.

"Not yet, babe. Not until you are so needy you can't think straight," he replied, his cool breath flitting across my hot skin, making me shiver.

His cock breached my entrance.

"Yes!" I cried loudly, but Luca wasn't ready to let me have my way.

He pulled out and continued his torture, teasing me until I couldn't take any more. I was about to come, but I wanted to do it when he was buried inside me.

"Please, I need it, I need you, fuck me, Luca, please…," I cried, the words tailing off into mumbled nonsense.

He was driving me wild, just as he'd planned.

I could've cried when he pulled away, sitting back on his knees. He grabbed my legs and lifted them high into the air, turning his head to press kisses to the top of one thigh, then the other.

My breathing was coming so rapidly and I was unable to form a coherent sentence, I mumbled "please," over and over. I was shaking, my need so strong. I had to have him or I'd go mad.

Pushing two fingers deep, he thrust.

"So tight, so wet," he murmured. "I'm going to fuck you now, babe. The first time of many times tonight," he whispered, brushing his lips against my ear.

Thank god!

The world shrunk down until nothing existed but him. I was so sensitive everywhere, that even his breath on my earlobe made me shudder with excitement.

As he lined up his cock, I wiggled, impatient to feel it buried deep.

The torturing devil chuckled.

"Don't come until I tell you!" he commanded then thrusts hard right to the hilt.

"Yes!" I cried out. Finally, he was right where I needed him.

Oh, that felt so good! I almost came then but remembered he had said not to. I took deep breaths, fighting my release, and trying to adjust to the intrusion.

Then he started to move, and it was like he couldn't stop himself. It was flipping amazing! He pounded into me so hard and fast that I knew I really couldn't hold out much longer.

He was desperate now himself, plunging deep into me at a relentless pace, rubbing, tugging, and twisting my nipple.

"Come, sweetheart!" he shouted, and I did. Like a fucking tsunami! My pussy milked his cock as he continued to thrust another few times before he too shouted out his release.

"That's my good girl!" he said, as the waves of pleasure died down, making me smile even as I gasped for breath. He slowly withdrew his cock, and we kissed again. My pussy already felt empty without him.

Reaching up, he undid the tie, before collapsing beside me and pulling me close.

"That was utterly amazing. I knew it would be," he said with a chuckle.

My body felt like jelly, and I couldn't help smiling at my completely sated, blissed-out state. I lay on his chest as he kissed the top of my head.

Suddenly, he went very still, barely breathing.

"Babe, I'm sorry, but I got so carried away I forgot to put on a condom. I'm clean though, I promise!" he said.

"Me too," I replied. "And I'm on the pill!" I added quickly.

"Okay, great. I love feeling us together with nothing

between us, but I can use a condom from now on if you prefer?" he asked, his gaze flickering over my face.

Luca was still worried about us. He obviously still expected me to reject him. Shame filled me. I'd played with his feelings long enough. It was time to come clean.

"I'm happy to continue without, Luca. I know I'm safe with you. I trust you," I told him, and I did. He might have been a player before we met, but I believed him when he said that was all over now.

"Luca, I need to tell you something," I said.

Concern flashed in his eyes, so I hurried on.

"I want to give us a shot. I decided that before you made the bet. I won't keep denying what's between us. It's special and I want to see where it goes."

His eyes lit up with hope, and I knew I'd made the right decision.

"What about my Bratva links?" he asked quietly.

I smiled and shook my head.

"I won't lie and say I don't still have my concerns about your criminal life but I refuse to let that stop me from exploring a life with you. As you pointed out, and whether or not I like it, we don't live in a world that's black and white. Most of us live in shades of grey. It's time I faced that reality. And I want to dance with you in the grey, Luca," I told him, tears pricking my eyes at the raw vulnerability I saw in his.

Smiling, I pulled his head towards me and kissed him deep, letting him feel my sincerity in every stroke of my tongue.

When we finally broke for air again, he grinned and rolled me onto my front.

"Time for round two," he whispered, his voice thick with desire.

Kneeling between my legs, he ran his hands down my

back and squeezed my ass. I loved it. I loved everything this man did to me. I couldn't get enough of him, and the thrill of our connection left me breathless.

"Up on your knees!" he commanded, and my heart raced at his authority.

I rushed to obey, knowing the night had only just begun, and with each moment, I was falling deeper into a passion I never wanted to end.

CHAPTER 24

LUCA

A WEEK LATER – GATHERING MY DEFENCE

I t had been one hell of a week. Whistling as I descended the stairs toward Marko's office, I couldn't wipe the grin from my face. My Little Miss Sexy Ass and I had just wrapped up another steamy session, and things between us were better than ever. Claire had finally given in, and we'd been inseparable since, spending every moment we could together—talking about everything when we weren't going at it like bunnies.

She'd left a short while ago with Vlad to see Bradley; she had a client up in court this afternoon. I couldn't shake the anticipation of her return. Every moment apart felt like an eternity. Tonight, as she joined the other women for Marcie's cocktail night, I wondered how much more of her wild side would emerge. I craved that side of her, the one that lit up like fireworks after a couple of drinks.

I pushed open the door to Marko's office, the scent of stale coffee and the hum of computers greeting me like old friends. Still riding the high, I strolled in, my grin impossible to hide.

"You look happy," Marko said, glancing up from his computer.

Dropping into the seat beside him, I grinned, my fingers tapping restlessly against the armrest, my pent-up energy needing an outlet. "I am. And once I clear my name and we deal with the MP, I'll be even happier."

"All going well, that won't be long," Marko said. "I'm still digging into how the MP figured out who you were. We'll get to the bottom of it."

It was a dilemma.

Marko's office, cluttered with monitors displaying streams of data and walls plastered with graphs and photos, felt like the nerve centre of our operation—a place where plans were hatched and secrets were unearthed. If the guy wasn't Bratva, I swear he'd be a top analyst for MI5. Maybe even one of their agents.

The name's Bond, Marko Bond.

I snorted, spilling coffee down my shirt. Dabbing at it with a blank piece of paper.

"What the fuck is wrong with you?" Marko asked, looking at me as if I'd lost the plot.

Sniggering, I shook my head but didn't respond.

Instead, I changed the subject, getting serious. "Did you manage to get anything yet?"

It had taken a while, but Marko had finally found proof that the cameras in my building on the night of Julie's murdered were indeed tampered with. He'd been working to recover the deleted security footage ever since.

He nodded. "I'll bring it up on-screen and we'll view it together."

As we waited for it to load, he filled me in on the latest with Simpson—a guy we were keeping alive because he might prove useful, despite the fact the perverted arsehole should have been killed months ago.

"Fucker's been lying low. He knows we're watching his every move. He's even stopped his little rendezvous with the rent boys he loves so much."

Thank fuck. Bile rose in my throat as my mind assaulted me with images I'd seen of him in compromising situations. I hated the slimy little weasel. He was married with teenage sons, but that didn't stop him from regularly attending sordid sex parties where he got far too friendly with young boys not much older than his sons. The guy sickened me.

Just before I met Claire, we'd discovered the alliance between the Malia Boys and Broxys. After their attack on our estate and drug lab, we found they were backed by a London lawyer named Nigel Simpson, working for a Glasgow lawyer, Aiden Mathieson.

Mathieson had been quietly orchestrating our problems for years, driven by a vendetta against Miki's dad, Alexi, who had exposed Mathieson's banker father's criminal dealings. When his father committed suicide in prison, Mathieson set out for revenge, funding gangs and running a human trafficking ring, building a powerful little empire for himself. Somehow, he'd learned about Alexi's involvement in his father's demise. By that time, Alexi was dead, and Miki was pakhan, but that didn't stop the fucker from extracting his retribution.

Once we learned he was the one responsible for our troubles, we pulled Mathieson's empire down like a house of cards, thanks to Eilidh, Miki's fiancée, who had been investigating him. She understood the risks all too well; her father had been killed by the same corrupt cops Mathieson had in his pocket. Eilidh's intel helped us gather evidence that brought Mathieson's operation crashing down, and we managed to grab him before the police did. But the bastard's heart gave out under interrogation before we could extract anything useful.

Marko hacked into one of Mathieson's accounts and set up an alert for any activity. Months later, a transfer popped up —this time to a woman named Melissa Martin. At the time, she was just another lead, but through her, we uncovered the MP's connection to Mathieson: they were half-brothers, sharing the same father and a deep-seated grudge against us. It wasn't until later that Melissa became Marko's fiancée.

When I went undercover as the MP's bodyguard, I thought my disguise—blond hair, fake tattoos, and a Scottish accent—was foolproof. But somehow, he figured out who I was. We knew there was always a chance my cover might be blown, but we never imagined it would happen so soon—or that he'd go as far as killing one of my exes to frame me for her murder.

The MP was a lunatic, and we needed him out of the picture—permanently.

"Here we go," Marko said as a grainy black-and-white image flickered to life on the screen.

"It's a shit system they have, and I haven't been able to clear it up any better than this," he continued, squinting at the footage as we both leaned in closer.

We watched the video intently, taking note of the comings and goings from the basement car park. Then I saw what I was looking for.

"There," I said, my voice barely above a whisper. Marko quickly froze the image.

"That's Joey McDougall. One of the MP's bodyguards. A right arsehole," I said, anger simmering beneath the surface as Marko snapped a screenshot of the man's face.

We spent the next couple of hours combing through the

rest of the footage. By the end of it, we had identified our killer. The bastard had been in the car park of my flat not long before I returned home. He'd shown up carrying a large holdall, one big enough to contain a body—or more likely, a restrained person. Julie. Within twenty minutes, he'd exited again, and this time the bag didn't look quite so heavy.

Now we'd identified the likely culprit, we needed to link him to Julie and find more evidence because the images alone wouldn't be enough.

It didn't take long for Marko long to hack into his mobile and unearth numerous texts between him and Julie.

They'd been dating, having met after she got out of rehab. From what I gathered, she'd been at the MP's garden party on the day of the heist while I was undercover. I hadn't seen her, but she must have spotted me, recognised me despite my disguise, or perhaps noticed something about Leon Peters, my alter ego, that reminded her of me. Maybe she hadn't given it much thought at the time, but after the MP was arrested and I went off the grid, she might have mentioned it. They could have easily connected the dots.

Something had clearly gone wrong between her and McDougall, as several texts revealed him calling her a cheating slut. That was the motive.

So, Joey McDougall was the rapist and murdering bastard directly responsible for Julie's death, and he was going to pay.

"Let's tell Miki what we found. We need to find this guy," Marko said.

Marko and I strode into Miki's office, the air thick with urgency. Miki was hunched over a stack of documents, his brow furrowed in concentration. He looked up as we entered, sensing the gravity of the moment.

"What's going on?" he asked, setting aside his work.

I took a breath, ready to lay it all out. "We found our suspect in Julie's murder. Joey McDougall, one of the MP's bodyguards. He was in the car park of my flat just before I got home. He had a large holdall with him, and it didn't look so heavy when he left."

"Got any proof?"

"Absolutely," Marko confirmed, stepping forward and opening his laptop to pull up the images we'd gathered.

"Good work. Miki said, smiling in approval as he scanned the footage.

"Can we tie him to Julie?"

"Yeah. I hacked his mobile, there are a lot of conversations between the pair," Marko stated.

"McDougall and Julie had been dating, having met after she got out of rehab. She was at the MP's garden party on the day of the heist. We suspect she might have seen something, and he could have found out about our past," I told Miki.

Miki leaned back in his chair, the weight of the situation settling in. "Motive?"

I nodded. "We're working on it. The initial messages to Julie were passionate before things went dark. His jealousy and anger are evident in those texts. They paint a clear picture of a volatile relationship."

Miki's eye narrowed in thought and he steepled his hands. "If he's our guy, we need to move fast. I don't want him slipping through our fingers. We need him alive. He's your way out of this, Luca. But we can also use him to hammer yet another nail into that fucking MP's coffin.

I felt the adrenaline surge through me, a familiar rush of determination. "Let's make it happen."

Marko exchanged a glance with Miki, and I could see the gears turning in their minds. "Alright," Miki said, leaning forward. "Let's find out where McDougall is hold up, and

Simpson; we'll use both of these arseholes to get the MP to break his bail conditions. He won't be able to fuck us up so easily while he's stuck in a prison cell. We need him remanded and dealt with once and for all."

As we discussed the plan, my thoughts drifted back to Julie. The rage I felt simmered just beneath the surface. She didn't deserve this—none of it. And I would ensure that those responsible paid.

CHAPTER 25
CLAIRE

THE SAME DAY – NAVIGATING THE
SHADES OF GREY

The last week with Luca had been nothing short of extraordinary, the best of my life. It felt like a dream I didn't want to wake up from, each day filled with an intoxicating mix of laughter, desire, and a happiness I hadn't felt in years. Mornings were softer, the world a little brighter, and I found myself smiling for no reason other than the thought of him. We spent our time wrapped in each other, sharing moments that felt stolen from reality.

The thrill of being with him hadn't faded; it had only grown stronger, making every goodbye feel like an unwelcome intrusion. Luca had a way of making me feel seen and cherished, as though every part of me—the good, the guarded, the messy—was exactly what he wanted. I'd never known a connection like this, one that burned with both passion and comfort, pushing me to let go in ways I hadn't thought possible.

But as perfect as it felt, the undercurrents of change tugged at me, a slow acceptance that the lines I'd always drawn were blurring. I was no longer just the barrister who clung to the law like it was an unbreakable creed; I was his, and that came with complications. Each time Luca confided in me, every moment he'd shared about his world, stirred something deep within—a mix of pride, worry, and a growing willingness to understand his reality.

The days had passed in a haze of courtrooms and whispered phone calls, while the nights overflowed with passionate encounters and exchanges that left my heart racing. I felt different, changed, as if the weight I'd carried for so long had lightened in his presence. I'd catch myself replaying our moments together—his lips on mine, his hand trailing along my skin, the way he looked at me like I was his whole world—and it made everything else seem distant, less significant. Even here, surrounded by the rigid decorum of the courtroom, fidgeting with my pen as I waited for the next case, I couldn't help but drift back to thoughts of him.

My phone buzzed against the polished wooden table, pulling me from my reverie. I glanced at the screen, and my heart leapt at Luca's name. His timing felt like a gentle reminder of his presence in my life.

"Hey, you," I answered, a smile spreading across my lips.

"Hey, beautiful," he replied, his voice smooth and reassuring. It was as if the world around me faded away, leaving only the warmth of his words. "I wanted to give you an update. We've made progress on the case."

"That's great! Tell me everything," I urged, my heart racing at the prospect of good news.

He recounted his findings, his tone filled with excitement. "Oh my god, Luca. That's amazing. Just what we need," I squealed in delight before realising where I was and lowering my voice. "We should let the prosecution know. This will blow their case out of the water. All we have to do is provide a shadow of doubt, and that more than fits the bill."

"Not yet, babe. We're going to try to use him to ensure

the MP gets remanded so he can't cause us any more grief while awaiting trial," he said.

I frowned, feeling a twinge of frustration. I'd prefer to simply get Luca exonerated now, but I understood the importance of keeping the MP from being a problem. I couldn't shake the unease at the thought of him retaliating.

"Alright, but we should disclose this information soon. I'll tell Bradley in the meantime. He'll be over the moon."

"That's my good girl," Mr Sexy Kisser said, and my breath hitched. I hadn't realised I had a praise kink until him.

As we exchanged a few more tender words, my heart soared. The connection we had forged over the past week was unlike anything I had ever experienced before. Our moments together had been intense—electric—a blend of passion and warmth that left me breathless. The nights spent sharing laughter and whispered secrets contributed to a joy I hadn't realised I was missing.

The Clerk entered, signalling that the court session was about to resume.

"I have to go," I said reluctantly. "But I can't wait to see you later."

"Me neither. I'll be thinking about you," he replied, his voice a low murmur that sent a thrill down my spine.

I was thrilled with Luca's news; it meant he wouldn't face a lengthy court case that could jeopardise his reputation and expose his lifestyle. The bonus of avoiding too much time in front of Lady Frost was a relief, though I knew I'd have to deal with her in the future. Just the thought of her smug, icy expression made my jaw clench. If anyone had a chance of getting him hurt, it was her.

As I chewed on the end of my pen, waiting for my client's case to be called, I couldn't shake the nagging thoughts about Luca and the lengths he might go to in order to protect himself. The courtroom buzzed around me, the low hum of whispered conversations blending with the creak of leather chairs, but my mind was elsewhere. I pictured Luca and his Bratva brothers, the unspoken understanding between them, their fierce loyalty to each other. I had always believed in justice, in the law—yet now, I found myself grappling with the reality that sometimes, justice was a slippery concept, especially in the world he inhabited.

What would they do to ensure McDougall co-operated? I didn't think they'd kill him; after all, he was crucial for Luca's defence. But I could easily picture the pressure they might exert to keep him in line—strategies that went beyond mere persuasion. The idea of intimidation lingered in the back of my mind, a concept I had once found repugnant. Yet, as I sat there, I felt a disquieting sense of acceptance. This was their world, and perhaps I was starting to grasp that the ends sometimes justified the means.

Maybe it was a terrible thing to ignore, but I found myself unwilling to stand in their way. The law had always seemed so black and white, yet I was beginning to see the reality was far more blurred than I'd ever imagined. My life was becoming entangled in shades of grey, forcing me to confront the unsettling truth that the rules of the game had shifted. Navigating this murky terrain was not just a matter of legality; it was about survival—and my growing connection with Luca.

CHAPTER 26
LUCA

After extracting Joey McDougall's location from that little weasel, Nigel Simpson, the three of us met up with Ash, Romi, Vlad, and Trigger. The atmosphere crackled with anticipation, thickening as we prepared to confront the bastard. We probably didn't need to go en masse, but uncertainty loomed—McDougall could very well be waiting for us with backup. It was odd that he was hiding out here instead of the country estate with the MP. The MP had to know we'd track him down; after all, McDougall had been Julie's most recent boyfriend, and the police would have wanted to question him. Or at least they should have, if they weren't all in on framing me. So, was he lying low to avoid the police, or was this some sort of trap set by the very people who had tried to ruin me?

Tension coursed through my body, igniting a heightened awareness as I scanned the area, my instincts screaming at me to remain vigilant. The building loomed in the distance—a decaying wooden railway structure, its paint peeling and splintered like the remnants of a forgotten past. It sat alone on an unused track just outside of London, its size imposing yet shrouded in neglect. The larger section had once housed snowploughs, their metal frames rusted and lifeless, now mere echoes of their former purpose. The smaller part resembled a neglected office, cluttered with debris that told tales of abandonment.

Surrounded by overgrown trees on two sides and an open field on the other, the place felt isolated—an ideal hideout. Or a perfect trap. I couldn't see anything alarming, but complacency had no place here. With McDougall linked to the MP, we weren't taking any chances. My heart thudded in my chest, a reminder that the stakes were high, and failure was not an option.

Slipping into our bulletproof vests and dark, inconspicuous overalls to avoid drawing attention, we approached cautiously, weapons in hand. Guns weren't our weapon of choice in Britain; few were in circulation. Knives or knuckles were the preferred tools of our trade, but since the attacks orchestrated by the MP, we had adapted, equipping ourselves with handguns.

Trigger positioned himself high in a tree, ensuring he had a good vantage point, his sniper rifle ready. Once he signalled he was in position, the rest of us crept toward the building from different directions, avoiding the field. If this wasn't a trap, we aimed to catch McDougall off guard.

We reached the door without incident and paused, straining to listen. Silence enveloped us, thick with tension, before Vlad kicked it in. The element of surprise was on our side, but it wasn't needed. The place was empty except for McDougall, sprawled out on a filthy old sofa, an empty bottle in his hand and a bag of coke lying on the scratched wooden coffee table nearby. Fucking bastard was high on drugs and booze!

A battered metal bucket sat near the sink in a small

kitchen area off to the side. I grabbed it, filled it with icy cold water from the tap, and threw it over him. He stirred but didn't fully wake, so I doused him again. This time, the shock brought him around enough to register our presence.

"What the fuck?" he spluttered, bleary-eyed, before his gaze locked onto mine, recognition dawning in his eyes. "You!" he exclaimed, attempting to jump to his feet in a futile effort to run.

"Sobered up now, I see," I said, stepping in as Vlad moved in front of him, yanking him back down onto the sofa. The coward was in no state to fight. He might have been employed as a bodyguard and had a penchant for hitting on women, but I knew his type—brave when surrounded by others, but weak when faced with true power.

"Good, because I have questions, and you're going to answer them," I stated, feeling the weight of the moment settle in my gut, my resolve hardening. I had to know everything about Julie's death—who was responsible and why. The anger coiling within me craved release.

"Why did you kill Julie? Did the MP put you up to it, or was it your suggestion?" Anger boiled within as I confronted the male who'd murdered her.

"I'm saying nothing, you fucking bastard," he spat.

"Answer the questions. Otherwise, you're not going to like what happens," I told him, my voice low and dangerous. I wanted the truth, and I was prepared to extract it by any means necessary.

He laughed, a hollow sound. "I'm not scared of you." His eyes darted around the room, but I saw the flicker of fear behind his bravado—a coward trying to mask his terror.

The smile never reached my eyes. "It's going to get rough if you don't start talking."

"Fuck you!" he sneered, but I could sense his confidence wavering.

I nodded to Ash, and he brought an old wooden chair into the centre of the room. Vlad and Trigger seized McDougall, forcing him into the seat and binding him with rope. Normally, we'd take the bastard to the Crematorium, better known as the C, where we had a special room built underneath for interrogations. But that was a one-way trip, anyone we took there, didn't come out. We needed this fucker alive, at least for now, so we would extract the answers here.

"Now, talk. Why did you kill her? Did you do it because the MP asked, or was there more to it?"

He fell silent, but his snigger told me he wasn't taking me seriously. That would change. I punched him in the gut, and he grunted.

"Is that all you've got?" He smirked, his voice full of false bravado.

Another punch landed, and he wheezed.

"Tell me!" I commanded, punching him hard in the face, his head jerking to the side.

"Aargh! You fucking bastard." He spat blood.

As I prepared to strike him again, Ash restrained me, whispering in my ear. "Luca, calm down. Let's not mark him up where it can be seen. It won't help our plan if he looks like he's taken too much of a beating." I nodded, taking a deep breath to calm myself. The irony of Ash telling anyone to calm down wasn't lost on me; it was usually him who needed restraining. He'd come a long way in managing his own anger.

He looked scared now, glancing between us. "What are you guys whispering about?"

"Ash here wants to start burning you, but I prefer other

methods myself." I smirked at him, feeling the darkness within me stir.

"Fuck off! The MP's going to fucking ruin you guys. You think you're tough? Wait until you see what he can do." He laughed, but I grinned back, a predator toying with its prey.

"Are we going to have to do this the hard way, Joey? Please tell me we are?"

"I'm saying nothing, you fucker," he said, but his eyes showed a slither of fear.

"Oh, you'll talk. No matter what it takes," I told him, my voice dripping with menace as I pulled a knife from my pocket. It glinted ominously under the dull strip light overhead.

He gulped, the bravado slipping away.

"I only did what I was told!" The coward practically shouted in fear as his eyes followed the knife.

"You killed her," I said, my voice low and dangerous. "You tied her up, drugged her, and raped her before you slit her throat and left her to bleed out on my bed. You're a fucking bastard. And over what? Jealousy? Money? Both?"

I nodded to Ash, and he punched the bastard in the gut, the sound of McDougall's grunt of pain making me smile.

"She was a fucking whore!" he spat out, the words forced as he tried to hold back his pain.

"That's no way to talk about a woman," I chided, shaking my head. The bastard needed a lesson in respect.

"The cheating bitch got what she deserved," he spat, and Ash punched him in the gut again.

"Well, maybe it's time you got a little of what you deserve," I told him, my voice deliberately menacing as I cut open his T-shirt, the fabric yielding to my blade.

"What the fuck are you going to do?" Fear laced his voice, a tremor that excited my dark instincts.

"Well, first I'm going to play. Let you feel a little bit of the terror Julie must have felt that night. Then I'm going to ask the rest of my questions, and you'll tell me what I want to know, or I will continue to play until you do, or die, whichever happens first." I smiled, the wicked glint in my eyes matching the intensity of my words. Of course, I had no intention of killing him, but he didn't need to know that.

He gulped in fear, eyes widening as the knife made its way toward the skin of his exposed chest.

"Wait, no, fuck. I'll tell you, whatever you want to know. I'll tell you," he screamed, desperation flooding his voice.

"Yes, you will. But not until you've had a little taste of a knife sliding through your skin, just like it did through Julie's. Gag him," I instructed Vlad.

"No…" McDougall screamed, but the sound was muffled as his ruined T-shirt was wrapped around his mouth.

Over the next few minutes, I slowly cut into him, making shallow cuts that brought him pain, just as my dad and Alexi had taught me. And enjoying every second of it. This man would feel at my hands, all the fear Julie must have at his.

Tears flowed down his face as he screamed behind his gag with each small laceration I made. When he finally pissed himself, I decided he'd had enough.

"That was for Julie. Now answer my questions or you'll get more for your part in framing me for her murder. Understand?"

He nodded, and satisfaction flowed through me. A short while later, I had the answers I wanted, and he was still alive —for now.

Leaving Vlad and Trigger to watch over him, the rest of us returned home to put the final touches on our plan to lure the MP into a trap of our own.

CHAPTER 27
CLAIRE
A FEW DAYS LATER – ATTACKED

The firm's conference room buzzed with conversation and clinking glasses, the familiar hum of ambition and success surrounding me. I lingered near the back, holding a glass of champagne, listening as Donald Turner—Old Man Turner to everyone—gave his retirement speech. He'd built Turner and Hanson into one of the most respected law firms in the city, and tonight was his swan song. Partners, associates, and barristers crowded the room, all here to celebrate the legacy of a man who had spent his life defending the law.

"It's been a privilege," he began, his voice carrying authority, commanding the room's attention as he'd commanded the courtroom for the past forty years. "I've seen this firm through its highs and lows, and now it's time to pass the mantle on to younger folk."

He raised his glass toward his grandson, Damien Turner, who stood proudly beside his mother, Margaret. "Damien, you've proven yourself time and again. Our youngest partner yet. You're going to take this firm to new heights, and I'll be watching with pride as you do."

"Grandfather," Damien said in his crisp, upper-class English accent, lifting his glass in response. He looked around the room with a smug smile, soaking in the praise. The epitome of a privileged upbringing, he wore his entitlement like a badge of honour. He was exactly where he wanted to be, where he believed he was destined to be—partly because of his talent, but mostly because of his family name. I watched, feeling a mix of envy and determination. Damien was on the fast track, but I'd fought for every inch of my success.

"And Claire Benson," Turner continued, his gaze shifting to me. "One of our brightest. With the results you've been delivering, it won't be long before we're celebrating your partnership, too."

The applause that followed warmed me, a comforting validation of the years I'd spent proving myself. I raised my glass, catching Old Man Turner's eye. "Thank you, Mr Turner. I've learned from the best."

He nodded, his smile crinkling the lines of his well-worn face. "And now, it's my turn to step aside, leave the office behind, and spend more time on the golf course. So, if any of you fancy a round or two, you know where to find me."

The room erupted in applause once more, a fitting send-off for a man who had dedicated his life to the firm. As he stepped back, I was swept up by the buzz of congratulations, colleagues offering praise and encouragement. For a moment, everything felt like it was finally falling into place. This firm had been my world for years, and making partner wasn't just a title—it was validation, proof that every late night and sacrifice had been worth it. I had fought for every opportunity, and the dream of partnership was inching closer to reality.

Eventually, the crowd began to thin as the night wore on.

I excused myself and headed back to my office. I still had some paperwork to wrap up before I could call it a night, and I wanted to leave, knowing I'd cleared my desk for the weekend. I typed up my final report. it was Friday night, and I was longing to get home. Vlad would be bored sitting outside waiting for me all of this time.

As I finished tidying up my desk, I pulled out my phone and texted Luca.

Hey honey, I'm just finishing up now. Miss you. x

His response came quickly, laced with his usual warmth.

Miss you too, babe. Can't wait to have you back in my arms. x

I smiled at his words, a rush of anticipation swelling within me. I glanced at the clock, feeling that familiar excitement of knowing I'd be home soon. Just as I was about to gather my things and leave, I heard footsteps approaching my office.

There was a knock at my door. I looked up, expecting to see one of the other associates. Instead, it was Damien, leaning against the frame with an easy smile, his tie loosened and eyes hazy from too much champagne. There was a cockiness about him that always rubbed me the wrong way.

"Evening, Claire," he drawled, stepping inside and closing the door behind him. He didn't just shut it; he locked it, the click of the mechanism sending a ripple of unease through me.

"Evening, Damien." I tried to keep my tone light, though the alarm bells in my head were already ringing. "I'm just finishing up."

Smirking, he took a few steps closer, and I could smell

the alcohol on his breath. "You know, I've been meaning to catch you alone. Thought I'd take my chances one more time. Drinks? Dinner? Or maybe we could simply skip those and go straight to mine?"

Damien's words hung in the air, and I felt a flutter of uncertainty in my stomach. It wasn't the first time he'd asked me out, and I'd always politely refused, keeping our interactions strictly professional. "Thanks, Damien, but you know my rule. I don't mix business with pleasure."

His smile faltered, darkening with irritation. "That's a shame, Claire. You don't seem to mind mixing business and pleasure when it comes to your Russian."

The words hit me like a slap. I stared at him, caught between anger and disbelief. "That's none of your business. You should leave."

But he didn't. He moved closer, his presence suffocating in the confined space of my small office. "I don't like being told no, Claire. Not when I know you've already got a taste for bending the rules."

His tone sent a shiver down my spine, and I took a step back, my mind racing. "Damien, I'm serious. This isn't appropriate."

He ignored me, his eyes fixed on mine with a predatory intensity. Before I could react, he lunged, grabbing my arm and pulling me toward him. I twisted, trying to break free, but he was stronger, and the alcohol had dulled his sense of restraint. He pushed me against the desk, his hands rough and insistent, fumbling at my blouse.

"Get off me!" I shouted, shoving at his chest, but he pinned me in place, his weight crushing against me. His hand snaked up, gripping my wrist painfully as he tried to force my head back for a kiss.

I fought against him, clawing and kicking, but his grip

tightened, and panic surged through me. This couldn't be happening. I twisted my body, managing to free one arm long enough to drive my knee up, catching him in the groin. He let out a grunt of pain and staggered back, giving me just enough space to scramble away, my breath coming in ragged gasps.

Damien's face contorted with fury as he straightened, his hand clutching where I'd kneed him. "You bitch—"

The door burst open, and suddenly Luca was there, eyes blazing, his presence filling the room with a terrifying fury I'd never seen before.

"What the fuck do you think you're doing?" Luca's voice was low, dangerous, as he advanced on Damien.

Damien backed up, fear flashing across his face, but it was too late. Luca grabbed him by the collar, slamming him against the wall with such force that Damien's head cracked against the plaster. I watched, still shaken, as Luca's fist connected with Damien's jaw, the sound of bone hitting bone sharp and brutal.

"Luca, stop!" I shouted, my voice breaking. But he didn't hear me, or maybe he just didn't care. He landed another punch, and then another, each one driven by a fury that seemed unending.

I rushed forward, grabbing Luca's arm, trying to pull him back. "Luca, please. That's enough!"

He paused, breathing heavily, his eyes wild with rage. Damien slumped to the floor, dazed and bloody, his bravado shattered. Luca released him, but not before leaning in close, his voice a low growl. "Come near her again, and I will kill you. Got it?"

Damien nodded, clutching at his jaw, his arrogance replaced by fear, and I knew he'd remember Luca's words long after the bruises faded. Getting to his feet, he stumbled out of the office, and I breathed a sigh of relief.

Luca turned to me, his expression softening, and in that moment, all the adrenaline that had been keeping me upright finally drained away. My legs felt like jelly, and I sank back against my desk, trembling. Stepping closer to me, he took me in his arms and held me.

"Are you alright, babe?" Luca asked, his voice gentle now, full of concern as he murmured the question against my hair.

I nodded, though I didn't fully trust my own voice. "Yeah, I just… I didn't expect him to…"

Luca reached out, brushing a strand of hair from my face, his touch grounding me. "Let's get you home."

I stood shakily, gathering my things with Luca's help.

"What are you doing here? I thought Vlad was taking me home as usual?" I asked, my voice a little steadier now.

"Thought I'd surprise you. I was just heading back home from work myself when you texted me and made a detour. Trigger's waiting in the car. I sent Vlad home for the night," he said, holding me close into his side as we slowly walked to the lift.

As we passed Damien's office, I glanced inside. Damian was there, hunched over in his chair, a cloth held against his bloodied lip and reddened jaw—the aftermath of Luca's wrath. Fury, fear, and disgust filled me. What would come of all this? Neither of us would report the incident to the police; I wouldn't want Luca to get into trouble for beating Damien, and Damien wouldn't want a sexual assault charge against him. But that didn't mean he wouldn't seek some form of revenge. The reality was, as a partner in the firm where I was employed, I would have to interact with him regularly. Could we truly maintain a professional working relationship after this? Would this incident jeopardise my future here? As I gnawed on my lip, a knot of anxiety twisted in my stomach. I couldn't shake the worry that my career was now hanging by a thread.

Luca followed my gaze, sensing the turmoil brewing within me. He pulled me closer, his arm tightening around my shoulders in a protective gesture. "Don't worry about him right now. Let's focus on getting you home and safe. Everything else can be dealt with on Monday." His voice was firm, grounding me amidst the chaos in my mind. The warmth of his presence offered a flicker of reassurance, but the weight of uncertainty lingered. I needed to find a way to navigate this mess without compromising everything I had worked for.

I nodded, leaning against him as the lift doors opened. Once inside, the silence was heavy, broken only by the soft hum of the machinery. I felt Luca's eyes on me, a mix of concern and something deeper, something I wasn't ready to confront.

As the lift descended, I replayed the events of the night in my mind, the horror of Damien's attack juxtaposed with the fierce protectiveness Luca had shown. It left me feeling raw and vulnerable, but also grateful.

"I'm so glad you arrived when you did," I finally said, breaking the silence. "I'm not sure what would have happened—"

"I know," Luca interrupted, his voice low and steady. "But he won't touch you again. I promise."

The lift doors opened, and we stepped into the parking garage. Trigger was waiting, leaning casually against the car, but when he saw us, his eyes widened with concern as he took in my dishevelled appearance.

"Is everything alright, Miss Benson?" Trigger asked, his tone professional, but I could see the worry etched in his features.

I nodded, forcing a smile. "Just a little altercation at work."

Luca opened the door for me, and I slid into the back seat, the leather cool against my skin. He climbed in beside me, closing the door with a decisive thud that cut off the world outside.

As Trigger started the engine, I turned to Luca, searching his face for reassurance. "Thanks for saving me, Luca, for having my back in there. I'd like to think I could have handled the situation myself, but if I'm truly honest, I'm not so sure I could." Admitting something like that to anyone else would normally have made me feel vulnerable, but this was Luca. With him, I felt a strange sense of safety blooming in my chest, one I hadn't anticipated. It was a welcome change, knowing I could lean on someone without losing my own strength or resolve.

"You don't need to thank me. I'll always have your back, Claire, and I'll never let anyone hurt you. Not now, not ever," he replied, kissing the top of my head.

His words and the warmth of his lips sent a shiver down my spine, igniting a fire in my chest that both thrilled and terrified me. In the cocoon of the car, with Luca beside me, I realised just how deeply I needed him—and the lengths I was willing to go to keep him in my life.

As we drove through the city, the streets blurred past, but I felt anchored by Luca's presence, his promise wrapping around me like a shield. Yet, the reality of what had happened with Damien loomed large, a reminder that the consequences could ripple through my life in ways I couldn't yet fathom. But I was the Ice Queen, and I would face whatever came with my usual steel resolve.

CHAPTER 28
LUCA

THE FOLLOWING DAY – BREAKFAST
IN BED

The early morning light seeped through the curtains, casting a soft glow across the room. I lay in bed, acutely aware of the warmth beside me. Claire's long blonde hair spilled across the pillow like a silken cascade. Her face was peaceful in sleep. A wave of affection surged within me, mingling with the remnants of last night's adrenaline. After the incident with that Turner guy, I had held her close, offering comfort in the only way I knew how. The heat of our bodies had entwined, melting away the tension, and we'd found solace in each other.

I watched the rise and fall of her chest as she lay sprawled across me, and the situation I'd found her in the evening before replayed in my mind. When she'd called, I'd been on my way back from work myself after a meeting with the manager of one of our restaurants. I'd known she'd be working later so she could attend the after-work drinks for the retiring partner, and I'd been content in the fact that Vlad was waiting for her outside. But when she'd called to say she hadn't left yet, I'd got Trigger to head there so I could surprise her. And I couldn't be more glad I had.

It hadn't occurred to me that Claire would be in danger in the office where she'd worked for the last few years. A place where she should have been safe. The fact that one of her colleagues would dare to attack her galled me. The man was a problem. His image invaded my mind. Damien Turner—his bruised face hopefully a reminder not to touch my woman, or any woman for that matter. Though I doubted it.

Someone who would try to force himself on a woman was an A-grade arsehole in my book. That thought filled me with a primal rage, just as seeing her dishevelled appearance and frightened look after he'd tried to attack her had made me nearly lose it completely. If she hadn't been there, hadn't pulled me back, I would have killed the guy. I'd taught him a bit of a lesson, but I doubted it was one he'd remember for long.

As we'd left the office, I'd noticed the glint in his already swelling eye. I'd seen the look before. The one that promised revenge. I would need to keep a close watch on the bastard because I had a feeling last night's incident wouldn't be the last.

Body tense, I bit down hard on my growing anger, not wanting to wake my Little Miss Sexy Ass up yet. After the day she had yesterday, and with the worry she must be feeling over the future of her employment at Turner and Hanson, she needed her rest.

I hated the idea of Claire needing to work there with that guy again. The thought of that bastard being anywhere near her sent another pulse of anger through my veins. But I knew how hard she'd worked to get where she was, and how much she'd set her heart on becoming one of their partners in the next couple of years. So, if she wanted to remain working there, I'd do all I could to ensure her safety from now on.

Vlad had been shadowing Claire since her car had been

vandalised in the prison car park. Until last night, he'd kept her safe. However, at her request, he'd been discreet about it. That ended now. From today, I'd ensure he made his presence known, dogging her every step as a warning to anyone else who might try to harm her. Whether or not she liked it. Although, after the experience of yesterday, I suspected she wouldn't fight me on that any longer.

I reached out, brushing a strand of hair from her forehead. She stirred, her eyelids fluttering open. For a moment, she simply gazed at me, her blue eyes soft and inviting, as if I were the only thing in her world that mattered. It made me feel powerful and vulnerable all at once.

"Morning," she murmured, her voice thick with sleep, yet it sent a jolt of desire straight to my core.

"Good morning, beautiful," I said, leaning down to brush her lips with mine. "How are you doing after last night?" I asked, concern lacing my voice as I noticed the slight trace of worry in her eyes as she peered up at me.

"Last night was intense," she said, her voice barely above a whisper, but I could hear the underlying tension.

"Yes, it was, but it's over now and you're safe. I'll make sure of it," I said, my hand drifting up to gently stroke the back of her head.

She nodded, a slight smile lifting the corners of her mouth, but I could sense the shadow lingering in her mind. "Usually, I can take care of myself. My mum brought me up to be independent. I've done several of the classes Derrick runs for women in self-defence, and I have to admit, they helped last night. But I was still vulnerable. That's not something I am used to feeling. Not me, the Ice Queen, who can shut a man down with just one look. If you hadn't arrived when you did, I'm not sure if I could have continued fighting him off. It was a humbling experience to know that I can't always rely solely on myself after all."

"That's not a bad thing, Claire. You're strong, but it's okay to rely on the help of others now and then. It doesn't detract from your capabilities or make you any less independent. Believe me, I know. In my world, I've had to grow strong too and rely on that strength and my wits to keep me safe. But there are times when even that isn't enough, and I've needed someone to have my back. That's usually been Miki and the rest of my Brotherhood. But recently, it's also been you, and I can't tell you how much that means to me."

She kissed my chest and sighed. "You're mine now, Claire, and I won't ever let anything happen to you. Not while I have a breath left in my body. I will always have your back and you can rely on me for anything," I told her, letting the sincerity come through in my voice.

I could feel her smile against my chest, and in that moment, the heaviness of the night before lifted.

"You know, I never expected to wake up like this," she said, glancing around the room as if it were a new adventure.

"Waking up next to me is a privilege," I replied, teasing her with a wink.

"Right," she laughed, her eyes dancing with mischief. "What are you going to do to convince me of that?"

"Hmm." I pondered, pretending to think seriously as I pushed her hair behind her ear. "How about I start with this?"

With that, I rolled her onto her back, leaning down to capture her lips in a heated kiss. It was soft at first, a gentle exploration that quickly ignited into something deeper. Her hands slid around my neck, pulling me closer as I pressed my body against hers, the cool sheets contrasting sharply with the heat radiating between us.

When I broke the kiss, I looked down at her, breathing

heavily, feeling the urgency of desire pulsing through me. "What do you think?"

She grinned, her cheeks flushed. "I think you're becoming an addiction."

"Well then, I'd better give you your next fix."

With a swift movement, I climbed atop her, the weight of my body pressing her into the mattress. She laughed, a sound that filled the air with a lightness I cherished. I leaned down, kissing her again. This time, it was hungry, desperate—a culmination of our fears and the lingering echoes of last night.

Claire's body responded to mine, arching up against me. I felt her breath hitch in her throat. The intimacy of our connection enveloped us, for the moment drowning out any remnants of anxiety that dared linger.

Our movements became a dance—timed, passionate, and electric. I relished every gasp and sigh, in the way her body fit perfectly against mine, as if we were two pieces of a puzzle that had finally found their match. As we lost ourselves in each other, I felt a possessive surge rise within me. A primal need to claim her, to ensure she knew she was safe here with me.

Moments passed, the outside world fading away, and all that remained was us. I held her gaze as I explored every inch of her body. My lips trailed down her neck, her collarbone, worshipping her in a way I hadn't thought possible. She was more than just the Ice Queen; she was my icebreaker, melting away the coldness of my past and filling the void with warmth.

When we finally succumbed to the heat between us, it was a moment of pure bliss—a culmination of everything that had brought us to this point. I buried my face in her neck, inhaling her scent, a mix of vanilla and something uniquely her.

In the aftermath, as we lay tangled together in the sheets, I traced idle patterns on her skin. My mind still circled back to Damien. The thought of him stirred my protective instincts, a reminder that this peace was fragile. Claire was strong, but I couldn't shake the feeling that our fight wasn't over.

"Hey," she said softly, drawing me back from my thoughts.

"Yeah?"

"I'm yours, huh?" she asked, her grin taking on a wicked gleam.

"You are," I grinned back.

"And are you mine?" she questioned, but I could see she already knew the answer by the teasing glint in her eyes.

"Definitely," I replied, wondering where this was going.

"And would you do anything for me?" She twirled a lock of her hair, pouted, and batted her eyes.

I chuckled, hoping her playfulness would lead to naughtiness. "Of course."

"Well, I thought you'd like to serve me breakfast in bed."

Oh. "Sure, babe, what would you like?" I asked, moving out from under her.

"Where are you going?" she asked.

"To get you something to eat. Do you want some toast? Or something more substantial?"

"Oh, definitely something more substantial, but I don't think you understand what I have in mind," she replied, kneeling up, the bed sheets pooling around her.

My jaw dropped, and the semi I'd been sporting since I'd woken, shot to full mast.

The glint in her eyes was wicked as she tugged my hips towards her and her mouth descended. My eyes widened in a shock for a second before my mind processed what she'd been implying. God, I was a lucky bastard.

"Well, eat away, you need your sustenance after all," I told her, my voice strained as I tried hard to maintain control through the ecstasy of her exquisite attentions mouth around my cock.

As she lapped, sucked, and licked me to release, I held her head gently, fighting the urge to thrust my cock into the back of her throat, unwilling to do anything other than enjoy how much she wanted me.

My knees buckled, and I just barely caught myself from collapsing as the last of my cum shot into her throat and she gave my sated dick one last lick before pulling her mouth off with a loud slurp.

"Hmm, now that's the best breakfast in bed, I've ever had," she said, grinning wickedly as she licked the final drops of me off her lips.

The sight went straight to my groin and my cock was suddenly awake again. "Time to return the favour," I told her, pushing her back onto the bed. "Time to melt the Ice Queen," I teased, a grin tugging at my lips.

She rolled her eyes but couldn't suppress a smile. "And yet, you can melt me so easily."

I chuckled, the sound echoing in the quiet room. "It took a while to figure out how, but now that I know. I'll be keeping this delectable little body of yours so hot with need, they'll have to start calling you the Flame Queen. There will be no doubt in anyone's mind that you could spontaneously combust with your passion for me at any second. In fact, you'll be so hot that you'll scorch people with the heat from your body, instead of that icy look you usually give them."

"You're such a fool." Her laughter mingled with a sigh as she snuggled closer, resting her head against my chest. I savoured the moment, tracing small circles on her back with my fingertips, relishing the feel of her skin against mine. It was a luxury to have her here, to feel her warmth and the steady rhythm of her breath.

She giggled as I dived between her legs, intent on eating my own breakfast. Soon, her giggles had turned to breathy moans.

A few hours later, sated after our mutual breakfast had turned into yet another full-blown sex session, we dozed, wrapped up in each other, enjoying the peacefulness of a lazy Saturday morning.

Claire sighed and shifted in my arms. She was thinking about the incident with that fucker again. I could practically hear the thoughts whirling around her head.

"You're thinking too loud, babe," I said, forcing my eyes open.

"Sorry. I'm still processing everything, I guess. I hate that I have to face with him again. How are we going to manage to work together after that?"

"Yeah, about that." I paused, gathering my thoughts. "I don't like it either. I'm going to look into him."

Claire lifted her head, a spark of concern in her eyes. "Luca, I appreciate the thought, but—"

"No buts," I interrupted, my voice firm. "You deserve to feel safe, and I won't let some piece of shit threaten that. I won't interfere or tell you not to work there, but I want to know just how much of a threat the man is. From now on, Vlad will be with you to ensure he can't threaten you again. Hopefully, he will have learned his lesson and that won't be a concern in the future. But for now, we're not taking any chances. Understood?"

"Yes, sir!" she said with a cheeky salute. My eyes blazed with lust.

"Sir… hmm, I like that. Brings all sorts of wicked thoughts to mind. We'll have to see what we can do with that later tonight," I said, licking my lips and winking.

She giggled. "You're incorrigible." She shook her head at me, but I could see the speculative glint in her eye. I wasn't the only one interested in exploring that particular kink. Role play hadn't been something I'd ever been into before, but suddenly the idea had me hard again. Unfortunately, such explorations would have to wait, as I had a meeting to attend.

After reluctantly extracting myself from Claire's warm embrace, I showered and dressed before kissing her goodbye.

"What are your plans for the rest of the day?" I asked.

"I'll stay in bed until lunch, then grab something to eat. After that, I'm going to find a nice comfy spot in that fabulous library you guys have here, curl up, and read Gracie's book. Maybe I can get a few pointers from the book boyfriend for you," she teased.

"Ha, ha. I'm better than any book boyfriend," I said, unable to keep the trace of indignance from my voice.

She laughed. "That's what they all say!"

I pouted at her and her eyes softened, her smile turning wicked again. "But in your case, it's true."

"Glad you think so, I was beginning to think I'd have to throw you back onto that bed and teach you the error of your ways," I said, kissing her on the top of the head and valiantly avoiding doing exactly that.

"I'll be sure to remind you of that fact again later tonight. Have a good day and when you're reading Gracie's book, I know who you'll be picturing as the lead guy," I told her with a wink as I strode out of the bedroom, adding a touch of swagger to my walk.

Her laughter rang out behind me. "You wish!"

Oh, she'd pay for that! A good spanking was in order and that would fit nicely with a little sir, naughty girl, role play.

Humming a tune in happy anticipation of fulfilling that scenario tonight, I climbed into the back of the SUV where Miki and Ash were waiting. Ash was grinning and whispering into his phone, no doubt talking to Gracie.

"Great day to go for a pub lunch," I said, grinning.

Miki snorted and raised his eyebrows at my happy demeanour and I could tell he was about to tease me over my obvious infatuation with my Little Miss Sexy Ass just as I'd often done him when he'd first succumbed to Eilidh's charms.

"Shut it!" I told him and he laughed but said nothing. His chuckle lingering in the air as we made our way into London and our highly anticipated meeting with the O'Briens.

———

As we stepped into the bustling family bar and restaurant owned by Sean's family, my eyes quickly scanned for threats as they always did, and I was glad when everything appeared normal. In fact, there was a cosy, welcoming feel to the place that brought a smile to my lips. I liked it immediately. The smell of food was strong, and banter of the clientele loud, reminding me of the strength and loudness I associated with Sean and Finn. I liked it immediately and the warm, friendly atmosphere boded well for this alliance being something beneficial for all concerned.

Miki smiled next to me, and the tension I'd hardly noticed he was carrying loosened. The scent of hearty Irish fare made my stomach rumble, and I looked forward to sampling some if everything went according to plan.

Sean greeted us at the door. "Great to have you here,

come meet my da," he said, hustling us over towards a large, formidable figure behind the bar.

"Da, our guests have arrived," he said to the man before turning back to us. "This is my da, Cormac O'Brien," he said, pride evident in his voice.

"Mr O'Brien, I'm Luca, this is Mikhail Rominov, his brother Ash and their cousin, Romi," I introduced us all.

"Cormac, please," he replied, a grin splitting his face as he stepped up to shake our hands.

"And this is my son Sean and nephew Finley," he introduced the pair.

"Cormac, Sean, Finley, it's good to meet you all," Miki said, before turning his attention to Cormac.

"Luca has told me of how helpful your lads were to him when he was in need. He also suggested we might have a chat," Miki said, obviously eager to get things moving on.

"A chat is just what I was hoping for. Shall we go to my office?" Cormac responded pleasantly.

"Sean, Finn, you two stay here and keep the other lads company while Mikhail and I have our chat," he directed before quickly adding, "If that's alright with you, Mikhail?"

"Of course, and it's Miki to my friends," he replied, a trace of challenge in his voice as he stared at the man who might become our newest.

"Well, Miki, a friendship is exactly what I seek," Cormac said with a firm nod, the gleam of understanding and respect in his eyes as he returned Miki's gaze a relief. Things were going well. "Let's go talk, then we can all enjoy a good meal afterwards. The rest of you lads, take a seat, have a drink and get to know one another."

He waved us toward a table at the back of the room and we sat down.

"I'll get us some whiskey," Finn said.

"Coke for me, I'm driving," Romi shouted to him.

He nodded before hurrying around behind the bar, returning quickly with a bottle of whiskey, several glasses and a can of coke for Romi.

"Cheers," Sean said as he poured us each a couple of fingers of the golden nectar the Irish loved so much.

Lifting the drinks, we replied, "Nostrovia!" as we downed took our first sips. The burn in my throat felt refreshing, I wasn't usually a fan of whiskey but this was good stuff.

"It's great to see you again, Luca," Sean said.

"You, too, guys," I replied.

"When's your court case?" he asked.

"In a few weeks, but I'm hoping it might not get that far," I told him.

"Good, court's a fucking nuisance," Finn said.

"It's not something I've dealt with before, as you know, and I hope it isn't something I need to deal with again once this is all over," I told them, praying that would be the case.

"Here, here," they both said, raising the glasses to me.

I smiled at the pair, both of whom looked a little rough around the edges, but had an undeniable spark of loyalty and fire. The sort of blokes you wanted in your corner. I liked them.

"Heard you guys had a bit of trouble of your own, how did that go?" Ash asked.

"Sorted," Finn said, a hint of a smirk on his lips. "Just a couple of posh lads who thought they could play rough in our pub. Naturally, we had to teach them the error of their ways."

"One of them ended up in hospital, which was how we ended up on remand. But hey, they started it. We just finished it," Sean added.

Finn leaned in, a conspiratorial look on his face. "A bit of friendly persuasion from some of our lads and they dropped the charges," he grinned.

"Glad to hear you both came out on top," I replied, lifting my glass.

"Here's to not letting anyone walk over us," Ash said, before downing his drink.

"Sean, Finn, can you give me a wee bit help in the kitchen?" a woman called.

"Sure, Ma, I'll be right there," Sean shouted back.

"Duty calls. You two lads enjoy your drinks. We'll be back soon," Finn said before the pair disappeared.

I turned to Romi who'd been sitting quietly, observing the pair as we'd conversed. Keeping my voice low. "So, what do you reckon? These O'Briens' seem solid enough. I like them anyway."

"Me, too," Ash added.

Romi nodded, his brow furrowed as he considered. "They're not afraid to get their hands dirty, and they've got connections. I think it's a smart move."

I glanced at Sean and Finn, who were currently delivering meals to a large table of customers who seemed to be celebrating a child's birthday. They laughed and bantered with the party and the sight heartened me. "They seem like decent blokes. They'll be good for us."

Ash, sitting across from me, raised an eyebrow. "But can we trust them? No offense, but they're Irish. You know how these things can go."

"True," I admitted, "but Miki's discussed the O'Briens with Jim and he wouldn't have accepted this meeting if he didn't see potential. Besides, they're not looking to muscle in on anyone's turf right now, just looking to take over what we inherited and don't want. So, it makes sense. These guys are here to stay, so it's best we become allies, not enemies."

Moments later, Miki returned, his expression serious but pleased. "We've struck a deal. The O'Briens are on board."

A wave of relief washed over me. "That's good to hear." We were another step closer to getting rid of all the illegal shit we did, except the white collar stuff and it couldn't come quick enough for me.

Cormac rejoined us, his smile wide and genuine. "You lads are now part of the O'Brien family. Come join me at the family table and we'll have that meal I promised."

Drinks were poured once again as we all settled down together in the O'Briens' private dining area at the back of the restaurant.

Miki raised his glass once more. "To new alliances."

"To new alliances!" echoed around the table, and for the first time in a while, I felt truly optimistic about what lay ahead.

As we settled into the meal, Cormac poured us his finest Irish whiskey, the smooth liquid gliding down my throat and easing the tension from earlier. Miki and Cormac excused themselves, disappearing into the back office for what I presumed were negotiations for our alliance.

"Now, what about that fight we were talking about?" Sean said.

"Alright, lads, let's make it happen. Finn, you ready to take on Vlad?" I asked.

"Always ready. Just tell me when and where," he replied with a cheeky grin.

"How about Glitz? It's our family club, and we can set it up for one of our quiet nights, probably a Thursday, in a few weeks' time. Plenty of space, and we can control the crowd." Ash suggested.

"Glitz sounds perfect. We've been meaning to check the place out. We heard it's stylish though, and a private club, are you sure you want to lower your standards and let us Irish in?" Sean teased.

"I'm sure we can do that for one night," Ash teased in turn.

"Well, I will look forward to spraying its walls with your man's blood." Finn laughed and winked.

"Don't get ahead of yourself. Vlad's been itching for a good fight, and he's never lost. I'm afraid he's liable to wipe the floor with you, Finn," Romi said.

"Yeah, my money's on him," Ash said with a nod.

"Don't bet on it!" Sean said with a chuckle.

"That's exactly what I intend to do," Romi chuckled in turn.

"Well, this will be interesting," Cormac said with a grin.

"Definitely," Miki agreed.

The easy banter continued as the afternoon ran into evening. Laughter and stories flowed freely, and I felt the weight of the future lift just a little. With both Glowacki and the O'Briens at our side, we could offload the areas we wanted to and still retain strong allies who'd have our back. Between our new alliance and my burgeoning relationship with Claire, life was looking up. All I needed to do now was fuck up Damien Turner, get rid of the MP, and regain my freedom.

And then, life would be peaceful at last and I'd finally get the holiday I'd been dreaming of and introduce Claire to my family. Or so I hoped.

CHAPTER 29
CLAIRE

MONDAY – THREATS AND INTIMIDATION

As I stepped into the office building on Monday morning, the weight of dread settled in my stomach. The air felt charged, thick with anticipation and unspoken accusations. I hadn't slept well last night, the thought of facing Damien Turner again making me uneasy.

"Are you sure you don't want me to come with you?" Luca had asked before I left this morning, concern etched on his handsome face. He'd been fantastic over the weekend, passionate, supportive, and caring. Everything I could want in a man.

"No," I had replied firmly, trying to hide the tremor in my voice. "I need to handle this on my own. Besides, Vlad will be there. I'll be fine."

The truth was, I didn't want Luca in the crosshairs of whatever chaos was about to unfold and it would only make matter worse if he was there. I knew he was itching to protect me, but this was my fight, and I had to face it head-on. If I was going to continue working with Damien, I needed to show him I still had backbone and that his little stunt hadn't dented my steely nature. Even if it had, just a little.

With my resolve in place and Vlad at my side, I felt a little more grounded, though the knot of anxiety in my chest refused to loosen. I made my way to my office, each step echoing in my mind. As I approached the door, I caught sight of Damien's office—shuttered and quiet. He was likely nursing his injuries. I wondered for the millionth time since Friday night what he'd told his mother. Surely he wouldn't tell her the truth. No, he'd make up some other story. But what? So long as it didn't involve me, or Luca, I didn't care.

Just as I settled into my chair, my phone buzzed with an incoming call. It was Margaret Turner's secretary, asking me to come her office. My stomach dropped. What did Damien's mother want? Whatever it was, it couldn't be good.

As I walked into her office, I braced myself for impact. The room was filled with polished wood and expensive art— everything about it screamed power and prestige.

A movement to the side caught my eye, and I glanced towards it. My stomach dropped further.

"Why are you here?" I asked Lady Frost who was sitting, arms folded, face neutral, watching me intently.

"I'm here as a friend, Claire," she replied, her slight smile and syrupy tone not giving me any comfort.

Of course, how could I forget that's it was her connections to the Turner's that got me my job here in the first place.

"Why don't you have a seat?" She gestured to the chair a few feet from her own.

A flicker of uncertainty filled me. What was going on?

She signed. "I've been a close family friend of both you and the Turner's for years, I came to offer my support."

Support? For what? And to whom?

My gaze flicked to Margaret, sitting behind her imposing desk, arms crossed, her expression a mixture of anger and disappointment.

"Claire," she said, her voice sharp, "sit down."

I took a seat, trying to maintain my composure. What had that bloody bastard son of hers told her? "Margaret, I don't know—"

"Don't." Her eyes narrowed. "Let's cut to the chase. What happened with Damien was unacceptable." Maybe he'd told her the truth after all. Or someone else had. Either way, relief washed through me.

"Your behaviour was intolerable." Wait, what?

My behaviour? I clenched my jaw, fury threatening to overcome me.

"Margaret. I don't know what he told you, but I didn't—"

"Save it," she snapped. "Damien just got engaged to a woman from a prestigious family, and your behaviour could have jeopardised that. If anyone had seen you attempting to take advantage of his inebriated state, and word got back to Lorraine's family, they might have thought he was cheating on her. That's not something they'd tolerate. I won't have you ruining his future marriage in an attempt to use him to further your career."

"Use him?" I felt my anger rising, hot and prickly. "That's ridiculous. He—"

"Enough! I don't want to hear any of your excuses," she said, her voice shrill with barely controlled fury. My eyes blazed in response and I took a deep breath, desperate to maintain my control. I was bloody raging at how the bastard had twisted the narrative, painting me as the villain in a story I never wanted to be part of.

"I never took you as the type who'd throw yourself at a man just to get on in life. Although with your ambitions, I suppose I should have." The look of disgust and the disdain in her voice cut through me.

"Not only did you try it on with Damien, but you were then discovered by your thug of a boyfriend, who beat my son, breaking his tooth and almost breaking his jaw. I'm appalled, Claire," she finished her tirade with a shake of her head.

"Oh, Claire, I'm so disappointed in you," Elizabeth said, feigning shock.

I narrowed my gaze at her, then Margaret. What were these two up to?

"Naturally, Damien doesn't wish to press charges against either of you," Elizabeth said quickly.

Press charges against us? That fucker!

"Not when he understands how it might have looked to that Orlov man. How it might look to Lorraine if she was also to mistake the incident."

"And we wouldn't want the firm to be the centre of a scandal. That wouldn't do anyone any favours," Margaret pipped in, her expression smug. "However, that's not to say we can just sweep everything under the rug, so to speak."

I could feel Elizabeth, Margaret's accomplice, in whatever was about to come, shift slightly in her chair, her expression unreadable but her eyes glinting with barely concealed amusement.

"Why did you do it, Claire? Did you think by seducing my son, the newest partner in the firm, you'd somehow be able to get a fast track to partnership?" Margaret continued, her voice laced with venom.

I shook my head about to deny things, but held her hand up, stopping me as she continued. "Because let me be clear— your actions have consequences. If you don't do what we say, you'll find yourself in a great deal of trouble."

"What do you mean?" I managed to choke out, a sense of foreboding washing over me.

"That thug of yours has enemies in high places, as I believe Elizabeth already explained to you. One of those enemies in particular has plans for him and his associates. You getting him out on bail caused his plans to falter, and he wants them back on track, and that means revoking his bail," she said, leaning forward, her tone conspiratorial.

"You're going to plant drugs in his car and then arrange for the police to find them. It's the only way to ensure he goes back inside where he belongs. After that, you'll withdraw any help you've been giving that lawyer of his, and steer clear of the man."

The audacity of her words left me speechless. Seriously? What the hell did they take me for?

"You can't be serious. That's illegal. Reprehensible."

Margaret smirked and waved a dismissive hand. "What's reprehensible is you attempting to sleep with a junior partner while you're with someone else."

"I bloody well didn't!" I retorted, clenching my fists to stop me from flying across her desk and punching her in the jaw. "I'm not going to do what you asked. Why does the MP want Luca to be put away so badly? Surely, he doesn't need him in jail to have him killed?" I had to know what the heck the MP had planned.

Elizabeth's gaze sharpened. "So, you know who wants this man dealt with then. Very good. I'll get right to the point. Luca Orlov is Bratva. The Bratva were responsible for the death of the MP's father, and he's been trying to get revenge on them for some time now. His original tactics proved fruitless and, in fact, resulted in his current problems. So now, he is taking a less subtle approach. Incarcerating the Orlov man sends a message to the Bratva, letting the individuals within the organisation know that they are not untouchable. The MP may be down, but he's not beaten."

"But isn't framing Luca enough to do that?" I asked, determined to find out all I could about the MP's plans.

"It was until you got the man out on bail. Now, he's decided to take a leaf out of the Bratva's book and ensure the police discover their less than stellar activities. Planting the drugs in Mr Orlov's car is just one of the steps he's taking to make that happen."

Oh hell. That meant the Bratva had more trouble to come.

"Do this and we will not only forget all about the incident with Damien, but you are guaranteed your promotion next year when Hanson retires," Margaret said, smugness in her voice.

They really thought I would do anything to get a partnership? Truly? Well, hell no! I might have been relaxing my previously strict moral code and be willing to overlook some things, to dance in the grey with Luca, but I wasn't going to compromise my integrity entirely.

I shook my head. "Not happening!"

Elizabeth sighed. "You are so like your mother."

"And proud to be!" I spat out.

"Quite, but she didn't always know when to act in her own best interests either and look where it got her. I just hope you won't be quite so foolish," she said.

A chill raced down my spine. "What are you implying?"

"Nothing at all. Just giving you a friendly warning," Elizabeth replied, her smile devoid of warmth. "You wouldn't want your life to end in the blink of an eye, like it did for your mother. I suggest you think long and hard about the choices you make moving forward. It would be a shame if you found yourself facing unexpected consequences."

Fury ignited within me, a fire burning away the fear.

"How dare you?" I shot back, my voice rising. "You think you can intimidate me? You're wrong. I will not do this. Not now, not ever."

Margaret's eyes flared with anger. "You think you have a choice? You don't. I'll ruin your career before it even begins. You'll regret this, Claire."

I stood up, the chair scraping against the floor as I pushed it back. "Fuck you, Margaret. And fuck you, Elizabeth. I won't be part of your twisted games."

Elizabeth blocked my exit. "This conversation never happened. If you think to disclose our discussion, just remember what we said."

"Get out of my way!" I glared at the woman who'd been my mother's best friend for years.

Had she only implied my mother's death was something other than an accident to scare and intimidate me, or was there a more sinister explanation for the night her car ran off the road during a snowstorm? Bile rose in my mouth, and I shuddered at the thought.

Fighting to maintain a semblance of control and not let just how much she'd rattled me show, I held her gaze until she finally stepped aside.

I yanked the door open to find Vlad on the other side looking concerned.

"I know you said to wait for you here, but I heard raised voices. Everything alright?"

"Fine. Take me home please," I replied, and he nodded, his gaze still fixed on the women in the room.

"You'll receive my resignation by email in due course," I shouted over my shoulder as I stormed from the room.

I was going to get Marko and Luca to help me look into that. If I found out it wasn't an accident and that Elizabeth had something to do with it, I'd make the bitch pay.

CHAPTER 30
LUCA
LATER THAT DAY – REASSURING CLAIRE

walked into the bedroom, immediately spotting Claire pacing back and forth. "I got your message, babe. Are you okay?" I asked, concern lacing my voice.

The tension in the room was palpable as Claire stopped and faced me, her eyes filled with a mix of fear and determination.

"Luca, I need to tell you what happened," she began, her voice trembling slightly. "Those women, they threatened me. They tried to intimidate me into planting evidence against you."

I felt a surge of anger, my fists clenching at my sides. "Who? What happened?

"Margaret Turner and Elizabeth Traynor. When I arrived at work this morning, Margaret's secretary called me to go and see her. When I got to her office, Elizabeth was there too. She's a friend of the Turner's, has been for longer than she was friends with my mum. It was her that got me the position with Turner and Hanson." she explained.

"What did they say?" I asked, my voice low and controlled.

"Damien told Margaret I'd thrown myself at him when he was drunk and you'd found us in a compromising position and misunderstood the situation, blaming Damien for it and beat him up."

"That fucking bastard!" I cried in fury. "How could she believe such a thing? why would a beauty like you need to throw herself at anyone?" I asked appalled.

"Apparently, in order to seduce him into fast tracking my partnership," she replied, sounding sick at the thought.

"You'd never do that. Don't these people know that?" That bastard Damien Turner would answer for this.

"I guess not, or maybe they do, and it's convenient for them to believe the story. Maybe they even concocted it themselves. Who knows?"

"Anyhow, the guy's getting married to some society bitch and is afraid she'll hear of his so-called liaison with me and break off the wedding. So, they are going with this version of events. They said they were willing to avoid a scandal and further problems if I planted drugs in your car and had the police find them."

"What? They wanted you to risk your integrity to frame me?" My voice shook with barely controlled rage.

"Yeah. They said the MP wanted you back inside but also he was planning to bring your Bratva activities to police attention and not just by planting the drugs on you. You need to let Miki know,"

"I will. What else did they say?"

"They said if I did it they'd forget about the incident with Damien and even ensure I got my partnership next year when Mr Hanson retires. They hinted at physical harm, if I didn't. Even suggested my mum's accident might have been something more sinister," she replied, her eyes glistening with unshed tears.

I crossed the room in a few strides and took her in my arms. "Claire, you did the right thing by refusing. I'm proud of you for standing your ground."

"Do you think it's true what Elizabeth implied about my mum's death?" she asked, the break in her voice almost breaking my heart.

"I don't know, babe. But I will get Marko to look into it. And if it is, I promise you, we'll find who was responsible and make them pay," I vowed.

She nodded, but I could see the worry still etched on her face. "I'm really concerned about what the MP is planning, not just for you, but for everyone else. He's determined to bring the Bratva's activities to the attention of the police. I don't know what he's capable of, but it scares me."

I hugged her tightly. "I'll handle it, Claire. I promise you, I'll protect you. The MP won't get away with causing us anymore harm."

She looked up at me, her eyes searching mine. "You really think we can stop him?"

"Yes," I said firmly. "We're putting our own plan in motion tomorrow night and that should make any of his plans harder to accomplish until we can rid ourselves of the bastard once and for all. And you were right to resign. The bastards don't deserve you. I know you had your heart set on becoming one of their partners, but there are other opportunities out there for you. Better ones. You'll see,"

"Now, why don't I run you a hot bath and you can relax and forget all of your worries for now while I go and talk to Miki and get Marko looking into your mum's accident?"

A small smile tugged at her lips. "Thank you, Luca. A bath sounds good right now, I don't know what I'd do without you."

"You'll never have to find out," I replied, kissing her forehead. "We're in this together."

———

A short while later, I returned to the bedroom, carrying a tray of food. Claire was just coming out of the bathroom, looking all relaxed and sexy wrapped in a fluffy white towel that barely covered her. My mouth went dry, and my libido awakened at the sight. I stood there, staring. She gave me a slow, sultry smile when she noticed me openly ogling her. I gulped and cleared my throat.

"I brought us some dinner and wine. I didn't think you'd feel like joining everyone in the dining room as usual," I told her.

"That was thoughtful of you thanks," she smiled and approached the small living area I had. My room was a glorified suite, really. When I'd lived here as a child, we'd lived on the estate in a cottage which afforded us privacy while still being close to the Rominov's.

When my parents had returned to live in Russia permanently, I hadn't wanted to remain there alone and preferred staying here with the other guys. So, the place was now used as a guest house for when they, or other members of the family, visited and there wasn't enough room in the main house.

Up until now, this room had been adequate for my needs, especially since I had my own flat in the centre of London too. Now, though, sitting at my tiny two-seater table, eating with Claire, I figured I'd need to rethink my living arrangement.

After what happened with Julie, I hadn't been back to the flat and wasn't planning on ever returning. Once I was exonerated of the crime, I'd get someone to dump the bed and then get the movers in to pack everything up for me and put it into storage until I decided what I wanted to do with it.

"That was lovely. Nonna has outdone herself again," Claire said.

"She's the best," I agreed. Nonna was what we called Maria, the housekeeper here at the Rominov estate. She was Miki's mother's nanny in Italy and then when she married Miki's dad, Nonna had moved to Russia with her to become their housekeeper. Then later she followed us all to the UK. Since we all grew up with her looking after us, she insisted we call her Nonna. She was like a grandmother to us and we loved her deeply. She was also the best cook I'd ever known.

"This is nice. Spending time like this together. Very domesticated," Claire said, a twinkle in her eye. "I could get used to being treated like this. Hot baths, lovely food, pleasant company. Almost makes a girl not want to leave," she said, sighing contentedly.

"Almost?" I asked, getting up and stalking towards her. "And what would make that almost, into an absolutely?" I asked as I grabbed her and pulled her into my arms.

"Oh, I don't know. A girl has more needs than simply food, comfort and conversation." The glint of playful mischief in her eyes felt like an invitation.

"You're right, of course. I am neglecting those other needs. I will have to remedy that," I told her before claiming her lips. My kiss devoured her, leaving her breathless.

I smirked. "Is that a good start, Little Miss Sexy Ass?"

Claire chuckled and rolled her eyes at my nickname for her, as she always did whenever she heard it.

"Hmm, I think you can do better," she replied.

"Indeed, well, my sexy lawyer, challenge accepted."

Sweeping her up into my arms, I whipped off her towel

and threw her onto the bed. her laughter filled the room, warming my heart and ratcheting my libido up another notch further.

My cock thickened and jerked at the sight of her laid out before me.

"What do you have planned for me?" she asked, batting her eyes coyly.

"On Saturday, when I left to go to my meeting with the O'Briens, you said you would be reading Gracie's book that afternoon, and I suggested you would be picturing me as the lead guy in her book. Do you remember that?"

"Yes," she said, sounding a curious as to where I was going with this.

"You said "you wish!" under your breath," I said, giving my voice a stern, headmaster tone.

"Didn't you?"

"Wasn't sure you'd heard that," she said, biting her lip as she tried hard not to grin.

"Oh, I heard it, and I've been meaning to punish you for your cheek ever since."

"You have?" she asked, her voice breathy with excitement.

"Oh yes, and I think now is the time to do it."

Her eyes lit up, and her breath hitched.

"You were a very naughty girl. Weren't you?"

She nodded, chewing on her lip, excitement in her eyes, her breathing speeding up. I smirked, my Little Miss Sexy Ass didn't just have a praise kink it seemed. My cock jerked. I was going to enjoy this even more than I'd anticipated.

"Use your words, Claire," I commanded.

She bit her lip and slowly shook her head, refusing to comply. The mischievous little grin she sported enough to make me come on the spot.

I tutted and shook my head. "You are being a very naughty girl again now, too."

I sat down on the bed. "Lie across my lap," I demanded.

She lifted her chin in defiance and looked at me, still resisting.

"Now!" I shouted, and she jumped to comply.

"That's better," I said, stroking my hand over her bottom. God, I loved those squeezable, spankable cheeks.

"Are you ready to be a good girl and accept your punishment?" I asked my voice thick with lust. My cock was hard, poking her belly as she lay on top of it, causing the most exquisite torture. Fuck, this was going to be as painful and pleasurable for me as it was for her.

"Answer me, Claire," I said, squeezing her cheeks, then dipping a finger through her folds. She was wet and needy already. I licked my lips in excitement.

"Yes," she said with a breathy gasp.

"It's yes, sir, Claire," I said, my hand coming down hard on her bottom.

"Yes, sir!" she cried out, and I groaned in delight.

"Good girl," I cooed, stroking where I'd just slapped, before spanking her again.

"Ah!" she cried, her body jerking with the intensity of it.

"Yes, Claire. That's it. You're taking your punishment so well. Such a good girl, aren't you?"

"Yes, sir!" she cried again.

I continued on, alternating giving her a few more quick hard slaps, with playing with her pussy. When we were both panting hard, her bottom a lovely shade of red, her pussy dripping and my cock ready unable to take any more, I pulled her up to sit on my lap.

"God, you are the sexiest, most amazing woman I've ever

met," I told her before, kissing her deeply and turning her to straddle me. "Now, be a good girl, and sit on my cock!"

She obeyed immediately, lifting her body up, notching my cock at her entrance then taking me inside her in one quick movement. She moaned as her bottom hit my thighs, the sting in her bum heightening her pleasure. "Ride me!" I told her, slapping her already stinging sexy arse. "Yes, sir!" she screamed, using my shoulders as leverage to plunger herself up and down on my cock, over and over again.

When she began to tire, I spanked her again. "Don't you stop until we both come," I growled, taking her hips and helping her continue on.

A few more thrusts was all it took and her pussy clenched hard, she screamed my name, as her core milked my cock. I groaned her name unable to hold back any longer and my release swept over me.

"I love you, babe." The words slipped out without thought. I glanced quickly at my Little Miss Sexy Ass, hoping my confession hadn't scared her off. Our relationship was so new, and she'd fought me for so long that I couldn't bear to lose her because I'd been unable to hold my feelings back.

Claire looked at me, her eyes brimming with unshed tears, and I gulped, torn between hope and dread. She didn't speak; instead, she leaned in and kissed me deeply. I prayed those tears sprang from joy—longing for the day she'd feel safe enough to whisper those words back to me, to join me in this reckless leap of faith we were taking together.

CHAPTER 31
CLAIRE
THE FOLLOWING MORNING – THE THREATS CONTINUE

"So, what have you got planned for today?" Luca asked the following morning.

"I need to go over to my house later and check the mail. I'm expecting my new bank card in the post. But first I'm going to email my resignation off to Turner and Hanson, then I need to get my CV in shape so I can start looking for a new job, I guess," I sighed.

"You can always take over from Bradley, babe. You know Miki's already asked you and Brad would love to train you up as his successor."

"I know, but I'm still not sure I'm ready for that. I'll think about it," I told him and I meant it. I'd quiz Brad on things when I saw him next.

"Yes, please do. We are moving out of our more illegal activities a bit at a time and soon there will be little chance of any of us needing a criminal lawyer. Well, so long as we don't get caught out with the white collar stuff, but that's unlikely. Marko is exceptionally good at what he does, and the chances of anything being traced back to us are extremely slim. Even if it did happen, we wouldn't expect you to get involved. We'd ensure you never had anything to do with that side of the business, so you'd never have to worry about getting your hands dirty," he said.

I nodded.

"Great, I'll see you tonight," he said, leaning in to kiss me goodbye before playfully swatting my bum. The tap brought back memories of last night's role play, sending a shiver of delight through me as my body remembered the sting of his hand. My pussy clenched so hard I almost came on the spot.

Shock coursed through me. My god, what was that? I'd never expected to enjoy spanking, but that first time had opened my mind to it, and now I couldn't get enough. Adding the role play had only intensified the pleasure. My body still hummed with the memory.

Smiling to myself, I quickly dressed and opened my laptop. A few short, clipped sentences of resignation flew from my fingers, leaving me with a mess of emotions. Sadness that my partnership dreams with Turner and Hanson were over. Disgust over the incident that had led to this. Anger at their manipulation and intimidation. Hurt that years of friendship and mentorship had been a lie. And worst of all, disillusionment in the people and systems I'd always believed in.

I updated my CV and sent it off to several firms that might be interested. With every email, my heart wavered— caught between the heaviness of starting over and the possibility of new beginnings. I'd promised to think about taking over from Bradley, and I would, but it didn't hurt to explore other options.

Later in the afternoon, I went in search of Vlad, finding him in the kitchen devouring some of Nonna's leftover pie. "Can you drive me over to my house? I want to check my mail."

"Sure," he said, scoffing the last bit.

When we reached my house, we parked in the drive at the side. The moment I stepped out of the vehicle my heart sunk at what I saw. The mess. Someone had sprayed the front door of the house with paint. "Bitch. You'll pay!"

Anger surged through me at the sight.

Vlad's arm grabbed mine. "Get back inside the car until I check around the house," Vlad said, his voice just as calm as usual, his eyes scanning the area once again for threats. Without argument, I did what he said, but I was fuming. I was sick of the threats. This thing with that bloody MP had to stop.

I sat in the car and watched Vlad cautiously move around my home. A few seconds later, he was back.

"All clear. This is the only damage," he said.

I sighed in relief. He took a photo and sent it to Luca. Then rang Miki to send the cleanup team.

As we stepped inside, I berated myself for not getting a better security system. All I had was the camera on the doorbell at the front—now sprayed over. I pulled up the footage on my phone: a figure, likely male, dressed in dark clothing with a hood pulled up, approaching from the side before spraying the camera—then nothing. Typical.

"Send a copy of that to Marko," Vlad said. "He might be able to enhance it."

I nodded, forwarding the footage. I doubted it would reveal anything useful, but Marko was the tech wizard, not me.

After that, we quickly went inside, I grabbed the mail, and we headed back to the Estate. I'd always loved my little cottage on the corner of town. It's where I grew up with Mum, and later Gracie, filled with pictures and memories. It had always felt safe. But until the MP was out of the way, I wouldn't be back. And when I finally returned, I'd get top-of-the-range security. It seemed that being a part of Luca's life meant I'd need it.

Once, the thought of this would have filled me with dread and given me another reason to stay away. But now, it was just another hurdle because I'd realised something in the past few weeks: Luca was the only man for me. No amount of moral dilemmas, threats, or danger would drive me away.

CHAPTER 32
LUCA
THAT EVENING – FRAMING THE MP

The derelict railway building loomed over us, a skeletal reminder of a past era, its broken windows gaping like missing teeth. Cold air whistled through the cracks, carrying the faint metallic tang of rust and the stale scent of old oil.

I was here only a week ago, making Joey McDougall talk and giving him a taste of my knife in revenge for Julie. Since then, we'd had our people watching him closely—he was crucial to the next part of our plan.

"You know what you have to do?" I checked. He nodded, and I yanked him up by the scruff of his neck.

"Don't fuck this up, or I'll fuck you up. Got it?"

"Yeah… yeah!" His frantic head bobbed in a rapid rhythm with his words, his body shaking with fear.

Joey was nothing more than a pawn, though he didn't know it. I passed him his mobile.

"Call him and remember to stick to the script," I warned, my voice dripping with menace. "And put it on speaker!"

"They're here. I've got them," he said.

I could hear the MP's glee in his reply. "We're on our way." He hung up, and I smiled. He was coming just as we'd hoped.

We'd had Nigel Simpson contact the MP to inform him that the rumour was we'd found out about McDougall, and we were after him. As expected, the MP ensured the guy's location was fed to us through an informant, unaware we already had him in our clutches. He then contacted McDougall, telling him to expect us and that he'd send a few guys over to help capture us. Once that was done, he would call the MP, who we anticipated would come himself to finish us off—an opportunity like that was just too good to waste.

The couple of guys he'd sent were already in our custody, leaving us with nothing to do but wait. I flexed my grip on the pistol I'd taken from one of them, the cool metal a steady reminder of what had to be done. The MP's arrogance would be his undoing; he'd underestimated us at every turn, believing he could take on the Bratva without facing consequences. Tonight, we'd show him just how wrong he'd been.

Miki crouched beside me, his eyes scanning the entrance for any sign of movement. The lines on his face were sharper tonight, tension radiating from him. This was personal. The MP's attacks had struck deeper than business; they were a direct hit at Miki's pride, his control, and, of course, his sister. Taking the bastard down wasn't just about securing our safety —it was about retribution.

"Think he'll definitely show and not just send more of his men?" Ash asked, keeping his voice low. The only sounds were the distant hum of traffic and the occasional drip of water from the crumbling ceiling.

Miki glanced our way, his expression unreadable. "He'll

show. Arrogant bastards like him always do. He can't resist the chance to gloat. He thinks we're already under his control; he has no idea he's walking into his own trap."

The plan hinged on the MP's ego, on his need to see his enemies brought low before him. We'd spun a story he couldn't refuse—Miki, and I, tied up and ready for him to exact his revenge. There was no way he'd miss out on that.

When he arrived, he'd enter the office where Joey had been hiding out, and we'd have him.

A flicker of headlights cut through the darkness, illuminating the graffiti-covered walls. I tensed, pressing closer to the cold wood as three vehicles crawled up the gravel path—the MP's convoy. I counted the men spilling out —six, maybe seven—moving with the cautious, alert manner of those who sensed danger but hadn't yet pinpointed its source.

The MP stepped out last, dressed in his usual tailored suit, an outfit that looked utterly out of place in a dump like this. He adjusted his cufflinks, a small gesture of arrogance that made my blood boil.

He strode forward, eyes sweeping the area with disdain. Joey stood at the door of the office to meet him, just as planned.

"Where's Luca? Where's Miki?" The MP's voice echoed through the quiet of the night, loud and impatient.

From our hidden spot, Miki nodded. The moment had arrived. We moved in unison, stepping out of the shadows with our guns raised, blocking any route of escape. The MP's men reacted, hands twitching toward their weapons, but they hesitated, outnumbered and caught off guard. The element of surprise was ours, and we weren't wasting it.

The MP's eyes narrowed as he took us in. A smirk twisted his mouth, but the flicker of surprise couldn't be hidden.

"Well, well. Leon, or should I say Luca? Slumming it in the gutters with the rest of the Bratva, I see. Is this what you've been reduced to?" He laughed, still maintaining his air of superiority.

He tutted, shaking his head. "You should have stayed as Leon; he had a bright future with me. Now, Luca, you will be the first of the Bratva's top circle to die."

I ignored his attempt to bait me, my focus locked on him. He was here, in front of us, exposed. Every ounce of anger I'd bottled up over the months—every slight and underhanded move he'd made—surged to the surface. "This ends tonight," I said, my voice steady but edged with the cold fury that came from months of planning, from waiting for this exact moment.

"You plan on killing me?" he smirked. "I've already left a special document with a friend, letting them know that if I die anytime soon, the Bratva will be behind it. They're to ensure a certain Chief Constable gets all the information on you."

"Oh, we have no intention of killing you. We've got friends who'll be more than happy to do that and keep us out of it," Miki said, his voice laced with menace. "You're done."

The MP laughed, the sound sharp and mocking. "You think this is over because you've got me cornered in some abandoned shithole? You're a fool, Miki. You always have been. I've got judges, police, politicians. You think I haven't been planning for this?"

I stepped closer, gun trained on his chest. His eye twitched, and his expression tightened.

Miki jerked his head up—a sign. I turned and shot Joey in the chest. He fell to the ground, dead.

"What the fuck?" one of the men standing nearby murmured in shock.

The MP's bravado faltered, if only for a second, but it was

enough. He looked around, searching for a way to regain control, but found none. His gaze flickered from Joey's body to us. "You think you can scare me? You're just dogs on a leash. And I cut the chain."

Miki's voice cut in, sharp as a blade. "This isn't about scaring you. It's about ending things and making sure you never cross the Bratva again."

His men shifted uneasily, the tension thickening the air between us. I could see the calculation in the MP's eyes, weighing his options. He wasn't the type to go down quietly; he'd drag anyone he could into the abyss with him if he could. He wouldn't get the chance.

"You're done," I repeated, my voice leaving no room for doubt. "All your schemes, your betrayals—it ends here. You're going to jail, and once you do, you'll die inside, just like your dad."

That finally got to him. His mask of arrogance slipped. Fists clenched, he lunged—reckless, desperate. I fired a warning shot into the ground at his feet, halting his advance.

"Take him," Miki said, and Ash and Romi rushed forward to grab him. He struggled, but was quickly subdued.

The rest of our guys disarmed his men, then gave them something to briefly knock them out before we moved on to the next stage of our plan.

We kept the MP awake so he could watch.

First, the fingerprints were wiped off the gun used to kill Joey, then it was positioned in the MP's hand before pulling the trigger again. A few of his men were arranged back in their cars while the rest were laid beside the MP with their guns drawn. The scene was set to make it look like the MP had killed Joey.

Since the railway was too far away for anyone to hear the

gunshots, we had one of our guys call the cops anonymously to report shots fired.

Not long after, the shrill wail of sirens filled the air, growing louder, twisting the MP's expression into one of fury and panic.

"Now we have our guy positioned with a sniper rifle to blow your fucking brains out if you so much as twitch before the police get here," Miki told him coldly.

"I'll kill you. All of you," he shouted as we prepared to leave. But he didn't move.

The arrogant bastard probably thought he could bribe his way out of this mess, but that wouldn't happen. How did we know? We had our own guys in the police, ensuring they'd be on hand to take the call.

Just in time, the MP's men started to rouse from their drug-induced sleep.

With a nod from Miki, our men slipped away. Ash and Romi headed back to our car while Miki and I watched in silence, blending back into the shadows as the MP was forced to his knees, his hands wrenched behind him in cuffs. The police weren't gentle; they dragged him up, shoving him toward the nearest patrol car. He thrashed, spewing curses, but his bravado was hollow now—a desperate outcry from a man who knew he was no longer in control.

Miki gave me a nod—the kind that conveyed everything words couldn't. This wasn't just a victory for the Bratva; it was a warning. No one crossed us and walked away unscathed. The MP was about to finally learn that.

As we left the railway building behind, the echoes of the night's events faded into the distance. Outside, the city was waking up, oblivious to the events that had unfolded not far away. For the first time in months, I felt a strange sense of calm, as if a weight I hadn't even realised I was carrying had been lifted.

I let out a slow breath, the tension easing from my shoulders. It was almost over. The months of strategising, the sleepless nights spent plotting every move and every counter —all of it led to this moment. The MP had played his game, and he'd lost. Now we just needed to ensure that was his final hand.

CHAPTER 33
CLAIRE
THE FOLLOWING MORNING – CASE
DISMISSED

My heels clicked against the pavement as I stepped into the afternoon sunlight, my heart feeling light for the first time in what felt like forever. Luca was free. My Luca. The charges had been dropped, the case against him shattered by the truth, and now we could finally breathe. I had spent so long bracing for impact, waiting for the next blow, that the relief hit me like a tidal wave.

Hand in hand, we slid into the back seat of the sleek black car, with Vlad already at the wheel. He offered a quick nod through the rearview mirror, a silent acknowledgment of the weight lifted off us all today. I settled in, Luca's arm slung around my shoulders, feeling safe and content.

Luca was on the phone, dealing with a staffing issue at one of the restaurants he oversaw. I leaned back, relaxed, and let my mind drift to what was next—tonight. I had spent the entire morning battling my nerves as I faced my nemesis, Elizabeth Traynor, in court. But now, the rest of the day stretched ahead like a promise.

The city streets blurred as we drove, each familiar landmark passing by unnoticed. I was too lost in my own thoughts, anticipation buzzing in my veins. Tonight was ours. No more threats, no more shadowy fears lurking at the edges of our lives—just Luca and me, together, celebrating his freedom. A smile tugged at my lips as I thought about my secret surprise for him. The dinner I had planned—a quiet, intimate meal at the estate, in the summerhouse amid the vast gardens, hidden away from the outside world.

I had spent hours planning it all, ensuring every detail was just right. The caterers had been sworn to secrecy, the wines handpicked to match Luca's favourites, and the summer house would be transformed into our little sanctuary, away from everything and everyone. I wanted it to be perfect because he deserved perfection. We had been through so much together recently, and he had been my rock—taking care of me, looking after my needs, spoiling me, and keeping me grounded. Now it was time for me to take care of him and spoil him in return.

My pulse quickened thinking about my outfit. A black silky dress that clung to every curve, elegant yet provocative. High slits that hinted rather than revealed, and delicate lace that played peekaboo in all the right places. I could already picture the way Luca's gaze would darken when he saw me in it, the heat that would flare between us before the night had even truly begun. It was bold, daring—exactly the kind of statement I wanted to make.

Tonight was about showing Luca how much he meant to me. I needed him to know how glad I was that he'd persisted, not giving up on me. That after all the denials and rejections, all the hurt I must have caused him, and the changes that took place; I was finally, totally and completely all in. How could I not be? My Mr Sexy Kisser was the guy I never knew I dreamed of.

We'd fought so hard for this—battled through lies,

threats, and the weight of his lifestyle pressing down on us. I wanted him to feel just how fiercely I was his, how much I loved him. Because I did. That thought settled around me as comfortably as his warm embrace. So much had changed in me. The phrase "rocked my world" didn't quite capture what Luca had done; he'd stormed in like a tempest, dismantling my carefully constructed ice walls and replacing my fears with fierce devotion. He lit a fire within me, awakening a desire I hadn't known existed, and taught me that love could be a beautiful chaos—both frightening and thrilling in equal measure.

As Vlad navigated the familiar turns leading us back to the estate, I caught a glimpse of myself in the car's tinted window. I looked excited—alive. I couldn't wait to get back, to throw off the weight of the day and lose myself in Luca's arms.

Dinner first, followed by slow, sensual dancing. I envisioned teasing him with my body, his hands tracing every curve as if committing each line to memory. And then… the rest of the night stretching ahead, limitless and ours alone. I imagined how his hands would feel on my skin, the rough scrape of his stubble against my neck as he pulled me close.

I'd even had a makeshift bed set up for us, complete with new toys to explore: fluffy cuffs, a blindfold, and chocolate spread. I bit back a giggle at the thought of what I could do with that, and what I hoped Luca would do. I could almost feel those sexy lips, that amazing tongue enjoying my offerings. My body reacted with a shudder.

Luca glanced questioningly down at me, and I reached up to kiss his neck. His face broke into a wide grin, his eyes sparkling with understanding. He tried to act unaffected as I stroked the top of his thigh, but the bulge in his pants and the slight hitch in his breath—the only signs he was—betrayed him while he continued his conversation with the employment agency about hiring additional staff. I smirked, knowing I was playing with fire and desperately hoping for it to consume me. The Ice Queen had captured the Player, and the Player had melted her heart.

As the estate's iron gates came into view—towering and formidable yet somehow welcoming now that the worst was behind us—my pulse quickened. Luca still had some work to do, and I'd promised to pick out baby items with Gracie, but tonight couldn't come soon enough.

I was determined to remind Luca exactly why he had fought so hard—for this moment, for us. Because now, there was nothing standing in our way, and I was finally ready to confess my love.

CHAPTER 34
LUCA
SEVERAL NIGHTS LATER – THE FIGHT

As I got dressed for tonight's event, I couldn't help but reflect on the past week. Since I'd been exonerated of Julie's murder had unfolded like a dream, each day brighter than the last, illuminated by Claire's laughter and the warmth of her love. I found myself waking each morning with a sense of anticipation, a spark ignited deep within me. The weight of the past few months, the danger and uncertainty that had shadowed our lives, felt like a distant memory now. Claire had created something magical in the Summerhouse, a sanctuary where we could finally breathe without the weight of the world pressing down on our shoulders.

Her surprise dinner that night had been nothing short of enchanting. The way she transformed the space—twinkling lights, fragrant flowers, the soft strains of music playing in the background—made it feel as if we were the only two people in existence. I could still recall how my heart raced when she stepped out in that black silky dress, the way it hugged her curves, the high slits teasing with just enough skin to leave me breathless. I'd never seen anyone look more beautiful or alluring.

As we danced, her body moving against mine, I was enveloped by a profound sense of belonging. The kiss she'd given me after her confession—the moment when the words "I love you" finally fell from her lips—was etched in my memory. It was sweet and intoxicating, a promise that she was ready to let me in completely. Claire's vulnerability, the way her eyes sparkled with joy and tears, made me feel as if I was witnessing the true essence of her—the woman beneath the Ice Queen facade, finally revealing her warmth and passion. In that moment, I knew I wasn't just holding her; I was cradling her heart, and it felt like the most precious gift I could ever receive.

Each touch, each whisper between us, reminded me of the connection we'd forged amidst the chaos my world had thrust us into. I'd fought for her with everything I had, and now I felt a sense of triumph as I realised she had fought for me, too. From the first moment I met her, the walls I'd built around my heart, fortified by years of loss and heartbreak, that left me unable to form prior long-term attachments to a woman, had crumbled under her gaze, replaced by an unyielding devotion I never thought I could feel. She was my one and only.

Now, as I prepared for the night ahead—a bare-knuckle fight at the Rominov's private members club, Glitz—I couldn't shake the glow that came from knowing Claire loved me. It was an intoxicating feeling, like a high that pulsed through my veins, filling me with an eagerness I hadn't experienced in ages. I'd never been one for sentimentality, but this was different. Claire had awakened something in me, igniting a fire that had long lain dormant.

With one last glance in the mirror, I adjusted my tie. The

reflection staring back at me was more than just the enforcer of the Bratva; it was a man reborn, fuelled by love and the promise of a future with Claire by my side.

Little Miss Sexy Ass herself wrapped her arms around me from behind, and we locked eyes in the mirror. What I saw there—the love that now shone so openly in her gaze—filled me with a sense of elation that made my heart race.

Taking a small box from my pocket, I handed it to her. "A small gift to show you how much you mean to me," I told her, my voice steady despite the butterflies in my stomach.

Her eyes lit up like stars. "A present? You don't need to give me gifts, Luca. As clichéd as it sounds, your love is gift enough. Every moment with you is a treasure."

"Still, I wanted you to have this," I said, leaning in to brush my lips across hers, tasting the sweetness of her breath. "Now, be a good girl and open your gift."

"Yes, sir," she replied with a sexy little giggle that shot straight to my groin. I bit back the urge to throw her on the bed and spend the rest of the night exploring that special little kink of hers. Tonight was too important to miss. The fight wasn't just a show of strength between Vlad and Sean O'Brien; it was a celebration, a signal of the new alliance forming between the Bratva and the Irish Mafia. It was about building camaraderie, about trust.

Claire's fingers trembled with excitement as she carefully opened the box. Inside lay a delicate silver necklace adorned with a small emerald pendant, perfectly matching her stunning emerald dress.

"It's beautiful, Luca," she whispered, her voice thick with emotion. I clasped it around her neck, my fingers grazing her skin, igniting a warmth that spread through me.

"Not as beautiful as you," I replied, relishing the moment as her cheeks flushed with pleasure.

She reached up and kissed me, rubbing her body against me in the most delicious way.

"Behave. We have somewhere to be," I murmured against her ear before reluctantly pulling away and offering my arm.

"May I escort you to your carriage, my lady?" I teased, putting on a posh English accent.

Claire laughed, her joy infectious. "Yes, sir," she replied, and I groaned as my cock jerked at the sound. Tonight was going to be filled with torturous fun and games.

———

The night thrummed with anticipation as we pulled up to Glitz. The neon lights glowed against the dark sky, casting the club in an almost surreal, electric haze. This wasn't just any night; it was a private event designed to solidify the new alliance between the Bratva and the Irish Mafia—a gathering marked by power and skill. The evening promised something more than mere entertainment: a bare-knuckle fight between two fierce contenders—Vlad and Sean O'Brien—where pride and reputation were on the line, far exceeding any cash bet.

Claire slipped out of the car, her heels clicking against the pavement as she adjusted her slinky, dark green dress that hugged her curves and turned heads. The colour was a cheeky nod to the Irish, a playful dig at our rivals, and only Claire could pull it off with such understated audacity. I walked beside her, my hand resting possessively on her lower back, guiding her through the thrumming crowd.

Inside, the atmosphere was electric, buzzing with the tension of what was about to unfold. Smoke curled lazily towards the ceiling, intertwining with flashing lights and pulsing bass that reverberated through the walls. The room was packed—suits and designer dresses, high rollers and heavy hitters, all here to witness the kind of fight you couldn't get on pay-per-view. Bets were already being placed, whispers of odds and payouts floating between clenched jaws and eager eyes.

"Luca," Miki greeted me with a nod as we reached the VIP section. He lounged back in his chair, looking every bit the king surveying his court, a cigar in hand and a glass of whiskey resting on the table in front of him. The usual entourage flanked him—trusted men, lieutenants, and enforcers, each with a sharp eye on the proceedings.

I returned the nod, glancing at the crowd. "Good turnout."

"It'll be worth it," Miki replied, his voice low and casual. But there was an edge to it, a hint of something darker beneath his calm exterior. "Vlad's ready?"

I looked towards the corner where Vlad was warming up, fists clenched, muscles taut and gleaming under the overhead lights. His eyes were focused, every movement deliberate as he threw quick jabs into the air, loosening up, getting into the zone. I knew that look. Vlad was a wild bear, caged and waiting to be let loose. "He's got this," I said, confidence surging through me. "I thought Finn was going to be Vlad's opponent?"

"Sean apparently wanted to see if he could take him instead," Miki smirked.

As he spoke, Sean O'Brien's laugh cut through the crowd, a sharp bark of amusement that drew eyes and turned heads. He swaggered over, bare-chested, muscles rippling as he shrugged off a leather jacket. His cocky grin was all bravado, but it hid the intensity that fuelled him. "Hope your boy's ready, Luca," he said, eyeing Vlad with a mix of respect and derision. "I'm in the mood to break something tonight."

I met his gaze evenly, unruffled. "Better men have tried."

Around us, the crowd swelled, pressing closer to the

roped-off ring at the centre of the club. The noise was a low hum of anticipation, punctuated by the clink of glasses and the shuffle of feet as bets were exchanged. High stakes, high tension. This was more than just a fight; it was a display of dominance, a battle for respect that transcended the punches thrown.

The fighters stepped into the ring, and the room exploded in cheers and jeers. Sean bounced on his toes, his eyes locked on Vlad, sizing him up, looking for any hint of weakness. But Vlad was stone-faced, all business. He raised his fists, and the crowd went wild, a roar that shook the walls.

"Ten grand on Vlad," Miki said to one of his men, tossing a thick roll of cash. I watched as the money changed hands, everyone around us getting in on the action. The energy was infectious, a heady mix of booze, bravado, and the promise of violence. I felt Claire's hand brush mine, a silent connection amid the chaos, and I squeezed back, knowing she was watching, feeling every beat of the night.

The referee—a burly bloke with a no-nonsense look— gave the signal, and the fight was on.

Sean was quick, coming out swinging with a flurry of punches that forced Vlad to backpedal, but he blocked each strike with calm, calculated precision. Vlad's style was measured, almost methodical, like a chess player setting up his pieces. He ducked under Sean's right hook, coming up with a jab that connected hard, sending a ripple of impact that you could almost feel in your bones. The crowd erupted, the noise deafening as they reacted to each blow with shouts and groans.

"Come on, Vlad!" Trigger yelled, and I saw a few Bratva men on their feet, fists clenched as they cheered him on.

Sean regrouped, wiping a trickle of blood from his lip, his expression shifting to something darker, more feral. He charged again, his punches faster, more aggressive, but Vlad absorbed the hits, his body moving like water, fluid and unyielding. He was in his element, reading Sean's moves, waiting for the right moment.

Vlad landed a brutal uppercut that snapped Sean's head back, and the crowd gasped, a collective intake of breath as Sean staggered, barely catching himself on the ropes. For a second, it looked like he might go down, but Sean was tougher than that. He shook it off, spitting blood onto the canvas, his eyes blazing with renewed determination.

Sean rallied better than I'd expected and lunged at Vlad once more on the offensive. His blows rained down, a few meeting their target, others being deflected. It was obvious he was tiring, but he didn't let up.

"Christ, he's relentless," I muttered, feeling the tension coil in my gut. But I wasn't worried. Vlad was playing the long game, wearing Sean down, deliberately letting him tire himself out. It was only a matter of time before the Irishman broke.

Beside me, Claire was on edge, her eyes glued to the ring. I could feel the energy radiating off her, a mix of nerves and something else—admiration, maybe. She was seeing a different side of this world, the raw, unfiltered violence that defined so much of what we did. And yet, she didn't look away. If anything, she was captivated.

The fight dragged on, each man trading blows with a vicious intensity. The crowd swayed with every punch, caught up in the brutality of it, drinks sloshing and cheers ringing out. Miki was on his feet now, bellowing encouragement, while the O'Brien brothers watched with grim faces, their confidence slipping with every punch Vlad landed.

Sean swung wildly, missing by a mile, and Vlad

capitalised, slamming a hook into his ribs that made Sean double over, gasping for breath. The impact echoed through the room, and Sean dropped to one knee, his face contorted in pain. The referee moved in, starting the count, but Sean pushed himself up before it reached five, refusing to stay down.

Vlad's eyes narrowed, and he went in for the kill, feinting left before delivering a right cross that hit with a sickening thud. Sean crumpled, hitting the canvas hard, and this time, he didn't get up. The referee's count felt like an eternity, each number dragging out the inevitable, and when he hit ten, the room erupted in a deafening roar of victory.

The Bratva erupted, men jumping to their feet, fists in the air, shouting Vlad's name as if he were a conquering hero. Drinks were spilled, money exchanged hands, and the tension that had gripped the room all night finally released in a wave of triumphant chaos. Vlad raised his arms, bloodied but victorious, a grin splitting his face as he soaked in the adulation.

"Fucking brilliant," Miki laughed, clapping me on the shoulder. "I knew he'd do it."

I grinned back, adrenaline still pumping. "Never doubted him."

As the celebrations continued, I spotted Anton and Marcie off to the side, their exchange seeming quite heated. Marcie's face was flushed, her voice raised as she gestured wildly, while Anton looked like he was barely holding on to his temper. They were too wrapped up in their own drama to care about the fight, and when Marcie finally stormed out, Anton followed, leaving the rest of us to roll our eyes and get back to enjoying the win.

"They're a mess," Claire muttered, taking a sip of her drink, her gaze following Marcie's retreating figure.

"They'll sort it," I replied, though I wasn't entirely sure. Anton and Marcie's relationship was a storm that never seemed to settle, but tonight wasn't about them. Tonight was about us, about showcasing the Irish that we were a force to be reckoned with and always would be. It was about proving how beneficial an alliance between us could be and ensuring we forged a connection that would last.

Vlad joined us, a little worse for wear, but grinning like a madman. A rare sight. "That was fun," he said, wiping blood from his split lip, his knuckles bruised and swollen. "Pretty boy Sean's tougher than he looks."

"He won't be looking too pretty tomorrow," Miki joked, pouring Vlad a glass of whiskey. "But you did good. You always do."

"Cheers," Vlad said, raising his glass. "Next round's on me."

The revelry continued, and I caught Claire's eye, the warmth in her gaze igniting something deeper within me. I wanted this moment to last forever, a bright flash amid the chaos of our lives. As we clinked glasses, I couldn't shake the feeling that tonight was just the beginning of something extraordinary, the kind of night we'd all remember long after the fights had faded and the lights dimmed.

CHAPTER 35
CLAIRE

THE FOLLOWING AFTERNOON – NEW
BEGINNINGS

The soft morning light filtered through the thick curtains, casting warm patches of gold across the rumpled sheets. I stirred awake, my head pleasantly heavy, remnants of last night's revelry clinging to me like a soft blanket. Beside me, Luca lay sprawled across the bed, one arm draped lazily over his eyes, his tousled hair giving him an air of careless charm. Despite the slight pounding in my temples, I couldn't help but smile at the sight of him.

"Good afternoon," I murmured, my voice rough around the edges.

"Mmm." He shifted slightly, but didn't uncover his eyes. "Are you sure it's afternoon? Feels like the middle of the night."

"Believe me, it's definitely afternoon." I propped myself up on one elbow and glanced at the clock on the nightstand. "We really need to start taking it easier on the tequila."

"Tequila? Was it tequila?" he mumbled, peeking out from beneath his arm. "I thought it was champagne. Or was it both?"

I laughed softly, the sound mixing with the dappled light

in the room. "Both, definitely. And you were quite the dancer last night. Who knew you could dirty dance like that, Mr Orlov? You weren't part of a male stripper group at any time were you? I've got to admit, I enjoyed it immensely and I'm sure that Miki and the guys will enjoy reminding you all about it for a long time to come."

Luca groaned, "God, don't remind me. I'm never going to live it down. I don't know what came over me, you were just too sexy to resist."

A laugh burst from me, making me wince from the pain in my head. "So, I'm to blame for your raunchy antics am I?"

"Definitely. And I might have to punish you for it later tonight. When I can see straight enough to do it," he mumbled teasingly.

I smirked, looking forward to it. Teasing Luca like this was fun. "You were pretty damn sexy yourself, I'm surprised you didn't attract more admirers."

Luca chuckled, running a hand through his hair. "They were there, trust me. But I only had eyes for you."

My heart warmed at his words, and I felt a rush of affection that chased away the morning haze. "Well, it's nice to know I wasn't just imagining it. Besides, I'm pretty sure you made quite the impression with your 'intense mafia man' vibe."

He grinned, his green eyes sparkling with mischief. "Always a winning strategy."

"I noticed Sean trying to copy some of your moves with that young woman he was all over." I laughed, that had been funny to watch.

"What can I say? Learning from the best," he sniggered and winced.

"Come here you. Quit your teasing, my head can't take it

right now," he said, amusement lacing his voice as he shifted to allow me to snuggle in close.

As we settled back into a comfortable silence, my mind drifted to the conversation I'd had with Bradley earlier that day. The weight of my decision to accept Miki's offer settled comfortably in my chest. I was finally stepping into my own as a lawyer, breaking away from the shadow of my prior mentors—none of whom turned out to have been worthy of the role—and forging my own path. The prospect of running my own legal firm filled me with excitement, and I could hardly believe how much had changed in just a few short days.

"What's going on in that pretty little head of yours?" Luca asked, his voice a low rumble, pulling me from my thoughts.

"I was just thinking about my plans," I admitted, turning onto my back and staring up at the ceiling. "I officially accepted Miki's offer. I'll be the Rominov's lawyer after Bradley retires."

"Really? That's great!" His enthusiasm was infectious, and I felt a swell of pride at his support. "So, what does that mean for you?"

"I'm going to open my own firm and specialise in corporate and family law," I said, my voice filled with newfound determination. "I'll still include criminal defence when absolutely necessary, but I want to steer clear of that world as much as possible."

"Smart move. You don't want to get pulled back into the chaos," he agreed, rolling onto his side to face me. The slight shift in the bed sent a spark of energy between us, and I licked my lips. "So, where's your new office going to be?"

"For now, Miki said I can set up a temporary office here while I look for a suitable place in central London," I explained, my voice light with anticipation. "I'll be taking over Bradley's company, renaming it, and hopefully keeping his staff. They know what they're doing, and one of them specialises in family law, so it's perfect."

"Sounds like you've got everything planned out," he remarked, his eyes gleaming with admiration. "What else?"

I took a deep breath, excitement bubbling within me. "The Rominovs have so many businesses and investments, especially now that they're starting families. I'll be busy updating wills and managing estates for a while, but I'm actually looking forward to it. It's a new direction, a fresh start."

"Couldn't think of a better person to handle all of that." Luca's gaze intensified, his voice dropping to a whisper. "I can't wait to see you shine in your new role."

I felt a flutter in my stomach at his words. "And once I'm up and running, I'm planning to take on a partner or two to help, especially with the corporate side of things until I get myself up to speed in that area. I'm hoping to lure a couple of old friends from law school into joining me."

"Sounds like a solid plan," Luca said, a teasing lilt to his voice. "Just make sure they know what they're getting into."

"Trust me, they will," I replied, a mischievous grin breaking out on my face. "I'll have to interview them first, of course, but I think one of them will be perfect. I'll get Marko to check them out thoroughly before I make any offers, though."

"That would be best," Luca said, lifting himself up on one elbow, his expression suddenly serious. "And what about us?"

I turned to face him, my heart racing. "What do you mean?"

"I mean, we need to talk about moving in together," he said, his gaze steady. "Once we've taken that holiday and you've met my family, I want us to start our life together. I know we're both a bit hungover right now, but I've been thinking about this a lot."

"You're right. We've talked about it. I didn't think we'd be ready so soon. but I suppose we're already living together even if we haven't quite made it formal yet," I said, my breath hitching at the thought of our future.

Luca smiled, his expression softening. "Well, let's do that. We can both sell our places and find a home together. Or you can keep your cottage and rent it out if you prefer to do so. But I want to build something with you, not just a relationship, but a home. Plus, I think it'll be good for us to create something new of our own."

"I've already decided to sell my cottage," I confessed, my heart racing at the thought of us. "And I agree you should sell your flat too. Especially after what happened to poor Julie, it would never feel the same again. We can find something together that feels like home."

"Absolutely," he agreed, a gleam of excitement lighting his eyes. "And while we're at it, we can look at that plot of land next to the estate. I put in an offer yesterday."

"You did?" I felt a rush of warmth at the thought of us building our life together, side by side. "What are you planning?"

"I'm hoping we can build something special. Miki's on board because he wants everyone to stay close, especially with all the babies on the way," Luca said, his voice earnest. "New generations, new homes. It makes sense."

"Plus, we'll have the space we need for our own future," I added, a dreamy smile creeping onto my face. "It sounds perfect."

Luca reached out, tucking a loose strand of hair behind my ear. "And I think it's important to keep everyone nearby for protection. The Rominovs and those who form part of their extended family—like me—have a strong bond, and it'll only get stronger as we start our families."

My heart fluttered at the mention of families. I couldn't help but envision what life would be like for us, surrounded by laughter and love.

"But those are all plans for the future. Tonight, I think we should celebrate," he declared, his tone playful.

"Again? Last night wasn't enough for you? You can handle another night out so soon?" I teased, delighted at the prospect of a date night.

"Oh, I can handle, it, you and anything else that comes my way," he smirked his eyes sparkling with mischief and sultry promises making me shiver in anticipation of things to come.

"And I've got it all planned. Just the two of us. Dinner at that new restaurant I know you'll love, followed by a suite at a nearby hotel. I want you to feel special."

My cheeks flushed at the thought, and excitement bubbled within me. "You really planned all this? I'm thrilled. Oh, I'm going to wear that little gold dress Sara made. It feels perfect for tonight," I gushed excitedly.

Luca's expression turned even more sultry as he leaned closer, his breath warm against my skin. "You'll look stunning in it. I'll look forward to having such a beautiful woman on my arm as we celebrate a new beginning."

"Together," I added, a grin spreading across my face as I revelled in the moment. "It's a new beginning for both of us."

"Exactly," he replied, pressing a soft kiss to my forehead. "And after that, we'll head to the Caribbean to holiday with my family. We can take a break before diving into our plans."

"I can't wait," I said, feeling a rush of anticipation. "It'll be a much-needed escape before we begin this new chapter. I mean, who wouldn't want to relax on a beach after what we've been through? I'm more than ready to enjoy some sun sea sand, sex." I beamed. "Oh, and to meet your family, of course," I added the afterthought.

Luca chuckled softly. "I'm just glad we're doing this together. I want to build a future with you, Claire."

As I met his gaze, a surge of certainty washed over me. I couldn't imagine my life without him. "I want that too, Luca. I really do. I love you."

"I love you too, babe," Luca replied with a gentle kiss.

With smiles that promised more lazy mornings and future adventures, we settled back into the warmth of each other. Plans buzzed through my head, and despite the remnants of last night's revelry, nothing could dull the excitement of what lay ahead, wrapping us in a cocoon of bright possibilities.

———

Under my gorgeous gold dress, I wore a delicate gold lace bra, without the matching knickers, and hold-ups. Luca told me not to wear any knickers, and, as much as I wasn't used to going commando, I'd followed his instructions. The feeling was odd, foreign—but somehow thrilling. Just before we arrived at the venue, Luca handed me a gift. "Slip these on," he said. So, instead of gold lace knickers, I was wearing a little pair of 'vibrating panties,' as the box had so innocently called them.

Wearing something like that out in public felt a little outrageous, but when Luca commanded, I found myself unable to resist. We'd played this game before, and tonight, I knew I was in for a ride.

During dinner, Luca wielded that remote like a weapon, teasing me relentlessly. Every press of the button sent a shock straight through me, my body reacting instantly, only for him to stop just before it became too much. He repeated this pattern until I was practically trembling, trying desperately to maintain some outward composure so no one at the restaurant would catch on to our game. But it was a delicious form of torture, one I hadn't known I'd come to crave.

Luca, of course, revelled in my torment, his eyes glinting with amusement every time I squirmed in my seat. Months ago, I'd have never allowed myself to indulge in such wickedness—rigid control had ruled my life. But Luca had torn down those walls, and with them, my inhibitions. Now, there seemed to be no limit to the desires I was willing to explore with him.

He knew exactly what he was doing, taking me right to the edge before pulling me back, over and over. It was maddening and utterly intoxicating. The anticipation of what he had planned once we were alone in the hotel room had my pulse racing, and I could hardly wait to see how far he'd push me tonight.

Once cocooned inside the room, Luca wasted no time in showing me what he had in store.

Champagne was poured over my tits and licked off, a trail of it dripping down between my breasts and onto my stomach, he followed it with his tongue licking it up as he went.

I giggled as he poured some into my belly button before sucking and licking it out. Slowly, with a wicked gleam in his eye, he moved down my body and poured more over my mound and does the same there. Then more through my folds. I gasped at the cold tingle that accompanied it. He chuckled, bending down and licked it up. My pussy clenched with excitement. After the torture it had endured, this was more than it could take and I came with a squeal.

Luca brought the bottle to my mouth, making me drink and then took a swig himself before he pressed first his lips, then the neck of the bottle against my entrance, slowly pouring a little of the liquid inside me, quickly lapping it up with his tongue.

"Claire flavoured champagne. I need to bottle it. I want it with every meal," he said with a teasing chuckle.

Fuck, Mr Sexy Kisser was such a bloody he deviant, and I loved it.

"Up," he commanded, lifting me into his arms, our naked bodies rubbing together deliciously as he moved us to the hotel bathroom and into the large jacuzzi bath. The bubbling water was warm and sent shivers over my body, heightening its sensitivity.

Luca, positioned me kneeling, then climbed in behind me. Leaning down, he squeezed my arse. "God, you have the best ass, babe. These cheeks are mine," he growled, running his palms all over them before giving them a light smack, and I shuddered in delight.

He bit my bum cheeks, one after the other, sucking hard on them, and I knew he was giving me a love bite there, marking me, marking my ass as his.

Some people might hate that, and there was I time I would have, not anymore. Now, I delighted in the act of possession. It was as sexy as hell!

Riding his cock, tits bouncing, murmuring his name, rocking against him in desperation, I revelled in the sensations that only he could elicit.

I had no idea how he managed to make every time feel more electrifying than the last, but somehow, he did. Each time we came together, it was like he knew exactly how to push me further, make me feel more. God, I was never going to get enough of him. Every touch, every kiss, everything about Luca consumed me completely.

How I ever thought I could keep away from him now seemed laughable. How I'd managed to stay away for so long after our first kiss? A mystery. One thing was certain—there was no going back. I couldn't leave him, not when his gaze alone could light me up inside. Luca was mine, just as much as I was his. Bratva soldier or not, this man was my dream, and I wasn't letting him go. I'd fallen hard and there was no denying it, no worrying over it, just acceptance now.

I looked into his eyes and knew that was where I belonged. "I love you, Luca," I whispered.

His breath hitched, and I saw all the love I felt for him reflected back in them.

"I love you too, sweetheart!" he said, grinning before kissing me long and hard until my pussy clenched, ready for more action. The things that man's kisses can do to me.

"Round two?" he asked.

"Hell yeah!"

CHAPTER 36
LUCA

A FEW DAYS LATER – IT'S FINALLY OVER

The news anchor's voice droned on, but I barely heard her over the sound of the blood rushing in my ears. There it was—confirmation that the MP was dead. Killed in his cell by the Irish Mafia, just like we'd planned. The screen flickered with images of the prison, the headlines crawling across the bottom of the screen.

Former MP found dead in jail; suspected foul play.

I leaned back in my chair, satisfaction settling in my chest like a weight finally lifted. The bastard had been a thorn in our side for too long. But now? He was gone, and with him, the last threat to our safety. Relief rippled through me, sharp and cleansing—not just for me, but for Claire. For all of us. We were free of him.

"They did a good job," Miki said, his voice gruff as he turned away from the television, arms crossed over his chest.

I nodded. "Yeah, the Irish kept their end of the bargain."

"They'll get their reward when they take over the territory the Malia Boys and Broxys used to control. If Uncle Maxim agrees, they can handle our side of the drugs route too. That'll get us out of it and give them the foothold they wanted. Jim

MacArthur was right when he suggested aligning with Cormac."

Miki's mouth quirked up at the corner. "And we'll be one step closer to our goal."

I met his gaze, feeling the weight of what that meant. Going legitimate had been a pipe dream once—something too far off to believe in. But now? With the way things were going, it was becoming a reality. We weren't out of the game yet, but we were getting smarter. Cleaner.

"And the lab?" Ash asked, breaking the moment.

Miki shrugged. "Glowacki still wants control if he can bolster his numbers again. The Polish Mafia have been our allies for the longest, besides Glowacki's family now, so he gets the first shout. If he changes his mind about, we'll see. It's early days with the Irish. They seem trustworthy, but trust is earned. If they continue to prove themselves, maybe they'll take over the lab too."

If all went to plan, we'd be out of the drugs game within a year, two at the most. It was a good plan, but nothing was ever certain in our world. The MP had proved that. Let your guard down for even a second, and someone would come long to threaten everything.

The news shifted, rehashing the MP's fall from grace. I snorted at the screen as they recited the story we'd planned.

With Claire's help, we'd concocted a version of events that cleared me of Julie's murder, kept my Bratva ties hidden, and handed the prosecution a perfect narrative. Joey and Julie had been lovers. When Julie found out about the hunts, she gathered proof but didn't trust the police, so she came to me —the only man with enough power to help. Together, we sent the evidence to Interpol, staying anonymous for our safety. Once the MP and his men, including Joey, were arrested, they figured out Julie was the snitch and discovered our past connection and that I'd helped her. Out for revenge, they killed her and framed me for the murder. But when the MP failed to pay Joey as promised, Joey threatened to testify. The MP killed him to shut him up, breaking his bail conditions.

With these further charges against him, the MP's bail was revoked, and he ended up exactly where we wanted him—in jail, ripe for our allies to finish off.

Now that he was dead, there'd be no further investigation into me. I'd already given my statement. It was over. The authorities would move on, and our police contacts would bury the truth, leaving my Bratva connections hidden under layers of misdirection and corruption.

I glanced back at the screen, a sense of finality settling over me. The MP's death didn't fix everything, but it closed that chapter. The bigger threats were gone, but we still had to be cautious. Marko was already on it, monitoring emails, tracking anything that might point back to us. We had people inside, watching everything, making sure nothing slipped through.

It was time to move forward, to focus on what mattered— our future. Going legit had been in the works for a while, but now it felt more urgent. With Claire by my side and the Bratva family growing, safety wasn't just a priority—it was everything.

The thought of Claire brought a smile to my face. Everything I'd fought for, everything we'd built, was for her. For us. The future was finally within reach, and the life I wanted with her was no longer just a distant hope.

"You're thinking about her again," Miki's voice cut through my thoughts. "I can tell by that stupid grin on your face."

I didn't bother hiding it. "Yeah. Can't help it. She makes me happy."

Miki chuckled. "Good. You deserve it, Luca. It's about time you slobbered over a woman, like the rest of us."

"Except Anton," Ash added. "He's still holding onto his past. If anyone deserves happiness, it's him."

For the first time in what felt like forever, I agreed. We all deserved it.

"In other news," the anchor's voice cut in, "Margaret Turner, a partner at Turner and Hanson law firm, and her son Damien Turner, have been arrested following allegations that they were regular participants in the brutal hunts orchestrated by disgraced MP Timothy Evans-Hughe through his underground network, Darkest Desire Productions…"

Satisfaction surged through me, and a grin tugged at my lips.

Marko had unearthed the last pieces of evidence—proof that both of them had been part of those twisted hunts. The police were informed, and the charges were piling up. Neither of them would ever threaten Claire again. Damien had likely been the one to leave that threatening message on her door, his last pathetic attempt to scare her. My fists clenched at the memory, the rage still raw, even though we'd already won.

But it wasn't just about threats. One of the tapes showed Damien raping a woman, the tattoo on his arm unmistakable. He wasn't just a coward trying to scare us—he was a monster. A murderer.

My knuckles turned white as the fury surged again. That primal need to protect Claire, to destroy anyone who even thought about hurting her, simmered just beneath the surface. Always. But for now, Damien was where he belonged. Facing charges that would keep him locked up for life.

Claire wouldn't have to worry about him. Or his vile mother. They were done. Justice had been served.

I exhaled, releasing the tension from my body. The worst

was over. Now, it was time to focus on what mattered—my future with Claire.

"I'm done with this shit for now," I said, standing up and turning off the TV. "We've handled it all—the MP, Damien, the hunts. Now it's time to focus on us. On the family."

Miki grinned. "It's been a long time coming, brother. I'm looking forward to making plans that don't involve Bratva business."

He was right. We had big plans. The estate was expanding, new homes being built. Claire and I had already put in an offer on land next to the Rominov estate. Miki was thrilled—he wanted us all close, families growing together, protected by the Bratva.

For the first time in years, the future felt certain. I had Claire. I had my Bratva brothers. The family was growing, and we were ready to build something real. Something lasting. A life that wasn't just about surviving but thriving.

And for the first time in as long as I could remember, I wasn't looking over my shoulder.

EPILOGUE

LUCA

A FEW DAYS LATER

The early morning sun filtered through the curtains, casting a warm glow over the room. I stood at the window, taking in the estate that had always been my home, yet today felt different. Today, we were taking on a new role—godparents to Ash and Gracie's twins. It was a promise of family, love, and a future filled with laughter.

The world outside was calm, the gentle sway of the trees echoing the sense of peace that enveloped me. With Claire by my side, this place felt less like a stronghold and more like a foundation for our life together. A year ago, I would have never imagined such a profound shift, yet here we were, ready to embrace whatever came next.

As Claire stepped into the room, her hair tousled and wearing one of my shirts that hung loosely on her frame, warmth spread through my chest. She looked up at me with that soft, knowing smile, making the worries of the past fade away.

"Couldn't sleep?" she asked, moving closer, her arms wrapping around my waist.

I shook my head, pulling her in tight. "Just thinking about everything ahead of us—about today and being godparents. I can't wait to see Ash and Gracie's twins and share in that joy. And after the christening, I'm excited to take you on holiday to meet my family."

Her face lit up, and I felt the joy radiating between us. "It's all so exciting."

I brushed my thumb along her jawline, feeling the weight of my feelings. "It's just the beginning."

The memories of the chaos and danger that once surrounded me felt like a distant echo. With Claire, I had found a path forward, one where the Bratva was still a part of me, but it no longer defined my existence. She had shown me a different way of living—a life filled with love, hope, and the promise of tomorrow.

"Whatever challenges lie ahead, we'll face them together," I said, letting the conviction of my words settle between us.

She nodded, her expression unwavering. "Together."

As I kissed the top of her head, I savoured this moment. The past was behind us, and the future was bright, full of dreams waiting to be realised. With Claire by my side, I felt ready to embrace it all.

———

CLAIRE

I glanced at the screen, my fingers hovering over the keyboard as I sent off another email. "*Jane, don't forget to forward Marcie's contract for the Fashion Show to her clients before you finish up for the weekend. Have a lovely one.*"

My new firm was thriving—more than I could've dreamed. With every client I brought on, I felt another wave of satisfaction ripple through me. Accomplishment, purpose, control. All the things I once doubted were possible, now at my fingertips.

Marcie had signed me on to handle her business contracts, and Anton followed soon after. Their ventures were keeping me busier than I thought possible. Then there were Gracie and Eilidh, both knee-deep in their novels, already hinting at representation. Even Melissa, an up-and-coming photographer, asked me to manage her growing list of clients. Juggling creative rights, business deals, and everything in between—it was my world now, and I loved every second of it.

But in the back of my mind, there was always that lingering question—what would Mum think of all this?

It's been over two years since she passed, and sometimes it felt like the world was moving too fast without her. So much had changed. I wished she could see it.

I knew she'd be disappointed in Elizabeth's choices, but what would she have thought of Gracie and me? Our partners were criminals—yes—but they were good men, men we loved. I believed that with all my heart.

Mum had always been on the right side of the law, a police officer through and through, steadfast in her morals. But I liked to think, in time, she'd have seen what I saw in Luca. She would've seen the goodness beneath the hard edges, the love that grounded him. I think she would've understood—understood the life we chose, the people we loved. God, I missed her. Every day.

News of Elizabeth Traynor's retirement had spread

recently, a hasty retreat from her Crown Court Judge position to avoid the fallout from her dealings with the MP and connections to Margaret and Damien Turner. Good riddance. As long as I never had to see her again or face her in court, I couldn't care less. Marko had assured me there was no reason to believe my mum's death had been anything but an accident, and I hated that the conniving bitch had made me think that it might not have been. I'd never forgive her.

I glanced at the clock. Gracie's twins were being christened today, and I was over the moon to be their godmother. Luca would be standing beside me as their godfather—a surreal thought. A year ago, I never could have imagined being part of something so meaningful.

It was still early days for Luca and me. Babies weren't on the horizon yet. Maybe one day. For now, I was more than content being a godmother and babysitting for the new additions to our ever-expanding family. Everyone seemed to be moving into a new phase of their lives, and as I thought about everything we'd overcome, a warm sense of belonging settled deep inside me.

I smiled at my reflection, smoothing down the soft fabric of my dress. Today wasn't just about the twins, it was about celebrating all that we'd fought for, all that we had yet to experience. Standing by Luca's side, I knew we could face anything.

I stepped into the room where Luca was waiting, looking as impossibly handsome as ever. He glanced up from his phone, and the intensity in his eyes still sent a rush of excitement through me, the same pull that had been there since the beginning.

"Ready?" he asked, his voice warm and low, full of that familiar depth that never failed to make my heart race.

I crossed the room to him, a smile playing on my lips. "More than ready."

He grinned—a slow, knowing smile that made my stomach flutter. God, I'm so glad I gave him a chance. A year ago, I might've laughed at the idea. But now? Now I knew, without a doubt, he was mine, and I was his. Exactly the way it should be.

Who would've thought the so-called Ice Queen would fall for a Bratva enforcer with scorching intensity? But life had a funny way of bringing the unexpected.

As Luca wrapped his arm around my waist, guiding me out the door, I looked up at him and smiled. Our future was unwritten, but for the first time in my life, I wasn't afraid of it. We had faced so many challenges already, and each one had only strengthened our bond.

Whatever came next, we would face it together. And for me, that was everything.

ABOUT THE AUTHOR

Jax Knight is a fledgling author who finally gave in to the voices in her head, letting them come to life in her first dark contemporary romance series.

Jax lives in Scotland with her husband and son. She enjoys martial arts, reading and coffee and can often be found hiding away in a corner, glued to her Kindle or with her head buried in a book while sipping a Mocha.

A sucker for sexy, protective villains with morals and feisty, fun females, all her books have them aplenty and a guaranteed happy-ever-after!

Ash is her debut novel and the first of six books in her Bratva Blood Brothers Series.

If you'd like to keep up with all of her new releases and more, please come and join her newsletter or follow her on social media to stay up to date!

ALSO BY JAX KNIGHT

Bratva Blood Brothers

Ash

Romi

Miki

Marko

Luca

Anton

9 781916 562851